MYRIKAL

HOLLI ANDERSON

Appropriate for Teens, Intriguing to Adults

Immortal Works LLC
1505 Glenrose Drive
Salt Lake City, Utah 84104
Tel: (385) 202-0116

Cover Art by Mackenzie Seidel
mackenzieseidel.weebly.com

Formatted by FireDrake Designs
www.firedrakedesigns.com

ISBN 978-1-7324674-6-0 (Paperback)
AISN B07M6GKJ5J (Kindle Edition)

This book is dedicated to my dad; the toughest old cowboy I've ever known. You'll always be my superhero. I love you.

PART ONE
RUSS AND KARLY

⚡ 1 ⚡

Russ crept silently down the long, dark alley lined by dilapidated buildings. Similar to all the other dilapidated buildings in Manhattan. In every city. Everywhere. He remembered a time when this place had been pristine. When the noise of traffic in the streets and people rushing about would have covered up any sound he and Karly inadvertently made. He glanced at his wife, dressed all in black like him, stepping carefully over broken glass a few feet to the side of him. When the world broke almost a decade ago, she'd been his rock— the only reason he'd kept going instead of giving in to despair like so many others had.

Motioning with his hand, Russ directed Karly to stand guard as he continued forward toward the stairs leading down below the crumbling building. Light seeped through the small crack at the base of the door—real light, not like the flickering, yellow glow from a candle or torch. Whoever ran this place must have had solar panels. He shoved that thought to the back of his mind for later.

Although he was almost certain the door would be locked, he tried the doorknob anyway. People rarely left doors unlocked anymore. Russ pulled out his lockpick kit and made quick work of the deadbolt, knowing he would lose his element of surprise when the inhabitant of the basement space heard the lock click.

In one smooth, practiced motion, Russ pocketed his kit, pulled his gun, and threw the door open, squinting as his pupils adjusted to the light.

"What the…!"

Russ didn't give his target the chance to finish. Two bullets to the head silenced him and Russ was backing out the door and up the stairs before the woman in the room found her voice. She belted out an ear-splitting scream as Russ and Karly implemented their retreat. As the best assassins in Manhattan, they always had more than one route of escape planned. This time, fortunately, they didn't need to use one of their contingency plans.

"That was easy." Karly pulled off her mask and walked to the kitchen area of their hideout—one hideout of many. She pulled a flask out of the pack on the counter, screwed off the lid, and took a large swig before passing it to Russ.

"Yeah… too easy." He took the flask with a grim smile. The whiskey burned as it flowed down his throat. "The leader of a clan shouldn't have been so easy to get to. Even a small clan like his."

"Our client said it would be an easy hit." Karly sidled over to her husband and ran her fingers through his thick, dark hair. "He did his homework. He knew the target would be alone with his mistress tonight, away from his goons."

Russ breathed in deep and pulled his wife down onto his lap. "Easy or hard, it doesn't matter. All that matters is that tomorrow is payday for the Brannen and Brannen Assassination Experts, LLC."

Karly laughed deep in her throat and leaned in to kiss him. With her lips pressed against his she mumbled, "Time to celebrate."

⚡

CENTRAL PARK HAD BECOME a small city of tents and other makeshift homes overgrown with vegetation. Russ, gun in hand, watched astutely as Karly entered a yellow tent they'd set up as the drop-off point for last night's job. In and out in less than three seconds, she left the door unzipped as she exited, gazing down at a thin envelope in one hand and carrying a duffle bag in the other.

Russ smiled at her lithe form, the slight bulge of her strong bicep as she lifted the bag and settled the strap onto her shoulder. After all they'd been through together, including the end of the world, his heart still fluttered at the sight of her. Her willingness to do whatever it took to survive, the ease of which she took to the life of an assassin, and her cold-blooded heart that warmed only for him made her the only bright spot in a dark and dismal world.

He shoved his gun into the back of his pants and walked alongside her, the early morning chill cooling the exposed skin of his face. They walked in silence, heading toward the crumbled stairs of the defunct subway. The darkness engulfed them as they descended, stepping carefully over and around the debris. They stopped just long enough for Russ to pull a highly-coveted flashlight from his jacket pocket. A dim light barely pierced the shadows as he flipped it on. He growled. "We'll have to barter for some batteries soon, unless we're ready to resort to lanterns and torches."

"I heard the other day that there's this kid down on the square who's figured out how to refurbish batteries. We might have to give her a visit." She spoke in a low whisper. Not many people dared traverse the dark tunnels, afraid of cave-ins or lurking crazies, but it was still a good idea to keep conversations at a minimum. At least until they reached their destination.

They had a lot of safe houses underground. Russ ducked into one that used to be a small cafeteria. They'd reinforced it inside and camouflaged it outside to look like nothing more than a pile of rubbish. Once inside, he lit a lantern and turned the waning flashlight off. A big disadvantage to hiding out underground—no natural light. "Let's take a look in that bag." He reached for the strap hanging from her shoulder.

While Russ unzipped the tattered bag, Karly tore open the envelope, stepping closer to the flickering light of the lantern.

She read silently for a moment. "The client left a note."

"And…"

She cleared her throat and read out loud. *"Good job last night. Quick with very little mess. You seem to be as good as I've heard. There's a little extra payment for you in the bag. I look forward to working with you again in the very near future. I'll be in touch."* She looked up at her husband.

He'd removed the contents from the bag and spread them out on the cracked countertop. He lifted a package and smiled. "Z-packs. Five of them. These are worth a fortune!"

"Is that in addition to the penicillin we asked for?"

Russ nodded. "Yep. Everything's here. A case of freeze dried meals, a box of 9mm bullets." His eyes lit up. *"New* bullets, not reloaded."

"Any .380s?" She stepped toward him hopefully.

"Yeah." He held up a baggy. "And about a gram of gold powder." Money meant nothing anymore, but gold powder was still a tradable commodity.

Karly's mouth quirked up on one side. "Well, I hope he meant it when he said 'I'll be in touch'. He's the kinda client we definitely want to keep."

R uss and Karly slipped into their usual booth at the End of Times bar. The whiskey there wasn't half bad. It wasn't the same quality as the stuff before the 'quake, but it wasn't gut rotting like the stuff most other places served.

Only two other people knew that Russ and Karly were the killers known only as the Assassins Anonymous, or AA, and one of them was meeting them there in twenty minutes. Roman had been the middle man between them—a seemingly harmless, business-owning couple—and the dealers on the street they'd supplied drugs to before the whole world crashed. Their dojo had been the perfect front for their "business dealings." It was the ideal place to appear as though they were trying to help the troubled youth that came to learn Tae Kwon Do.

And the perfect place to recruit both buyers and sellers of their various "products."

They'd had to up their game after the apocalyptic earthquakes and resulting plague that seemed to have seeped out of the gigantic crevasses that opened up deep into the earth, but it had been an easy transition for them to go from drug dealers to killers. Their dispassion for anyone not them, mixed with a touch of narcissism, was the perfect combination to make cold-blooded killers for hire. Whatever it took to survive.

Roman wandered in and sat in the booth directly behind Russ

without making eye contact with either of them. The demise of cell phones and bluetooth technology made it harder to carry on a conversation incognito without looking like a crazy person just talking to himself. Roman pulled it off well. Because he *was* crazy. The drugs he took regularly before the 'quakes had started him down the road to insanity and the illness after the 'quakes drove him the rest of the way. Everyone in the city knew him as the camo-wearing man who roamed the streets talking to himself. Or, rather, talking to the voices in his head. They also knew he could somehow contact the AA where others failed.

Eyes never leaving those of his wife, Russ spoke just loud enough for Roman to hear him. "What've you got for us?"

Roman tilted his head to the side and paused in the diatribe he'd been muttering. "Hey… yeah… I know you, right? Yeah… I know you. You're *the one*. The *boss man*."

"Focus, Roman. What's the message?"

The waif-like server sat a glass of whiskey in front of the wild-haired man, knowing the tab would be covered. Roman cracked his knuckles one at a time as he smacked his lips. He reached a shaky hand toward the glass.

"No." Russ's stern voice didn't coordinate with the smile he presented to his wife, keeping up the façade to any on-lookers that he was just having a cordial conversation with her. "You can have the drink after you deliver the message."

Roman clasped his hands together and pushed them down to his lap. "Yeah… yeah. The message. A dude has a job for you. He'll leave the specifics… yeah… and first payment…" He tilted his head side to side again before continuing. "Uhh… yeah… at Saks. Tonight. 9:00."

THE OLD SAKS FIFTH AVENUE building had fared better than the surrounding buildings during the shifting of the earth. Of course, the windows were all broken and everything inside had been looted or destroyed by fire. But it was a good meeting place. Dark. No solar panels in this area. The building shifted often, pieces of the edifice dropping to the ground on a weekly basis. People stayed away.

Russ crossed his arms over his chest and leaned back, leering at his wife's butt as she bent over to squeeze into the tight space where the drop-off was. "*Woot woo*," he whistled.

"Shut up and come hold this metal bar up so I can reach the bag, you big oaf."

He couldn't see her face, but he knew she'd said it with a smile—or at least a pleased smirk. His shoes crunched on the broken glass and crumbling sidewalk as he stepped to her side and lifted the bar. Karly tugged on the straps of the bag with a grunt, then backed out of the cramped enclosure before straightening to a standing position.

Russ surveyed their surroundings and pursed his lips. "Let's get underground before we open it. I have a strange feeling we're being watched."

They took a circuitous route into the underground subway tunnels, making sure no one followed them. Karly slid the bolt across the closed door as Russ opened the bag. He read aloud from a note, "*Your next target is the teen son of the leader of the Willis Clan. I hope the rumors are true that you don't mind 'working' with minors.*" Russ chuckled and said, "Not at all, my mysterious friend. It's all about the payout."

"And…" Karly stepped up beside him. "What *is* the payout? It'd better be huge if they expect us to hit a Willis."

Russ continued to read. "*Our intelligence confirmed that the boy will be at a Rave tonight at Pier 34. In anticipation of your acceptance of this job, we've taken the liberty of paying you the required pre-payment, or half of the payment. The second half will be paid in full upon completion of the job. We feel we've been generous in our offer in order to make up for the short notice and trust that the amount will be more than sufficient to make up for it. We'll be in contact with you after the completion of this assignment."*

"Well…" Karly put her hands on her hips. "They're very sure of themselves, aren't they?"

Russ creased his brow and pulled a photo out of the envelope. "Yeah. They are."

"Let's see what their idea of *sufficient amount* is." She crouched next to the bag laying on the floor and pulled out the contents, spreading the items in front of her. "More bullets, both calibers. *Ten* Z-packs." She shook a bottle. "And looks like at least fifty penicillin pills." She handed a bag of gold dust to Russ.

He bounced it in his hand, thoughtfully. "Hmm. This feels like around ten grams." He looked up from the bag. "What else is in there?"

"Freeze-dried meals—the good ones. And a couple of breathable, black masks. A little black dress." She glanced at Russ. "And… this is just *half* of what they're paying us for the hit."

"Yeah." Russ raised an eyebrow. "Makes me wonder who we're dealing with here."

"But we're still gonna do it, aren't we." It wasn't a question.

Nodding slowly, he bounced the bag of gold up and down again. "Yep."

⚡

THE LITTLE BLACK dress came in handy. They couldn't exactly go barging into a rave in their usual black-masked attire and not draw attention. Karly looked every bit as young as the teenagers at the party even though she was in her mid-thirties. Russ leaned against a pillar and watched, his lips twisted into a half-smile. He knew the second she spotted her prey—her steps became more determined and she lifted the tight skirt of her dress enough to pull the small dagger from its sheath at her thigh.

The boy, no older than fifteen, smiled and raised his eyebrows as she bumped into him. Karly's lips turned up into a smile with just a hint of a snarl and the boy's eyes widened as she pulled him close, slid the blade between his ribs and punctured his heart. She was five steps away before his dead body hit the ground.

Russ walked in the opposite direction, away from the loud music and spinning, glow-in-the-dark whips and jewelry. He met up with his wife a couple blocks away. Her face bright with the thrill of the kill, he couldn't stop looking at her. The short black dress clung to her shapely body and exposed her muscular thighs. Russ bit his bottom lip, grabbed Karly's hand, and pulled her into an abandoned boat house. Another good thing about that dress—it pulled right off over her head.

⚡3⚡

K arly twisted away from the body as the puddle of blood spread beneath the exit wound in the dead woman's head. Her face turned pasty white before evolving to a sickly gray color. Russ stepped toward her, brows creased, just as vomit erupted from her mouth—all over his boots.

"What the hell, Karly?" He retched—he hated being a sympathetic puker—and jumped back, out of range of the splash zone.

She wiped her mouth on the sleeve of her shirt and sat back on her butt, resting her head on her folded arms atop her bent knees. "That freeze-dried meatloaf was better going down than it was coming back up."

"You okay?"

"Still a little woozy, but we need to get out of here."

Russ helped her up and kept an arm around her waist as they walked away from their latest "job." It had been six weeks since the rave job. They'd needed this one if for nothing more than something to occupy their time. Karly had been as irritable as a badger in a trap lately.

"Food poisoning, you think?" he asked.

She shrugged. "Maybe…"

He didn't like her tone. She was keeping something from him, he was sure. He ground his teeth together. His questions would have to wait until they reached the safe house.

⚡

ONCE BEHIND THE barred door of a basement apartment, Russ turned to his wife and demanded, "What's really going on with you?"

She sighed and looked down at her hands. "I… I think I might be… pregnant."

A small, unmanly sounding squeak squeezed through his tightening vocal cords. He ran his fingers roughly through his hair then shook his head. "What?"

Karly scowled. "You heard me."

"I didn't think that was possible…"

She rolled her eyes. "Improbable, yes. Impossible… apparently not."

"But…"

"I know," she interrupted. "We've been screwing without rubbers for a decade and nothing happened. Well"—she shoved him—"something happened this time."

He backed up until his legs hit something then he plopped down onto a ripped chair. He gasped for air as his chest tightened like a python's killing embrace wrapped around him. "What are we gonna do?"

"We're gonna do what we do best." She shrugged. "Kill it."

The pressure around his heart eased up only slightly and he nodded. "Yeah… yeah. That's what we'll have to do. But… how?"

"How should I know?" Karly yelled. "It isn't like there are any clinics we can run to anymore."

His face burned as frustration boiled up inside him.

Karly threw her arms in the air. "I don't know… Maybe you should just hit me really hard in the stomach."

"Do you think that'd work?" The thought of hitting his wife should have repulsed him, but, instead, a little thrill of excitement thrummed through his veins.

"Maybe…" She scowled. "Don't look so eager about it."

He bit his bottom lip. "Maybe we should go ask Doc. He might have some ideas."

"Yeah, okay, yeah. Let's do that." She grabbed her jacket from the counter and threw it over her shoulders.

The sun's rays never seemed to make it all the way to the surface of the earth anymore. Russ shoved his hands in his hoodie pocket as he glanced up at the dark sheet of clouds that had been an almost constant barrier to the sun since shortly after the 'quakes first hit. His thoughts bounced around in his head like a bag of marbles dropped from a third-story window as he and Karly walked through the streets of the deserted city.

There was more than one clan in Manhattan that would snatch Karly up in a heartbeat if they knew she was knocked up. Russ figured the same disease that had seeped up from the newly formed crevasses in the earth—the disease that had killed millions within a couple of weeks in the days following the 'quakes—had also been what had caused most of the women, or men, to become infertile. It was rare that anyone reproduced. And when a woman was found to be pregnant… Russ clenched his hands into fists. They'd take her for sure. Anything to increase their numbers. Rebuild the world to their own specifications.

He and Karly had refused to join any of the clans, becoming instead valuable assets to them. Their assassination business thrived in this world with no order. And they didn't have to rely on anyone but each other to survive. They'd never wanted a child even before the world had been broken. Children would slow them down. Be a burden. In this diseased and dilapidated world, it would be more than a nuisance. It would be downright deadly.

As expected, they found the man they called Doc in the remnants of a corner pharmacy. The empty shelves mocked them as they made their way to the back of the "store." The bald-headed man behind the counter whirled around at the sound of their footsteps. His face twitched and his head jerked toward his shoulder with a pronounced tick that always worsened when he got nervous.

"Heya, Russ, K… Karly. Haven't seen you around much lately." Twitch. Tick. Jerk.

"Doc." Russ nodded. "We… uh… we've been asked to do a job that we could really use your help with." Doc was the only other person besides Roman who knew their true identity. They'd needed his medical expertise a time or two.

The tick worsened, wrenching the older man's head in what had to be a painful convulsion. "You… you know I'm n… not in the business of killin', right?"

"I know, Doc. This ain't exactly our usual job. We just need some information from you."

"Okay." Nod. Twitch. "Okay. What do ya' need to know?"

"Well, let's say there's a woman that's with child. Only, she doesn't want to be. How would one go about getting rid of… uh… *ending* the pregnancy?"

"Oh," Doc's shoulders relaxed a fraction of an inch. "Depends on how far along she is."

"Let's say, not very far along. Maybe six weeks or so," Russ said.

Doc nodded. "It's mighty hard at that stage. You know… without endangering the woman."

Russ placed his hands on the counter and leaned toward Doc. "At what *stage* would it be safe and what process would one use?"

The old man stepped back and wiped his sweating hands on the once white smock he wore. "Well, none of it's *safe*, per se. But it's less dangerous if you wait 'til her belly's grown to where you can feel the uterus is maybe the size of a volleyball at least. Maybe a basketball."

He paused.

"And?" Karly huffed impatiently.

"Then you would stick a long needle in and infuse a big bag of solution into the womb. A highly salinized solution." He raised his eyebrows and looked at Russ. "I could make you some. I have the ingredients in the back."

Russ pushed back from the counter and folded his arms. "How long would this solution be good for? The lady's stomach isn't quite as big as a volleyball yet." He forced himself not to turn and look at his wife's abdomen.

Doc's mouth twitched in what could have been either an attempt at a smile or another tick. "Oh, uh, six months. Maybe a year."

"And, what would such a solution cost, if we were to have you make it?" Russ asked.

"Maybe… maybe just a couple a Z-packs?" He raised his eyebrows.

Russ was in no mood to bargain. "Okay. Two Z-packs. I'll bring them by tomorrow. Have the solution ready first thing in the morning." He turned to go then spun back around, eyes narrowed. "And that price better include the needle and tubing needed to perform the procedure."

Doc nodded his bald head vigorously.

EARLY ON, when Karly became sick and tired of being sick and tired, they'd attempted her previous suggestion of causing trauma to her abdomen. Russ pummeled her with his fists until she begged him to stop. Well, a little longer than that. He'd found it oddly invigorating and had a hard time reigning it in even after he'd had to physically uncurl her body from the fetal position to continue the beating. She didn't speak to him for a week after that, even though it had been her idea. And then, she'd only spoken to tell him she didn't think it had worked. Her abdomen was colored with nasty bruises, but there had been no bleeding or other signs of miscarriage.

So they waited reluctantly. When Karly's pregnancy started to become just a little bit obvious, she went into seclusion. Russ carried on with their business, serving their clients on his own. Being alone increased the danger exponentially, but the danger of anyone finding out about Karly's condition was far worse. The thought of her becoming a brood mare for any of the clans made him sick to his stomach. He'd never find another partner in life to match the way she heartlessly carried out assassinations in one breath, and tenderly—and sometimes not so tenderly—loved him in the next.

They set a specific date on which to perform the infusion that would hopefully result in the riddance of the parasite growing inside of her. Russ made sure his schedule was clear that day and the following two days in case there were complications. He'd been avoiding even glancing at Karly's bloated abdomen. The undulations caused by the creature's movements made him want to vomit.

The day arrived. Karly laid on a bed with clean sheets, her volleyball-sized belly uncovered. Russ downed his third shot of whiskey in preparation for what he was about to do. He wiped the side of the protruding mound with betadine and uncapped the long needle. The size of the needle, attached to tubing that ran to a large bag of not-quite-clear fluid, made him wince. Maybe he should have one more shot of whiskey…

"Russ." Karly's shrill voice startled him out of his thoughts. "Just get it over with already. I'm ready to be rid of this parasite before I go stir crazy here."

"Yeah… okay." He drew in a deep breath and reached for her belly with his free hand. He pressed his fingers into the flesh until he could feel the resistance of the uterine wall. The creature inside kicked against his touch and it took all his concentration not to pull his hand away. "Ugh," he growled.

"Come on already!" Karly tensed and grasped at the bed sheets as he inserted the needle.

He knew he must be in the right place when the baby—creature, he corrected himself—jerked and moved away from the sharp object. Russ held it in place with one hand and unclamped the tubing with the other, letting the fluid flow into his wife's uterus.

The fluid dripped slower and slower until it almost stopped. The bag was only a quarter empty. "It stopped," Russ said.

"Well, squeeze it or something! Doc said the whole bag needs to go in."

"Okay… yeah." He furrowed his brow. "You'll have to hold the needle in place."

Wrapping his hands around the three-liter bag, he squeezed and watched as the liquid flowed into the drip chamber of the tubing.

"Shit! That hurts!" Karly pushed her back into the mattress and grimaced. "Cramping…"

"Want me to stop?"

"No!" She closed her eyes and panted.

When the bag was empty, Russ pulled the needle out and held pressure to the puncture site with a square piece of gauze. He held the pressure for fifteen minutes then taped the gauze in place with duct tape. "Do you think it worked?"

"The little parasite isn't dead yet, if that's what you're asking." She gestured to her engorged abdomen. "The little life-sucker is flailing like a fish out of water in there. And I have to pee."

$\lightning\, 4 \,\lightning$

I t didn't work." It had been a week since the infusion. Karly had endured excruciating cramps for days. But the baby still wiggled around inside her.

"What do we do now?" Russ asked.

"I don't know, but I know I'm tired of hiding out. We need to figure out another way to get rid of this thing." She gestured at her abdomen.

He turned his back to her, messing with the wires from the solar panel he'd rigged up to a lamp. "We might have to just wait until it's born, then kill it."

"No way can I handle this seclusion for another four months. No way." She put a hand on his shoulder and spun him around to face her. "Think of something else."

He sighed. "I have a job to do tonight. I'll do some research after I'm done."

"Don't come home empty handed."

His *research* consisted of going to a dive bar—that's the only kind that remained in the new society—and getting slurred-speech, staggered-step drunk. He purchased drinks for an aged bum and they struck up a conversation that eventually turned to Russ's problem. The bum came up with what the drunk-minded Russ thought was a genius idea. After making a couple of stops to gather supplies, he stumbled his way back to their latest hide-out carrying a rather full duffle bag.

The light flickered in the top floor apartment they'd made into their hideout. Russ scowled. *I told her not to waste the stored solar power. Who knows when we'll see the sun again?* "Karly!" he barked as he stepped into the living area.

"I'm right here, you idiot." She sat in a busted up recliner, curled up under a blanket. "What did you figure out?"

Forgetting about the light and wasted energy, he smiled and wiped a small bit of drool from his chin. "We're gonna electrocute the little bastard."

Karly raised an eyebrow. "And… how exactly are you going to do that without also electrocuting me?"

"Don't worry. I have it all figured out." He unzipped the bag and removed a hard-case with the letters A.E.D scrawled across the top. He grinned again as he looked her in the eyes. "Now, I'm not sayin' that it ain't gonna *hurt*, but it won't kill you."

"You're a lunatic."

"A lunatic that loves you and is gonna take care of our little problem tonight. Besides, you're one of the few who survived the plague after the 'quake. A little electricity won't kill you." He opened the case and pulled the long-expired defibrillator pads out of their package. He ripped the pads off and twisted the bare wires around the ends of two long, large diameter needles, securing them with electric tape. He plugged the AED into the one working outlet, figuring their solar power would give him more juice than the half-dead batteries inside the thing.

"Okay…" Russ looked around the room. "You should probably lay down for this."

Karly lay on her back on the floor, a dusty pillow under her head. "I get to hurt you for every pain I feel during this. Keep that in mind, sadist."

He raised his eyebrows and nodded. Desire boiled in his belly at the thought. "It's a deal." He handed her a stick. "Bite on this."

In his drunken state, he forgot to clean his wife's belly with betadine before inserting a needle in each side. His idea was to insert the needles into the creature's flesh and then zap it. He could feel that the creature was trapped between the two sharp objects, but he kept meeting resistance when he tried to push them into it. "Hmm. I must be hitting bone."

"Just do it," Karly said. "The fluid should conduct the electricity right into the little parasite." She pushed the stick firmly into her mouth and bit down.

He taped the wires down to the skin of her ever enlarging belly —he didn't want to be touching them when the electricity fired— and hit the power button on the AED. He hit the "charge" button and a robotic voice said, "Shock not advised."

Staring at the small box, mouth hanging partially open, Russ took a moment to remember an important instruction from his slovenly new friend he'd met at the bar. He tilted the AED to the side and smiled as he reached for a switch to turn the "auto" function off. He hit the "charge" button again and glanced at Karly as an increasingly high-pitched tone sounded to signify the charging electricity. He pushed the red "Shock" button and stared as his wife's body convulsed, arching up off the floor. The lamp flickered and then died, casting them into darkness.

Karly lay panting before him. He reached for her hand, noting the cool moistness of her palm. "You okay?"

She spit the stick out and took a shaky breath. "Yeah. I think." She squeezed his hand. "Don't do that again."

"Do you think it worked?"

"I don't know yet. I can't feel anything but tingling right now."

"What if…"

"Get these damn needles out of me!" she yelled. "We aren't doing it again!"

He narrowed his eyes and looked from her to the device. There was no way she'd just lie there if he tried to charge it again. He frowned and removed the needles from her uterus, taping gauze over the puncture sites.

As he pressed the last piece of tape to her skin, the creature inside her kicked or punched out, hitting his fingers with a strength that surprised him.

"Damn it," he mumbled.

$\lightning$

"SHE INSISTS that I find another way to get rid of the 'tumor' in her womb. Try something else. Says she can't stand to be isolated for another minute, much less for three more months." Russ tipped the small glass up and swallowed the contents. He closed his eyes as the burning liquid coated his throat. "I don't know what to do."

The ancient bum whom he'd friended during his last visit to the dive bar nodded his head as he sipped the drink Russ had bought for him. "Have ya' tried radiation?"

"Huh?"

"Radiation…" the bum belched.

Russ scowled. "How on earth would I do something like that?"

"Welp… I was thinking about the before-times, when I had prostate cancer. You reminded me of that when you said 'tumor'." His eyes closed and his head bobbed forward.

"Hey!" Russ shook the bum's arm. "What about prostate cancer?"

The bum jerked awake. "Oh… yeah. I had this treatment called *brachytherapy*. They inserted these tiny radioactive seeds into my prostate. Iridium, I believe. Stronger than the iodine stuff."

"You're suggesting I radiate my wife?"

"The thing about these seeds is, they only radiate the area you put 'em. Make sure you get 'em inside the sack with the 'tumor' and your wife should be fine."

Russ couldn't believe he was considering taking advice from this drunkard old man. Potentially dangerous advice. Possibly an answer to their problem advice. "Where… uh… where would I find some of these 'seeds'?"

"Buy me another drink and I'll show ya'." The bum wiggled his eyebrows at Russ.

"Okay." Russ waved the harried waitress over. Was he seriously considering this? He nodded to himself. He was. This had to be the answer. The little creature couldn't possibly survive radiation, could it? "Drink quick, though. I want to go get this over with. Doin' jobs without Karly is gettin' old."

The bum—whose name, Russ learned, was George—surprised him with his litheness. Russ followed him to an old, boarded-up hospital a few blocks away where the old man climbed a five-foot wall into a hidden alcove and pulled open what looked to be a barred window. Upon closer inspection, Russ saw that the bars had been hack-sawed and just appeared to be intact when closed.

George led him directly to an area in the basement that had "Caution: Radioactive Material" signs plastered everywhere. His new, old friend loaded him up with a lead container full of "seeds" and the large-bore needles and syringes necessary to inject them.

"How did you know where to find this stuff?" Russ asked.

George shrugged. "I used to deliver it. Most of it's gone in the other hospitals in the city, but, for some reason, people have left this one alone."

RUSS BURST through the door to their latest hideout with an enthusiasm he truly felt this time. "*This* is going to work! You will be back out in civilization, such as it is, within a few days!"

PART TWO
MYRIKAL AND BRANCH

⚡5⚡

She'd asked Russ—she wasn't allowed to call him "dad"—once why he'd named her Myrikal and why he'd spelled it so weird. She'd been around five or six and she'd known how to read since she was three. It just hadn't occurred to her before then that her name was actually a play on the word "miracle." His answer took her breath away. Not in a good, life is beautiful way, but in a just got kicked in the gut by an elephant way.

She remembered the disgusted look on his face, eyes narrowed, lips curled in a snarl as he snapped an answer at her. "It's sarcasm at its best. Because your life is a sick joke." His eyes glazed over and his voice dropped to a near whisper. "We tried everything to kill you before you were born. We didn't want you. Nothing worked, so we decided to finish the job *after* you were born. As I held my dead wife in my arms—dead because of you—I tried again to kill you. But… you… just… wouldn't *die!*"

In a quivering, quiet young girl voice, she'd asked, "Why did you keep me, then?"

Blinking, his eyes became clear again and he blew a sharp snort of air out his nose in derision. "I wouldn't want a weapon like you to fall into the hands of my enemies."

Now, at age twelve, she'd figured out the real reason. He was training her to be an assassin like him.

She pulled the scarlet-colored, tight-fitting one-piece suit up, slipping her arms into it and pulling it up onto her shoulders. She had three of the heinous suits. Just those. Nothing else.

Russ always wore black, normal pants, shirts, and shoes. He told her, "I want you to stand out. You'll be the mascot for this operation. You don't need to hide in the darkness, because no one's going to be able to kill you." He narrowed his eyes and nodded. "Yeah... let them see you coming. Let their fear consume them when they realize you're coming for *them*."

Myri sighed as she caught a glimpse of her hardened skin in the sliver of a mirror in her temporary room. It didn't look any different from other people's skin other than maybe being smoother. The obvious difference, to her, was the thickness. She pushed a finger into the exposed skin at her neck. It didn't feel like normal tissue. It was hard, like pliable armor, and returned to its original position and smoothness immediately upon removing her finger.

"Get a move on, girl," Russ growled from the doorless doorway.

"Yes, sir." She hurriedly pulled her jet-black hair back into a ponytail, running her fingers down the inch-wide strand of silver that ran from her right temple all the way to the tip.

"Stop messing with that abominable streak or I swear, I'll yank it out of your head."

She knew her subconscious habit of stroking the stiff, metallic strands drove her dad crazy, but she couldn't make herself stop. Myri dropped her hand to her side and looked down at the floor. "Yes, sir." She didn't think he'd be able to "yank" it out, but she didn't want to test that theory.

"Let's go."

She followed him out of the subterranean hideout and into the pre-dawn streets of Manhattan, wincing at the dim light from the not yet risen sun. She grabbed for the dark-tinted goggles that hung from the belt at her side and slipped them over her head. She repressed a sigh as they settled over her sensitive eyes, wincing again as her father growled and shook his head. He appreciated her eyesight when darkness surrounded them since she could see in the blackest of night, even in the unlit underground tunnels. That appreciation evaporated like a drop of water on a burning hotplate whenever she reached for the goggles. Any sign of weakness put him in a dark mood. A *darker* mood.

Squinting even with the protection, her eyes slowly adjusted and she rushed to catch up with her father. She wondered where their destination would be today, but didn't dare ask.

As she reached his side, he spoke without looking at her. "Do you remember what you learned yesterday?"

Of course she did. Her mind took in and processed information like a fabled computer from days gone by. She never forgot anything. The trick to answering his question was trying to guess which lesson he was referring to. And… she knew she'd get it wrong no matter what her answer. It was all part of her "training"—a way to toughen her up. Feelings would get in the way of doing a job right. He'd told her over and over again he had to make sure she had none left before she joined him in the family business.

Myri squared her narrow shoulders and looked at her dad's profile as they rushed down the trash-strewn street. "Never trust anyone. Don't show them all your strengths and never show them your weaknesses…" She ducked as he twisted and threw a punch aimed for her face. Throwing an arm up to block his follow-up swing, she twisted and dropped lower, sweeping his legs out from under him with one of hers. She stepped back, outside his reach, and continued, "Be ready, always on your toes, for a physical attack —even from your supposed allies. Everyone's an enemy."

He nodded, rubbing his arm where it had collided with hers. "Good. Now help me up." He extended his hand.

Shocked at his positive words, her mouth dropped open and she reached for his hand. Off balance and unprepared, her greater strength did nothing to keep her from flying over him when he grabbed her arm and jerked. She fell, spread-eagle, and scraped along the broken cement face first. Her instincts, from years of training, kicked in and she rolled into a ball just before her dad's booted foot slammed into her. *He knows it doesn't hurt me, 'cause I'm sure he wouldn't do it if it did.* This went through her mind before any thoughts of action—evasive or otherwise.

The hours and hours of grueling training kicked in and Myrikal rolled and stood in one fluid motion, caught her father's foot by the heel as it torpedoed toward her face, and pushed it into the air. Russ's planted foot left the ground, lifting a good two feet into the air as his body whipped backward in an awkward spiral. He landed with an *oof* on the flat of his back, all the air whooshing out of his lungs.

Myri covered her mouth with her hands and stepped toward him. "Da..." She swallowed. "Russ... are... are you okay? I'm..." She planned to say "sorry", but remembered how enraged he got whenever she apologized. Apologies were for losers and wimps.

He narrowed his eyes at her, then rolled over onto all fours, trying to draw in a breath. Her instinct told her to go to him. To kneel by his side, wrap a tiny arm around his shoulders, and comfort him. Make sure he was okay. He would never win a "World's Greatest Dad" prize, but he was all she had. All she'd ever known. He kept her fed and clothed and made sure she stayed safe.

Instead, she straightened her slumping shoulders, folded her arms, and cocked her head to the side, plastering a neutral expression on her face.

Russ finally gasped. He hung his head and took in several more deep breaths before pushing up to his knees. He lowered his butt to the ground and leaned on one arm. With a clenched jaw, he scowled at his daughter. "How am I going to get you to lose the freakin' compassion, Myri? You can't have *feelings* for your prey." He shook his head. "Assassins can't have blasted *feelings*."

"Sor..." she stopped herself and swallowed. If he wanted her to be tough and unfeeling, she'd show him tough... She stepped toward him, intending to kick him while he was down. His eyes widened. And… she couldn't do it. Instead, she plopped down next to him, knees bent up under her chin, and wrapped her arms around her legs.

"What if I don't want to kill people?" she whispered.

"You'll have to get over it." He sighed. "Look, they're all bad people. I only kill *bad* people." He groaned as he readjusted his position. "I think you broke one of my ribs."

She clamped her mouth shut on the apology she wanted to make. "But… what if you're killing good people?"

He laughed, one short, cynical snort. "In a world like this one —a world of survival where the only goal is to survive one more day—people are no longer *good* or *bad*. They just *are*. We are no better than wild animals. Is the wolf that kills the baby deer for food bad? Is the baby deer good? No and no. They just *are*. I am neither good or bad. The people I'm paid to kill are neither good or bad." He tilted her chin up so she had to look in his narrowed eyes. "I just choose to be the wolf."

$$\text{\Large \lightning 6 \lightning}$$

Russ stumbled through the door, dried blood caked to the side of his head. He'd been out on a job all night and Myri had started to worry (or hope) that he wouldn't come back. He slumped onto the ragged couch and closed his eyes.

"Here… let me clean that up." She knew better than to ask him what had happened. She reached for the duffle bag that contained the first aid kit.

"No. Leave it." He tipped to his side and stretched out. "Just throw a blanket over me. I'm exhausted."

Myri knit her brow but didn't argue. Asleep and snoring before she could cross the room, Russ jerked a little then settled in as she spread a blanket over him.

No training today, then. Myrikal smiled. Time to go exploring.

The wilds of Central Park intrigued her. Vegetation had sprouted in the city streets, finding purchase in cracks in the sidewalks and roads—even inside buildings. But Central Park had become a jungle, complete with wild animals. Mostly human wild animals. It was her favorite place to explore.

Myri ran, not as fast as she could, but close to it. She counted in a steady rhythm to see how long it took her to go the seven blocks to the old park entrance. Dodging around and jumping over garbage and people, she ignored the stares and occasional hollers from those who had risen early or who were still out after the night's activities. Running thrilled her. She ran fast. Her father had told her that she could almost keep up with an Olympic runner, whatever that was. He thought her speed was related to her strength. Strong leg muscles could just pump faster.

Two-hundred twenty-five. Approximately two-hundred twenty-five seconds. She smiled. And that wasn't even her fastest. Walking now, she turned off from the main trail as soon as she found a spot that didn't look like it had been disturbed anytime recently. She pushed through the overgrown vegetation, ducking under branches and vines.

"Help! Someone. Anyone. Help me!" The voice wafted quietly from a distance.

Myri stopped, cocked her head to the side and pushed her thick hair behind her ear.

"No one's gonna hear you, *branch hanger*." Different voice, followed by the laughter of at least two others.

"Guys," the first voice pled. "I gotta pee. Just let me down, please."

"Ha! No way! I wanna see ya' piss your pants. *Branch baby*."

"Well… that ain't gonna happen." The first voice quivered just a tiny bit. "I'll just hold it. I'll hold it 'til my bladder bursts."

"Let's throw rocks at him! That'll make him piss his pants!"

Myrikal pushed her way toward the voices and found the boys—no, wait, two boys and a girl—digging around in the underbrush, trying to find suitable projectiles to fling at their target.

She looked from them up into a tree where a boy about her age hung tightly wrapped to a tree branch with rope, some fifteen feet in the air. He caught her eye, raised his eyebrows, and mouthed, 'run.'

Shaking her head, she narrowed her goggled eyes at the boy she picked to be the leader of the pack. "Hey. Jerk-face. What's going on here?"

The boy with a mess of dirty-blond hair and a mud-smeared

face whipped around to stare at her. "Are you… did you… did you just call me a 'jerk-face'?"

Myri nodded and placed her hands on her hips.

The boy took a step toward her as his two companions gawked. "No one talks to me that way, little girl. Prepare yourself to join *Branch* up there. We'll see which one of you'll piss your pants first."

"I told you to run," the boy in the tree said.

The blond boy lunged for her and found himself clotheslined and laying on the ground less than a second later. His bully crew stared with disbelief.

"Dude, you just let a little girl demolish you," his pizza-faced companion laughed.

"Get her!" the boy on the ground growled.

The much bigger boy—he had to be at least fourteen—hesitated briefly before jumping for Myrikal. He grabbed her wrist. She whipped her arm around, breaking his grip, and grabbed his wrist, twisting his arm behind his back. He cried out in pain and the girl-bully looked down at the rocks in her hands before cocking an arm back to throw one. Myri caught it bare-handed and dropped it to the ground. Then, small-for-her-twelve-years-of-age Myri, *lifted* the boy a few inches off the ground and shoved him toward the rock-throwing girl. They tumbled to the ground, the boy sprawled on top of her.

Blond-boy pushed himself to his feet, eyes wide as he stared at Myri. "Who *are* you?"

"I'm Myrikal." She shrugged, meeting his gaze.

"Let's get out of here," he said to his friends as they struggled to stand.

The three hoodlums hurried off in the opposite direction from which Myri had come.

She looked up at the captive. "So, *Branch*, you want help getting down from there?"

The leaves rustled on the captive's branch as he broke out into full-bellied laughter. "That… was awesome."

Myri stared at him through her dark, scratched goggles, one eyebrow raised, long enough to take in several breaths. Then, she did something she rarely did. She smiled. A full-on, teeth-baring smile. "Yeah. I guess it was."

The boy's laughter halted and he screwed his face up as he wriggled. "And… I can't feel my hands now." A bird swooped over him and splattered the back of his head with a load of poop. He sighed. "Today is just not my day."

Myri, still with a twinge of a smile pulling at the corners of her mouth, climbed up the tree, pulling herself up with just the strength of her arms. She reached the boy and started to untie the ropes that bound him.

"Uh…" He twisted his head back to look at her. "Are… are you just going to let me drop to the ground? 'Cuz, I think I might break something—or several things—if I fall that far."

"Oh, yeah." Myri paused. "I'll hold onto your arm and lower you down to where it'll be safe for you to fall the rest of the way."

"I saw that you're strong and all, but I'm a bit of a chunky kid. You sure you can hold me?" His gaze flicked from her face to her skinny arms.

She snorted. "I'm sure."

"K. As long as you're sure, 'cuz I can't even hold my own weight," he mumbled.

Myri tossed her head to get her hair out of her face and, frustrated with the knots in the rope, grabbed it and ripped it in half. She reached for his wrist, her small hand only closing half way around it, and pulled the rope from around his body.

He let out a little squeal as he dropped, squeezing his eyes tight. The limb bounced as his weight hit their outstretched arms. Myri held firm. The boy looked down, feet dangling in mid-air. "Still too far. Don't let go."

Myri swung around the branch and hooked her legs over it, hanging upside down. That got him a few feet closer to the ground. "That's going to have to do."

"Okay. Okay. Hold on. G-give me a second." The boy hyperventilated.

"On the count of three," Myri said. "One. Two..." She released her grip and the boy squealed again as he dropped the seven or eight feet to the soft, vegetation-covered ground.

"Ow, ow, ow." He rolled up to a sitting position and grabbed his left ankle, eyes squinted shut. "You said you'd count to three!"

"I lied." Myri swung from the tree limb and landed with a graceful *shush* of the tall grass. "You okay?"

"Just twisted my ankle, but that's nothing compared to the injuries I'da got from those three rock-throwing jerks." His mouth twisted into a pained grin. "Thanks. I owe ya' one. One point for you, zero for me. I'll even the score, though... someday."

"You're welcome. No need to even the score." She held out a hand to help him up. "So, Branch, what's your real name?"

He grasped her outstretched hand and winced as she pulled him up. "Everyone just calls me Branch." Several inches taller than her, he looked down at her. "And what's your real name?"

"Myrikal is my real name."

"Your parents must really love you."

Myri frowned and shook her head. "Just the opposite, actually," she muttered.

Branch tilted his head to the side and raised his eyebrows. "Okay, then. Parents are off the list of polite topics to discuss. How old are you?"

"Twelve. How old are you?"

"Thirteen. You're kind of a shrimp. Why are you so strong?"

Leaves rustled and Myri looked up at the crow that had just landed in the tree above them. She looked back at Branch and shrugged. "Not sure."

He rolled his eyes. "Well, what is your theory about it then?"

"I don't know... I think it has to do with the multiple times my parents tried to kill me before I was born." She kept her voice flat without emotion.

Eyes wide, Branch opened his mouth then closed it. He swallowed and opened his mouth again before finally speaking. "Wh… what? They tried to kill you? Why?"

Myri put her small hands on her hips. "Obviously because they didn't want me." She jerked her head up and sniffed. "But it backfired on them. The only one to die was my mom when she gave birth to me."

"Why…"

"Don't even ask why my dad named me Myrikal," she warned.

He shut his mouth.

"What about you? What's your story… *Branch?*"

He ignored her question. "What's up with the goggles? And that silver streak in your hair?"

Myri sighed. "I was born with the silver streak. As for the goggles, the light bothers my eyes. But I can see great in the dark."

Folding his arms across his chest, he narrowed his eyes. "Hmm… do you have any other weaknesses?"

"Hmf," she huffed. "Like I'd tell you if I did!"

Branch nodded and smiled. "Fair enough." He glanced down and tottered a little as he put more weight on his hurt ankle. "So… what are you doing today?"

"Why do you want to know?"

He shrugged one shoulder and looked into her face again. "Just wondering. Maybe we could hang out or something."

Myri narrowed her eyes. "Okaaay. Maybe. First you have to tell me something about yourself. What's your story?"

"Fine, but can we sit down while we talk? My ankle feels like someone's poking it with a burning stick."

"Oh, yeah. Sorry." Myri sat and leaned her back against a tree.

Branch limped over and sat next to her. "My story isn't much."

"Tell me anyway."

He sighed. "Well, my parents are dead… I think. They left me with the Repopulation Clan and took off to try to find some food. They never came back."

"You live with a clan? What's that like?" Myrikal's dad insisted that the clans were all evil and only out for themselves.

"Yeah." He raised his eyebrows. "Don't you?"

She shook her head. "No way."

"How do you survive, then? Why don't you belong to a clan?"

"My dad and I survive just fine on our own." She wasn't about to tell him that her dad was an assassin and she was an assassin-in-training. She didn't want to scare off the one kid her age she'd really ever talked to. "So, why *Branch?*"

"Why should I tell you? You won't tell me why you're named Myrikal." He smiled as he said it, like he was just joking.

Myri ducked her head and pulled up a small sapling by the roots, flinging it into a tree on the other side of the small clearing. She whispered, "It was a joke. Kind of the opposite of how my dad really feels about me."

The smile faded from Branch's face. "Oh. That sucks. Sorry."

They sat in silence for several long minutes.

"My real name is Morgan," Branch said, startling Myri out of her brooding thoughts. "There was already a Morgan in the Clan when we joined—and no one can have the same name—so they started calling me Branch."

"Why Branch?" she asked again.

He rested his arms on his bent knees and rolled his eyes. "When I was younger it was my job to hold a tree branch out of the way when the leaders paraded through the entrance to our compound."

Myri snorted as she tried to hold in a laugh. "Good thing you didn't have to hold back the flowers or something." She smiled. "I guess it's as good a name as any. Better than mine, anyway." She bumped his shoulder with hers. "What's your job now?"

"Tending to one of the gardens." He perked up as he continued. "It's actually one of the better jobs because I can get up early and get everything done and then goof off for the rest of the day."

Before he could ask about her or her dad's "job", Myri jumped up and stuck her hand out to him again. "Let's go do some of that goofing off now. I don't get to do much of that."

⚡

"Myri, wait up!" Branch yelled between gasping breaths.

She turned to face him, running backwards. "You're slower than my dad—and he's *old*!"

He scowled and slowed even more. Myrikal stopped, hands on hips, and waited for him to reach her.

He limped up to her then stood bent over with hands on knees as he sucked in great breaths of air.

"You need to get in better shape," Myri said.

Glancing up at her from his stooped position, he grinned. "I don't see no sense in running unless I'm being chased."

"And how's that working out for you so far?"

Branch straightened up and drew in another big breath. He cocked his head to the side and said, "You know, not that great, actually."

"You might find yourself tied up to tree branches a lot less if you had some stamina."

"What's 'stamina'?"

Myri rolled her eyes. "The more you run or do other exercises, the more you're able to run farther and faster. That's just common sense."

He grinned. "Nothin' about me is common. Including my sense."

Myrikal laughed for the second time that day and it warmed her frozen heart.

7

"Myrikal, where the hell have you been?" Russ yelled.

"I was just out exploring." She'd decided not to tell her dad about Branch or the confrontation with the bullies. Branch had shown her where to find the entrance to his clan's compound, and they'd agreed that she would come there whenever she could get away. Branch would watch for her since she wouldn't be allowed inside the compound.

"You were gone much longer than usual. Did something out of the ordinary happen?" he asked.

She'd never really had to lie before, and she didn't want to start now, but she needed to protect her new friendship and ensure that Russ wouldn't clamp down on her already infrequent free time. "I ran farther than I usually do, so it took me longer to get back." Not a lie.

Russ scowled. "Well, it's past dinner time. Grab something quick. We only have a couple of hours of daylight left for training and there are some things I want to show you."

An empty freeze-dried meal pouch lay on the floor beneath his feet, so Myrikal knew her dad hadn't waited for her to eat. Not that she'd expected him to. She pulled one of the meals out of the duffel bag without even looking at what kind it was. Eating was a necessity, not a thing to enjoy or be picky about. She ripped the top off, added water, and quickly ate the non-descript pasta inside. The supply was running out. It wouldn't have lasted nearly so long if more than half the world's population hadn't died from the 'quakes and the resulting plague-like illness. As much as her dad detested the clans, they'd have to start bargaining with one of the farm clans before too long. That or starve.

Before stepping out into the cloud-covered sunshine of early evening, Myri situated her goggles over her eyes.

Russ ripped them off her face. "No goggles tonight. We need to start training your eyes to go without them."

Myri gaped at him, mouth slightly open. "But…"

"No 'buts'. We start retraining your eyes tonight. You can't have any weaknesses for your enemies to exploit." He shoved the goggles in his jacket pocket and pushed open the door, shoving Myrikal out before him.

The clouds dimmed the sun's light, but not enough. Myri shaded her eyes with her hands and squinted to let the least amount of light in as possible. Tears instantly sprang to her eyes and ran down her face. It didn't really hurt—pain wasn't a sensation Myrikal was familiar with—but it blinded her. She could barely make out the objects directly before her, let alone anything farther than a few feet away. Every item she tried to focus on looked like a glowing blob with tendrils of bright light extending from it in every direction. She reached for Russ's arm as he walked. He jerked away from her and walked faster.

Stumbling, eyes flowing like a faucet, and nearly blind, Myri caught up to him and focused on the large, glowing blob she knew to be her dad as she followed directly behind him. Her nimbleness came in handy as she stumbled multiple times on the buckled sidewalks and roads, but never fell, always able to keep her feet.

Ten or so blocks into their walk, Russ turned down a darkened alley and stopped. Myrikal ran into the back of him as her overwhelmed eyes adjusted to the reprieve of the shadowy dead end.

He whipped around and grabbed her by the arm, propelling her forward. "Go check out what those 'nice' people are doing up there. Be quiet. You don't want to scare them off. Then come back here to me."

Myri nodded and snuck down the alleyway without making a sound—a much easier feat now that she could see. It would have been easier if she hadn't been wearing the flaming red lycra suit, but there were plenty of things for her to hide behind. She slid closer and had to cover her mouth with her hand to keep an anguished cry from escaping. She crouched, still fifteen feet from the small crowd gathered around a makeshift cage. Myri watched in horror as the men and women surrounding the cage placed bets on how long it would take for the mangy, medium-sized dog to succumb to the twenty or so rats swarming him.

The dog bled from hundreds of rat bites and barely had enough life left in him to whimper at the onslaught. Several dead or seriously injured rats lay strewn about the cage. At least he'd gotten some good licks in before he'd become overwhelmed. Myrikal had to stop the despicable carnage. She stood and stepped toward the cheering crowd before remembering Russ. He'd told her not to let them see or hear her. He'd told her to come back to him after she saw what they were doing. She hesitated. Her tender heart warred with her desire to obey her dad. Obedience won out. She couldn't survive without him. She was only twelve years old. Maybe she could convince him to help?

She hurried back to where he waited at the mouth of the alley. "Da... Russ. We have to help him! Those people... monsters... they're torturing him. They're making *bets* on how fast the rats will eat him alive." Myri looked up into his eyes and repeated, "We have to help him."

Russ narrowed his eyes and shook his head. "There's no payment in helping stupid, worthless creatures." He raised his eyebrows. "Or people for that matter."

"But..."

He leaned down to look her in the eyes. "No, Myrikal. We

don't do anything for free." He pushed her toward the sidewalk. "I have other things to show you, let's go."

Digging her feet in to resist his next push, Myri turned back toward the tortured animal, intent to save him, her father be damned. She could see perfectly down the long, dark alley. As she stepped toward the caged-dog, pushing against her father's tight grip on her shoulder, she looked upon the dog, now motionless, eyes glazed over and staring at nothing.

A cheer erupted from the crowd, along with a couple of groans. "Thirty-seven minutes, twenty-one seconds." A man's voice yelled over the crowd. "Whose guess is closest, Mack?"

Myrikal stopped pushing against Russ's grip, slumped her shoulders and hung her head. She shaded her eyes—now tearing up from something other than the light—and stepped out into the street.

"You have *got* to toughen up, girl," Russ snarled. "Come on, bleeding heart, I want to show you a couple more things."

She didn't want to see what else he had to show her. Why had he wanted her to see that? To "toughen" her up? She followed him anyway. The sooner they got done with "training" the sooner she could barricade herself in her room and think about anything but what she'd just seen.

BENEATH EVERY VIADUCT in the city were camps of people, vagrants unable or unwilling to find other shelter. Many of them were mentally ill—a sad side effect of the trauma of the 'quakes and the deadly virus shortly after. Russ passed by several of these camps, muttering to himself things like, "not this one," "no witnesses here," and "maybe…"

"Ah… perfect." Russ stopped to the side of a viaduct, just where the crumbling cement started to form a hill.

Myrikal shaded her sensitive eyes and squinted, looking into the shadows under the bridge.

A filthy waif of a man in ragged clothes, beard nearly down to his belly button, paced, talking to himself. "Hungry. We need to eat. Fuel for the body, fuel for the mind." He stopped in his pacing and cocked his head to the side as if listening to someone speak. "Yep." He resumed his shuffling walk. "Gotta get some food."

The vagrant plucked something from his gnarled beard, studied it, then popped it in his mouth. Myrikal looked away, glad she couldn't see what he'd just eaten.

A group of three teens watched him from the other side of the viaduct, whispering and laughing.

Myri had no idea what Russ planned to do, but her stomach roiled in anticipation. It couldn't be good.

"Stay here," Russ commanded. He stepped loudly as he approached the vagrant, drawing the attention of the teens. "Hi, sir. You look like you could use a bite to eat." He held out a freeze-dried meal packet.

The skeletal man stopped mid-sentence and raised his eyebrows. He hesitated only a fraction of a second before grabbing the packet from Russ's outstretched hand. "Bless you, sir." He shoved the package of food into his tattered jacket.

Could it be that her father had a shred of decency after all? The blossoming smile on Myrikal's smooth face froze when Russ turned around and stepped toward her. The menacing sparkle in his eyes combined with the slight upturn of the corners of his mouth turned her blood to ice.

"Here," he handed her goggles to her, "put these on. I want you to see this good."

She reached for the darkened goggles. What had he done? Had he poisoned the food? She pushed against her chest as her heart pounded against her sternum. She didn't want to see this—whatever was about to happen. She glanced up at her father and winced at the demented glee in his eyes.

"Watch, Myrikal." He gestured toward the man.

Against every screaming intuition she had, Myri did as he commanded.

The teens glanced at them, then whispered among themselves. Myrikal heard every word as if they stood right next to her.

"Do ya' think they'll try to stop us?"

"Nah, even if they do it's just an old dude and a little girl— what could they do to us?"

"Come on, before the street-bum takes off. I don't feel like chasing him down."

Myri's stomach dropped and she took a step toward the trio. Russ put his arm in front of her to stop her. "Just watch."

The teens rushed the vagrant, tackling him to the ground. One of the boys held the food pouch aloft in triumph. "Got it!"

"Please," begged the man. "Please, we're… I'm starving—"

"Shut up, crazy!" The boy holding the food packet kicked him in the ribs.

The other two followed his lead and stood surrounding the vagrant, kicking him without mercy.

"This is wrong," Myri whispered. "We can help him. We *should* help him."

"No," Russ said. "We shouldn't."

Laughing, the boy with the food aimed one more kick to the man's head. "Let's go. We have other crazies to visit." He glanced at Myri and her father and smiled.

Myri wanted to go to the man, help him, but was paralyzed by the decade of obedience her dad had trained into her. Without him even asking, she ripped the goggles from her face and shoved them at him. "I'd like to go home now." Her soft voice quivered.

"Not yet." Russ put the goggles into his jacket pocket. "We aren't finished with today's lessons."

I'm finished, Myri thought. But she turned and followed him anyway.

⚡

MYRI REMEMBERED DISTINCTLY the first time she saw a kitten. She'd been three-years old, walking alongside Russ in the area of Central Park, and a fluffy, gray kitten bounded out of a bush and playfully attacked her foot. She sat and played with the animal for several minutes while her dad watched.

"Can we bring it home, Da… Russ?" she'd asked.

"No. It's worthless. Come on."

She'd frowned, but knew better than to beg or throw a tantrum. Unfortunately, the kitten didn't know better. It followed them down the path, swatting at Myri's feet as she walked. Russ stopped long enough to kick the kitten. It yowled until it slammed into a tree trunk, then it slid to the ground and lay motionless. Myri had cried silently off and on for days, and blamed herself for her father's ill treatment of the tiny animal.

She'd never stopped to play with another animal in her dad's presence since then, but she couldn't help but gaze longingly at them whenever she saw one. It was no different this time, as she followed her dad into the darkened recesses of the overgrown park, tears still leaking from her eyes from witnessing the brutal beating of the man at the viaduct. Her eyes adjusted to the decreased light and she relaxed the squint.

Russ stopped and motioned for her to have a seat on a fallen tree. He sat next to her and pointed down the trail to a small clearing. "Watch."

At first, upon spotting the mangy orange cat, her spirits lifted until she remembered the other "training" lessons she'd witnessed already that day. Her stomach filled with dread as a man and a woman lured the animal closer with a dead mouse.

The man held the half-squished rodent by the tail and drug it along the ground in short little jerks, murmuring, "Come on kitty, kitty, kitty. Come get it."

Myrikal wanted to close her eyes. She wanted to run. Sh

wanted to scoop the cat up in her arms and run far away from this awful place. But she didn't do any of those things. She sat next to her father and stared at the scene playing out before them.

The cat slunk closer to the man, eyes darting back and forth from him to the mouse. The cat pounced, slowed by its apparent near starvation, and the man grabbed for it, catching it by the loose skin on its back. The cat let out a loud *rowrr* and flipped, sinking its claws and teeth into the man's hand.

The man cussed and slammed his other fist into the cat's head, then he grabbed it around the throat and yanked, dislodging its pointed teeth from his filthy hand. "Stupid animal! Give me that knife!" he yelled at his female companion. "I'll teach you to bite the hand that feeds you."

Myrikal held her breath as the man strung the cat up by its paws and wrapped a piece of cloth around its head. He raised the knife to the cat's chest and a small squeak of protest escaped Myri's lips.

"Gonna' skin him alive. Stupid cat." The man raised his hand to his mouth and sucked on the small puncture wounds.

Myri squeezed her eyes shut, her fingernails digging into the bark of the dead tree.

Russ nudged her. "Open your eyes, girl. Watch."

She watched, some part of her cursing her enhanced senses. Her body trembled as the knife pierced the skin of the living animal. The sound of the dull blade ripping through its hide. The cat's heart racing. The copper scent of the blood dripping to the ground. The cat fighting, squirming, twisting against its bonds. And —most of all—the human-like screams coming from the tortured animal as the man took his time peeling its skin away.

Chunks of the tree on which Myrikal and her father sat tore away in her hands. She yanked away from him as he attempted to grab her arm. And she ran, bowling over anyone and anything unfortunate enough to get in her way. The sun had set, but still, she couldn't see through the horror-filled tears staining her eyes.

⚡

DUST FELL on her bowed head and trembling shoulders from the cracks in the wall and ceiling from the pounding it had taken by Myrikal's head. Rolled in on herself, her head rested on her knees, her arms wound tightly around her shins. She rocked back and forth, breathing in great gasps of the dust-filled air.

She didn't look up or even pause in her rocking motion when her father burst into the room. "What in the hell, Myrikal! I told you to—"

"Why?" She shot to her feet. Russ stumbled back a step, eyes wide. "Why did you make me see those things?"

"You… you keep asking why." He swallowed. "Why I kill people. Why it's okay to kill people." He straightened his shoulders and stared into her eyes. "I showed you that humans are bad and they deserve to die. This is why we are the wolves, Myrikal. We have to be the wolves."

The sun broke through a rare gap in the clouds and filtered down through the treetops to where Myrikal and Branch sat. Myri had snuck her goggles out of Russ's jacket pocket as he lay snoring on the couch after another all-nighter. Whether he'd been out on a job or just out drinking, she hadn't a clue. Nor did she care to know which.

She arrived outside Branch's clan's compound where she found him waiting. "Finally! I was starting to think you'd never show up!" He pushed off the wall where he'd been leaning.

It had been over a week since she'd saved him from the rock-throwing bullies and it was the first time she'd been able to slip away since then. "Sorry, my dad hasn't let me out of his sight until today. What's in the bag?"

His eyes lit up. "Let's go to the park and I'll show you."

They sat side by side on the thick layer of tramped down vegetation, thumbing through the small pile of paper gold. "Where did you find these?" Myrikal asked, eyes wide behind the goggles as she stared down at the aged comic book in her hands.

A mosquito landed on Branch's arm and he swatted it, a smear of blood and a few random bug parts all that remained after the direct hit. "Stashed in a busted up trunk under a huge pile of bricks and stuff from a wall that fell."

"Why were you digging in a pile of bricks?"

"I heard a kitten crying in there. Thought I might see if I could help it." He shrugged.

"Did you?"

"Help the kitten?" His face flushed a light pink. "Yeah. He's all grown up now. We're buds."

"Well, these comic books are amazing. I'm amazed they aren't water damaged." She flipped the page and began reading the first frame.

"They were inside thick plastic bags."

They sat in silence for the next few minutes, the rustling of paper and wind-blown leaves the only sounds.

"So…" Branch pulled at the grass, looking down at the open comic book in his lap, but his eyes still, like he wasn't really seeing it. "There's another reason I wanted to show 'em to you besides the cool factor."

"Why's that?"

"Because…" He turned his gaze away from her, the intensity of his grass-picking turning up a few notches. "I… uh… I think you're one of them."

"One of…" Myrikal looked at the back of his head then down at the superhero comic book in her hands. "A superhero?" She laughed.

Branch cleared his throat, still looking away. "Well… yeah You're invincible, right? Super strong. You run fast. You have super-senses…"

Myri shook her head. "Nah. I'm just a girl that has tough skin because her parents tried to kill her before she was born."

Branch looked at her now and rolled his eyes, tacking a dramatic sigh on at the end of the roll. "Seriously, Myri? Let's forget the other stuff and just talk about your skin, then. What's the most dangerous thing that's ever happened to you? Something that should have killed or seriously hurt you."

Tilting her head back against the tree, Myrikal ran her hand over the skin of her arms and avoided his gaze while she though about his question. Her whole life had been dangerous. Her dad, always saying that he wanted to "test her strengths," had put her in increasingly more perilous situations as she grew. She closed her eyes, picturing in her mind the last few "tests." Ever since she could remember, he'd thrown or pushed her off rooftops and bridges—successively higher each time. The last time, only a couple of weeks ago, had been a twenty story building. She'd survived, obviously, landing in a crouch. She'd been fine, not so much as a broken fingernail, but the cracked sidewalk had buckled beneath her, leaving a two-foot deep dent in the cement. Just a few days earlier he'd tried something new—at least, as far as she could remember. He'd most likely tried it when she was a newborn and he'd been trying to kill her, but she couldn't remember back that far. This new test had involved him shooting her repeatedly with different calibers of guns. He seemed angry that it didn't even cause her pain.

"Well?" Branch asked.

She shrugged. "The *most* dangerous thing? I don't know. What's more dangerous: being shot at close range by a high caliber gun, or being pushed off a twenty-story building onto the sidewalk below?" She wasn't being facetious by asking, she truly didn't know.

Branch's eyes widened and his mouth hung open for several seconds before he found his voice. "Uhh... those things really happened to you?"

"Almost every day." Myri sighed.

"Wh... why?"

"Why do you think?" she whispered.

"Your dad. He's testing you." Branch looked at her. "Right?"

Nodding, she flipped the page on the comic book. "Which is more dangerous?"

Branch shook his head. "They both should have killed you."

⚡

"Myrikal!" Russ shook the couch where she'd been sleeping. "Get up and get dressed. I need your help with something."

Myri rubbed her eyes and sat up. No light peeked around the old sheet hanging in the window. "What time is it?"

"It's night time." He scowled. "Just get ready. We're leaving in five minutes."

Dressed in one of the hideous, stretchy red jumpsuits, she braided her hair in one long braid down her back, fastening the end with a rubber band. "I'm ready."

With a quick nod of his head as the only acknowledgement, he stomped to the door, a large heavy-looking bag hanging from his shoulder. Myrikal followed him, wondering what important task needed to be completed in the middle of the night.

She'd learned to not ask too many questions, instead just dampening her own curiosity and following along with whatever her father wanted her to do. Hanging out with Branch recently had opened her eyes a little, though. He told her she should be asking questions. It was her dad's job to answer her questions. What was the worst that could happen? He could just not answer. He could get angry and yell at her. Nothing new there. He could lash out in anger and *try* to hurt her. But he couldn't hurt her, could he? At least not physically. And—this was probably the biggest epiphany that had come out of her friendship with Branch—if her dad kicked her to the curb as she'd always feared he would if she didn't behave exactly like he wanted, she now had somewhere to go. Branch's clan would take her in, wouldn't they?

Myri quickened her step to walk alongside Russ down the middle of the dark, litter-strewn street. She took in a deep breath and asked, "Where are we going? What do you need my help with?"

Russ huffed, his step faltering for a split second. "What's with all the questions?"

"I just want to know."

"Fine. I heard about a sunken ship out in the Hudson. There

supposed to be a safe full of guns, ammo—explosives maybe—down there." He paused and looked at her, eyes narrow. "It's too deep for anyone to get to without the proper equipment, which doesn't exist anymore. Plus, since the 'quakes, there are creatures down there that no normal person wants to face. I want you to go get it."

She opened her mouth to speak, but quickly closed it when she realized she didn't know what to say. She could swim, barely. Her dad wasn't the "take your daughter on fun outings" kind of dad. And she was pretty sure *he* didn't know how to swim. She'd been six-years-old the last time she'd been in a pool of water. She'd jumped in to save what she thought was a drowning dog, except the dog wasn't drowning, just swimming. She learned from the animal, and doggy-paddled back to the shore.

She swallowed. "How deep is it?"

Russ shrugged. "We're about to find out."

"What kinds of creatures?"

"It doesn't matter, Myrikal," he yelled. "They can't hurt *you*. No more questions."

Unable to see in the starless night, he stumbled around the deserted pier in the old industrial area. Myri could see perfectly and chose, for the first time ever, not to warn him of the obstacles in his path. Her soft heart won out and the touch of rebellion so recently sparked, fizzled and died after a close call where he stepped into a hole in the pier and almost tumbled into the water.

"Russ, watch out, there's a piece of metal sticking up straight ahead of you. Step to your left a couple steps and you'll miss it."

She took his grunt as thanks as he dodged to the left.

"Let me know when we reach dock number twelve," he said.

The post they'd just passed had a rusty number "10" bolted to it. She looked beyond it, eyes focusing on the "12" a good hundred or more feet away.

"It's this one," she said as they neared dock number twelve.

"Good," Russ grunted. "This bag's getting heavy."

"I would have carried it for you."

"I'm not so weak that I have to have my twelve-year-old daughter carry my stuff." He readjusted the strap on his shoulder and stomped down to the end of the dock.

"Almost thirteen," she whispered before following him.

Small waves lapped at the pillars of the dock as a cool breeze touched her skin. Russ dropped the bag and knelt to unzip it. He pulled a thick, super long rope out, instructing Myri as he did so. "I'm going to tie this end to the dock cleat. You take the other end and dive in." He wrapped the rope around the rusting metal cleat. "Swim straight out from the dock, about twenty yards, I'll tell you when you're there."

Myri nodded, watching as her dad tightened his knot.

"You'll dive straight down from there, to the bottom." He looked at her and raised his eyebrows. "Find the wreckage. Find the safe. Tie the rope around the safe then get your butt back here to help me pull it in."

Apparently, he was too weak to do *that* without the help of his twelve-year-old (almost thirteen) daughter. "But... how am I going to breathe down there?" she asked.

"Just think of this as another test. We're trying to see how long you can hold your breath." He leaned in close to her and narrowed his eyes. "I'm counting on it being for a long enough time to complete this mission."

The other end of the rope fell at her feet where her dad had flung it. She opened her mouth to ask another question, but Russ scowled and shook his head. "Go. Now."

All of the muscles in her body tightened. She looked down at the dark water and thought about taking off, even turned a tiny bit toward the pier as the fight-or-flight instinct warred with her well trained discipline. She swallowed down the unfamiliar feelings of fear and bent to grab the rope.

Myrikal drew in a deep breath and held it. She stepped off the dock and fell into the water feet first, nearly dropping the rope.

when the cold water closed over her head. She kicked her feet and shot to the surface. She doggy-paddled as she had when she was six, but thought, *I'll never get there at this rate.* She'd watched people swimming in the ponds at Central Park before, fascinated by the process. She tied the rope around her waist to free up both hands, then mimicked their movements, kicking her feet out behind her and arching her arms through the nasty water.

She sensed something large churning beneath her and swam faster. Maybe a river creature couldn't break her body, but it could swallow her whole. She wondered if she could break through one's stomach and out through its muscle and skin… scales… whatever. She let out a little squeal as something brushed against her leg. She didn't want to find out.

Preoccupied with what lurked beneath her, she heard but didn't react to her father's voice the first time he yelled, "That's good! Dive there!"

He got her attention with his second, louder yell. "Myrikal, stop! You need to go down now!"

She stopped, treading water, and looked back toward the dock. She'd come further than she thought. She took a deep breath in and held it, knowing it would be a while before she could take another one. The water closed over her head again as the depths pulled at her sinking body. She opened her eyes, part of her not wanting to see what lurked beneath the surface, but the bigger part of her *needing* to see it.

Instinctually, she turned to dive head-first, her feet kicking above her now as she pushed at the water with her arms. The rapid, strong movements of her legs propelled her into the deep much faster than she'd been sinking. Much faster than anyone else would have been able to swim. Still, it took a long time to reach the bottom, and, although she hadn't seen any creatures, she could feel their presence in the darkness around her.

Her vision held out even in the deep water, although not as clear as on the surface. The seaweed swayed in the river bottom, alerting her that she'd made it. Pressure bore down on her from above, uncomfortable, but not unbearable. Her lungs tugged a little, not because she felt short on oxygen, more like they were just used to breathing in and out at regular intervals and wondered why they weren't being allowed to do their job.

She turned a slow circle, straining her eyesight to its fullest extent. Something caught her eye in the distance, a shadow, a deeper darkness than that surrounding her. She swam toward it, hoping it wasn't a human-eating 'quake creature.

As she neared the shadow, she was able to make out the hull of a small ship. She kicked faster. The tugging in her lungs turned to a burning, the first indication of a need for oxygen. How long had she been underwater? Unaccustomed to feeling any form of pain, she had to talk herself out of panicking. She focused on the sunken ship, propelling herself toward it. The water distorted distances and she brushed the metal side with her fingertips before she real-ized she'd reached it.

The mild burning in her lungs spurred her on. She just wanted to get this over with so she could surface and breathe normally.

The ship was tipped on its side. Myrikal pulled up to the deck then pulled herself along the railing until she came to an opening leading down into the bowels of the ship. She gripped the edge of the opening as she lay parallel to the deck, peering into the dark-ness below.

Needle sharp, four-inch teeth snapped at her from a mouth that could have covered her entire face and most of her scalp. Myri's quick reaction made the creature miss her face, but her ponytail whipped through the water as she evaded the tooth-filled monster. Its mouth closed over her braid and jerked hard as it yanked its entire body furiously from side-to-side.

Myrikal almost drew in a breath, running on pure instinct as she twisted around to face her captor. Face-to-face with the snub-nosed creature, she reached for its glowing eyes. Two hand-like appendages grasped her wrists, wrapping all the way around them

She'd expected fins or maybe flippers, like a seal's. But these hands pulling her down toward the opening in the sunken ship were eerily human-like with opposable thumbs. Webbing between the fingers and long claws were the main differences. Myri pulled one hand free and tried to dig her fingernails into the thick, rubbery, white-gray hide of the creature. She wrenched her other hand free and braced her feet on each side of the hatch where the majority of the creature's body still hid.

Tearing at its jaws, she yanked her hair free then wrapped her arms around its torso and squeezed, pushing up with her legs. The rest of its body, at least twice the height of Myrikal, slid through the opening. A serpentine tail whipped out of the hatch and circled around her, pulling her closer. It raked at her legs with its clawed, webbed hind feet. Hoping that the creature's kill spots would be somewhat similar to a human's, Myri applied some of the tenets of the training her dad had forced on her since birth. Her arms barely fit around its chest, so crushing its internal organs wasn't going to be her easiest route.

Myri pushed up out of the grasp of its tail and flipped over its head, grabbing it by the bottom jaw and twisting as she torpedoed over and behind it. The creature's neck cracked and it instantly became a dead weight in Myri's arms. She released her hold and untangled her rope from around it and watched as it sunk to the deck of the ship, its eyes no longer emitting a yellow glow.

She made her way back to the ship railing and held on as she thought. What if there were more down inside the ship? What would her father do if she came back up empty handed even though she'd likely found the ship? He'd make her come back down. He'd remind her that the creature didn't even hurt her—couldn't even hurt her—so why was she being a sissy?

The burning in her chest tugged at her, nudging her to do something, whichever choice she made, so she could fill her lungs with air again. Maybe the creature had been alone. Maybe… She closed her eyes for a moment to gather her courage. She pushed toward the hatch and, before she could talk herself out of it, swam in head first.

Myri half-swam and half-pulled herself around the lower deck. At the very end—she had no idea if it was the front or the back end—she thought she saw what could have been a safe. As she drew closer, she became more sure. A sense of relief entered her chest as she made out the lock. She wiggled out of the rope loop she'd tied around her waist. She wrapped the rope around the thick metal box that was as tall as her and at least half that wide.

She had to have been beneath the water for at least thirty minutes. The burning in her lungs had changed to a dull ache.

Now what was I supposed to do? She shook her head. She'd never felt like this before. Like her head had been stuffed with cotton. Thoughts came slowly. Black spots danced before her eyes. *Back to the surface. I need air.*

Which way is up? Her spotty eyes landed on the rope, floating out from where she'd tied it to the safe. She grabbed the rope and held to it loosely with one hand as she swam, following it out through the hatch then up toward the surface of the river. The world spun around her as she ascended to the surface a hundred or more feet above. She focused her thoughts on the rope.

Don't let go of the rope.

She could no longer remember why she was holding to it.

Don't let go of the rope.

Flashes of light crossed her vision, even when she closed her eyes. The kicking of her feet slowed and the ache in her chest grew.

She finally broke the surface, her hand still gripping limply to the rope. It took her several seconds to realize what the cool breeze on her face meant. She drew in a deep breath. She coughed and spit as some of the dirty water of the Hudson chased the air into her lungs. Rolling to her back, she floated as she continued to take deep breaths until her fuzzy mind cleared and her vision returned to normal. The ache in her lungs disappeared.

The strength returned to her limbs and she swam alongside the rope until she reached the dock.

"Myrikal?" her father whispered.

"Yes. It's me."

"Good. I was starting to wonder if a 'quake creature got you after all," he said, his words laced with annoyance.

"One tried to." Myri pulled herself onto the dock and stood beside her father.

"Is that so?" He raised an eyebrow. "You'll have to tell me about it. Later. Did you find the ship? The safe?"

She nodded.

"Did you get the rope secured around it?"

She nodded again.

"Well," he huffed. "Help me pull it up, then."

She reached for the portion of rope he held toward her. "How long was I down there?"

"I'd say forty-five minutes to an hour." He cocked his head and looked at her. "Did you have any trouble? You know, from holding your breath for that long?"

The way his eyes widened just slightly and his cheek twitched sent a chill straight to her heart. "No. No problems," she lied.

"Oh. Well, good. That's good." A flash of anger sparked in his eyes before he turned away to concentrate on the rope.

That wasn't the answer he'd wanted to hear. Myrikal shivered.

⚡ 9 ⚡

"Weapons?" Branch asked, eyes wide. "What kind of weapons?"

"Guns, ammunition, explosives… I guess. He didn't really let me see everything that was in there," Myrikal answered.

"What does he need that stuff for?"

Myri shrugged, she wasn't about to tell him what her dad's "job" was. "My dad said it's for our protection. He's worried about the gangs that have been getting more and more aggressive." She couldn't look at him while she lied.

"What's wrong, Myri? Something's bothering you."

She looked around the crowded city street. "There are too many people here. Let's go somewhere more private."

"Okay," Branch said. "I know just the place." He picked up a small duffle bag and headed down the street.

She frowned and followed him. He turned down Fifth Avenue one of the more devastated areas of the city. He looked back at her and grinned. He dropped to the ground and crawled through a small opening into a crumbling building, pulling his bag behind him.

"Wait, Branch." She inspected the broken down walls, the crumbling bricks, and the decaying wood piled up around the opening.

He stopped crawling and looked back over his shoulder at her. "What?"

"This doesn't look very safe."

He rolled his eyes. "That's why it's a good place to talk. Nobody's gonna' come in here. It'll be fine. I've been in here before."

Myri sighed and followed him inside. After crawling through a rubble tunnel a few feet long, it opened up into a bigger room. A small animal scurried behind a stack of tumbled, broken shelving.

Leaning back against a pile of mannequins, Branch sat with his hands resting atop his bent knees. "So… what's bothering you?"

She looked down at her hands. She could trust Branch, right? He knew all her other secrets and he hadn't told anyone about those—not that she knew of anyway. "You have to pinky swear not to tell a single living soul." She thought about the stories of ghosts and wraiths wandering the tunnels beneath the city and added, "Or a single not-living soul."

"I totally pinky-promise, Myri. I won't tell a soul, living or dead." He held his crooked pinky out to her.

Looking him straight in the eyes, she hooked her pinky around his and said, "Repeat after me: I solemnly swear that I will never tell another soul—living, dead, or otherwise—what Myrikal is about to tell me. On my honor and my grave, I swear."

He repeated the words, the solemnity in his eyes telling her that he meant every word. She sighed. Her secret would be safe with him.

"Remember when you asked me if I had any weaknesses, besides the light bothering my eyes?" she asked.

He nodded, eyes widening.

"I found another one. Only, this one could prove to be much more of a problem."

"What is it?" Branch whispered.

Myrikal swallowed and looked down. "I… I can't hold my breath indefinitely. I was underwater for an hour, maybe less, while

I was retrieving the safe. I didn't think I was going to make it back up to the surface."

"Oh… drowning. I never thought about that. I guess even super-cells need oxygen to function. What happened?"

"My mind got all fuzzy and dizzy. I started seeing spots. I… I think I was almost ready to pass out."

"Wow. That's…" He laid his hand on her shoulder. "Thanks for trusting me enough to tell me. I promise I'll never tell anyone."

"I know you won't." Something above them creaked. She halted her smile mid curve. "Branch, I think we…"

They both looked up. Branch started to stand, but Myri lunged at him and pushed him several yards away. He landed with a crash against the remains of a display case, broken glass crunched beneath him. Her friend safe for the time being, Myri crouched and shielded her head as a section of the second floor crashed down on top of her.

"Myri?" Branch's hysterical, muffled voice penetrated the rubble pressing down on her.

"Stand back," she replied. Facedown on the floor, a heavy beam pressed down on her upper back. She maneuvered her hands beneath her shoulders, in a push-up stance, and pushed, shifting the metal beam and surrounding ceiling tiles and other debris until she could get her legs under her.

Clearing junk out of her way as she crawled, she made her way out from under the beam. She cringed as it shifted behind her causing another loud cascade of building materials to crash down.

Myrikal got to where she could stand. She gazed around her having trouble seeing through the cloud of dust even with her enhanced sight. "Branch? Are you okay?"

His voice came from the other side of the mountain of rubble. "Yeah. Yeah, I'm okay… mostly."

She moved toward the sound of his voice. "Mostly?"

"I'm kinda' stuck. I can't get my leg out from under this column that fell."

"Hang on. I'm coming." Myrikal carefully dug her way to her friend. She stopped frequently and changed her course as the piles shifted.

After moving a chunk of cement, she was able to shimmy her head and shoulders through the small opening. Branch's pale, grimacing face worried her and she pulled the rest of her body through in a rush. A chunk of cement and rebar broke loose from its precarious position near the top of the pile and plummeted toward her friend's head. His eyes widened and he wheezed out a short cry of alarm. Myrikal charged forward and batted the deadly boulder away from him as it came to within an inch of his skull.

Branch winced as it landed close-by. He looked from the chunk back to Myri and swallowed. "Thanks. Again." He looked back at his trapped leg. "Think you can lift that thing off me?"

Myri rolled her eyes and moved toward the column. "Get ready to scoot yourself forward when I lift it."

She slid her fingers under the column and lifted carefully so as not to cause an avalanche of building materials to come crashing down on top of them. Branch grunted as he pushed himself forward with the un-trapped leg. When he was clear, Myri set the column down gently and let out the breath she'd been holding.

"Are you hurt? Can you stand?" she asked. "We need to get out of here before the other ten floors collapse on us."

"I'm fine." Branch stood and winced slightly as he put weight on his injured leg. "How are we going to get out of here? I can't crawl through that little hole you came through. I'm a bit chunkier than your scrawny butt."

Myri looked toward the back of the building. "Do you think there's a way out back there?"

Branch shrugged. "I've never really explored this building before. I've only been in this area."

"Well, I guess we'll find out together, then." She nodded to the pile of rubble blocking their exit from the front. "That isn't stable enough to try to dig a bigger hole."

"Okay, but you'll have to lead the way. It's too dark in here for me to see where I'm going."

Myri hadn't realized how dark it had gotten since the cave-in. Light that had been streaming in through the gaps in the boarded up windows, was now gone—on the other side of the mountain of debris. She pulled her goggles down and let them hang around her neck. "Alright. Follow me, then."

They wended their way through the ruins of the former store, Myrikal picking her way slowly around the bigger piles of junk so Branch could keep up. She sensed when his movement stopped and she looked back at him. "You okay?"

"I… can't see." He lowered his head. "We might have to hold hands or something—I know, that's gross, but I don't want to get lost in here."

Myri didn't think it would be gross. Why had he even said that? Did he think *she* was gross? "Okay." She grabbed his hand and continued forward, a little faster this time.

They reached what she assumed was the back of the store where a crooked door hung on one hinge. A metal sign said "Employees Only". Still thinking about what Branch could have meant about it being gross to hold her hand, she ripped the door off its last hinge as she pulled it open. She let go of Branch's hand and moved the door to the side. She peered into the "Employee Only" room and sighed. A jumble of tipped over metal shelves and clothing racks met her gaze.

She grabbed Branch's hand again. "Sorry. You're going to have to hold my *gross* hand again. This place is a mess." She dragged him forward toward a small glimmer of light coming from the other end of the room.

"Wait… I… I didn't mean that your hand was gross. Nothing about you is gross, Myri." He stumbled as he tried to keep up with her.

"Well, what did you mean then?" She stepped over a metal bar.

"Umm… some, or most, kids our age think… well, boys think

girls are gross and girls think boys are gross." He shrugged. "I thought maybe you'd feel that way, too."

"No. That's just stupid. Boys and girls are just people. We're both gross and we're both… not gross."

He straightened up. "Yeah. You're right." He squeezed her hand.

A warm flush rushed up her arm. She wasn't used to personal contact with other people. Her dad rarely touched her—and then only during training, when he was teaching her how to fight. This kind of touch was much nicer. She smiled as she continued to work her way across the room.

She had to break some boards off the empty windows for them to climb through to the alley behind the store. The exit door was stuck and she didn't dare push it too hard, with the way the building was prone to collapse.

Back out on the relative safety of the street, she let go of Branch's hand and pulled her goggles back into place.

"You saved my life in there, Myri. Twice." He grinned. "I owe ya' another one. That's two more points for you. That makes the score: Myrikal-3, Branch-0. I have some catching up to do."

She grinned back. "Nah. Don't worry about it. Isn't that what 'superheroes' are supposed to do?"

$$\not{\,}10\not{\,}$$

Now that Russ had his stash of weapons, he was more paranoid than ever. They moved underground, into the tunnels beneath the city. Not many people dared even descend into the depths below—mostly just the crazies. And Myrikal and her dad. She didn't know if people were afraid of cave-ins, crazies, or… something else. She'd heard rumors of "others" being down there. "Others" was what people called the supposed monsters that had crawled out of the core of the earth through the crevasses left by the 'quakes. She'd never seen one. Except, she guessed, the sea creature that tried to eat her in the river, but she'd never seen one in the underground. And, Russ didn't seem to be scared of anything.

They made their new semi-permanent home in the cars of an old subway train. Myri loved it down there. She could see and didn't have to wear goggles. Russ let her have her own train car to herself. It gave her life a bit of normalcy, whatever that was in this post-quake world. Just having the same place to return to each day had a calming effect on her—knowing she had a "home" with her own space at the end of the day.

The bad thing about the weapons was that Russ wanted to practice with them. And practice, to him, meant trying them all out on his daughter. Which meant he spent more time tormenting Myrikal under the guise of "training." And tha meant less free time for her, less time she could spend with Branch.

"This ammunition isn't going to last me forever," Russ said. "You still need to learn the family business. You're going to be the world's greatest assassin, which means I can retire someday and just mooch off of you like you've been doing with me for the last thirteen years."

"Yes, Russ." Myri averted her gaze from her father's. She wanted to remind him that he wouldn't have the ammunition at all if she hadn't gotten it for him. But she didn't. She *really* didn't want to kill people, but every time she broached the subject with her father, he spent the next several days showing her the disgusting underbelly of the dark society in which they lived. She didn't know how many more acts of cruelty she could witness without jumping in to help—or losing her mind, becoming like her father.

Shadows danced around them as the flames of the torches her father needed to see by fluttered with their movement. They sparred in an open area in the underground, surrounded by mostly intact concrete. The depressed area where the train tracks lay gaped beside them as Russ threw sharp knives at Myri in rapid succession. She could have dodged most of them, as they appeared to her to be flying toward her in slow motion.

Russ, however, wanted her to do more than dodge and insisted that she block and catch some of them. "You won't always be in an area where there's room to dodge."

Myri blocked another knife with her forearm, sending it flying down to the tracks. "Why don't I just stand here and let them hit me? We know they can't penetrate my skin."

The next throw went wide, aggravation making Russ's aim off. "I've told you before. Appearances. You want your targets, and more importantly, observers, to see your skills. To stand in awe of you. Your target will be dead after your encounter, but the audience—they will go out and talk. They'll tell others about you and before long, all will fear you."

"So… it just looks cooler?"

"It looks tougher, Myrikal. It looks badass. Now quit asking questions. I want you to catch the next three and fling them back toward me. But don't hit me. Then we can be done for the day."

⚡

"I FIGURED these would fit your scrawny twelve-year-old body." Branch held up a pair of decent looking jeans and a hoodie with "NY" blazed across the front.

"Thirteen," Myri said as she eyed the clothes.

"Thirteen? Thirteen what?"

"I'm thirteen now."

"What?" Branch lowered the clothes. "I missed your birthday? When was it?"

Myri shrugged. "I'm not sure of the exact date. My dad just says I was born sometime in September."

"I'm gonna' go out on a limb here and assume that you've never celebrated your birthday before."

"You should really refrain from going out on anymore limbs…"

He rolled his eyes. "Ha, ha. Very funny. And, you're avoiding my question."

"You didn't officially ask a question, so…"

He huffed out a frustrated breath. "Have you ever celebrated your birthday in any way?"

"No. My birthday is also the day my mom died. So my dad would rather just pretend I was never born or something."

"Yeah, well. That's not how *we* do things. Wait here." He threw the pants and hoodie to her. "You should try these on while I'm gone. I'll be back in a couple minutes."

Myri smiled and held the clothes to her chest. She would never admit it out loud, but she was thrilled to have some real clothes. She just hoped they fit. She ducked behind a pile of garbage in the alley outside of Branch's clan compound. Instead of taking the hideous red suit off, she just slid the jeans on over it. They were a little loose in the waist but the length was just right. She had to roll the sleeves of the black hoodie up a couple of times, but that was okay. She loved it anyway. Today, black was her favorite color.

Branch met her out front, his hands held behind his back, just as she exited the alley. "Not bad," he said. "What'd you do with that red thing you always wear?"

She lifted the hoodie up to show him the suit underneath. "I didn't want to carry it around all day." Myri smiled. "Thanks Branch. I feel more normal now."

"You're welcome. Consider it your first birthday present." He brought his hands around to the front. "And this is your second." He held out several small, red fruits of some sort.

When she reached for it, he said, "They're kinda soft, so don't squish 'em."

"What is it?" she asked as she held the fruit in her palm.

"Strawberries." He cocked his head to the side. "Haven't you ever seen a strawberry before?"

Shaking her head, she poked at the fruit with her finger. "My dad isn't much for taking the time to find fresh food. We almost exclusively eat freeze dried goods that are over twenty years old."

"That's just sad." He shrugged. "That's all we used to eat, too. That's why the leaders decided to try growing some stuff. Not everything we try grows well, though. Not enough sunshine."

"They're kind of pretty."

"They're delicious. Try one. Just don't eat the green part."

Holding one of the strawberries by the leaves of the stem, Myrikal bit into the red part. It was sweet and tangy and delicious. She hurriedly ate the rest of it, biting as close to the stem as she could without getting the leaves in her mouth. "Branch! These are awesome!"

"I know, right?"

She held her hand out to him, the three remaining berries resting on her palm. "You should have one."

"Nope. I get to eat them whenever I want this time of year because they're in my garden. Plus, it's your birthday present. You eat them." He grinned.

This time she pulled the stem out and popped the whole strawberry in her mouth. "Thank you so much! This is the best birthday month ever!" She grabbed him in a fierce hug.

"Squishing me…" Branch panted.

She released him, face turning a shade of pink. "Sorry."

Branch shrugged. "You can hug me anytime. Just try not to kill me when you do."

She ate the last strawberry and licked the juice off her fingers. "What do you want to do now?"

With an excited gleam in his eyes, Branch answered, "Let's go fishing!"

Myri raised an eyebrow. "Don't you need, like, special stuff to do that? Like a fishing pole?"

He patted his pocket. "I have everything we need right here."

As they walked, she asked, "When's *your* birthday?"

"Oh, I turned fourteen in July. I saved some of the small birthday cake one of the mom's made me for you. But you didn't come see me that week, so I ended up eating it."

"You had cake? Like, real cake?"

"Yeah. Who knew wheat grows well in the shade? We just got our first harvest this year."

"Awesome." Myri looked down at her new clothes. "Why did you decide to get me some clothes?"

"Well, I was looking through the comic books again and noticed that most of the superheroes have disguises. They don't want people to know who they are when they aren't doing super-hero stuff. They especially don't want their enemies to know who they are." He looked at her. "Your red stretchy jumpsuit kind of stands out."

"But I don't have any enemies. At least that I know of. And

they can't kill me anyway. And forget the jumpsuit—my hair stands out. Not many people have a streak of silver in their hair."

"Yeah, I didn't think about that. I might have to get you a hat or something. You will have enemies when people see what you can do. Maybe they can't kill you, but they'll keep trying to. Plus, you don't want people bugging you all the time, asking for your autograph and stuff." He ducked his head. "Plus that red suit is hideous. Which reminds me, I got you one more thing." He reached in his jacket pocket and pulled out some sleek, black goggles that looked more like sunglasses and less like the swimmer's goggles her dad had given her.

She took them from him and turned them over in her hand, inspecting them. "These are great, Branch. Really great."

"Try them on. I found them in one of those abandoned stores you're always telling me to stay out of."

She stopped walking and closed her eyes as she pulled her old goggles off and replaced them with the sleek new ones. She adjusted the straps to fit them snugly to her head. The soft cushion around her eyes blocked all light and felt as soft as a kitten's fur against her face. "These are the best, Branch. Thank you so much." She left the old goggles hanging around her neck, tucked under her hoodie.

"Hey, it's the least I can do seeing as how you saved my life, like, three times." He turned and walked backwards while facing her. "Speaking of that, I think the clothes, goggles, and strawberries earns me a point. What do you say?"

Myri smiled. "Yeah. At least a point, maybe two."

"No, I don't want to be greedy. I'll take one point for saving you from a fashion disaster. That makes the score: Myri-3 and Branch-1."

They sat on the edge of a bridge, their legs under the bottom railing, and dangled their feet a few inches above the water. Branch pulled a length of fishing line with a homemade hook on the end out of his pocket. He found a thick stick and wrapped the line around it. "See? No need for a fishing pole." He skewered a wriggling worm onto the hook and dropped it straight down into the water before handing the stick and remaining line to Myri.

"Do you have another one?" she asked.

"No, but we can take turns. If you feel a fish bite, jerk the line up then start wrapping it around the stick to pull it in."

"Have you done this before?" She stared down into the water, remembering her encounter with the river creature.

"A couple of times."

"Have you ever caught a fish?"

He perked up. "Yeah! I've caught a bunch. Well, three or four."

"What did you do with them?" Myri asked.

"I took them back to the compound and one of the cooks roasted them. They were delicious."

"I've never eaten real fish before." Myri bounced the line up and down in the water.

"Oh!" The line tugged in her hands. "I think I got a bite!" She jerked the line up like Branch had instructed.

"Good job!" He leaned over the bottom rail of the bridge, eyes on the river. "I see him! Keep reeling him in, I'll grab him when he gets close enough."

"How do you know it's a 'him'?"

"I don't." Branch leaned his head and chest between the last two bars of the railing and reached toward the fishing line as the fish broke the surface. "Be gentle with the last couple of wraps, you don't want to bounce him off the hook."

"Okay." Myri concentrated on her task.

The fish dangled in the air, its tail fin smacking against the water. Branch leaned as far as he could between the two rails and reached for it. He grabbed the line an inch from its gasping mouth and pulled it up high enough that he could stick his finger in it mouth and out through the gills.

"Got it!" He turned his smiling face to Myri. "Good…" Whatever he'd been going to say was cut off with a surprised grunt.

A river creature, similar to the one Myri faced when retrieving the safe in the Hudson, leapt from the water. Its mouth snapped shut around the dangling fish and Branch's hand. Myri dropped the fishing line and grabbed Branch's arm and pulled, trying to free it from the monster's mouth.

"Ow! Ow! Its gonna' rip my arm off!" he yelled.

Myri didn't know what to do. The creature jerked violently on the end of Branch's arm, pulling him through the railing to where his body widened in the middle and he became stuck. Branch screamed. Myri panicked. She let go of his arm and climbed the bridge's railing, intending to jump in the river and pry the thing's teeth out of her friend's arm. She stopped half-way over, legs straddling the railing. She'd never be able to reach its mouth without climbing up it. The added weight might really rip Branch's arm off.

The screams of pain and fear coming from her friend's throat bounced around in her skull like a boulder. She pressed her hands against her head and let out a primal scream of her own. Her chest tingled. Then burned. The tingling, burning extended to her shoulders. Her arms. Her hands. Her fingertips. She held her hands out in front of her and her eyes widened. Her fingers crackled with energy. Little yellow sparks flew from her fingertips.

Branch took panting breaths between screams. Myri emitted a growl that turned into a roar of rage. She flung her hands toward the creature with an instinct she didn't know existed and released the energy from her body. Bolts of electricity blasted from her fingers into the river creature. Bits of charred monster guts and other various pieces soared through the air, landing as far as a half mile away.

The thing's head still clung to Branch's arm, his hand stuck out the severed neck hole. Myri jumped back down onto the bridge and grabbed him around the waist. She pulled him back through the railing then pried the thing's jaws off him and dropped the head into the water.

Blood poured from the puncture wounds in his arm just above his wrist.

"We need to clean this out and wrap it in something." Myri tore a sleeve off her new hoodie and dipped the end in the water. "This water is gross, but it'll have to do for now. We'll wash it better when we get to some clean water." She scrubbed the wounds, holding tight to his hand as he tried to pull away.

"That hurts!" Branch winced.

"I'm sorry. But it has to be cleaned. Who knows what kind of germs that thing had on its teeth?" She finished and wrapped the hoodie sleeve around his arm and tied it. "We should get back so you can wash it better."

"Myrikal." He stared at her. "Aren't you going to say anything about what just happened? About what you just did?"

"I… I don't know what happened. I've never done that before." She examined her fingers.

"Well, that explains why you didn't tell me you could." He cradled his injured arm against his body. "C… can you do it again?"

"I don't know." She shoved her hands in the front pocket of her hoodie. "I don't want to right now. It kind of scared me a little."

Branch nodded. "Okay. But you have to try again later. You have to. That's one more super power to add to the list."

She gazed down the length of the bridge. "Let's go. You need to take care of that bite."

He walked alongside her in silence for a minute. When they reached the torn up road, he stopped and put his uninjured hand on his hip. "Dang it."

"What?" Myri asked.

"I just realized you got another point. That makes the score 4 to 1. I'm never gonna' catch up at this rate." He hung his head in mock defeat.

11

Myri couldn't sleep. Every time she closed her eyes she saw that monster with its teeth clamped around Branch's arm. She hoped he'd done as she'd said and cleaned it better when he got home.

After tossing and turning for what seemed like hours, Myri got up and went to the train car that served as their living area and kitchen, between her and her dad's sleeping cars. She found the as yet unpacked duffle bag where they kept their bug-out kits in case they had to leave in a hurry. Her dad snored one car over. Myri unzipped the bag and rummaged around in it until she found the first aid kit. She grabbed a package of gauze wrap, some tape, a couple of clean cloths, and a bottle of filtered water mixed with alcohol. She started to put the kit away, then thought about the dirty river water again. She pulled out the bottle of penicillin and counted out fourteen pills before putting the rest back.

She took everything back to her room and placed it in a backpack. She wrote a note for her dad, knowing he'd be awake before she got back.

Russ, Going for a walk. Be back soon. M.

She left the note in the shared car where he'd be sure to see it, knowing he'd still be furious that she left without permission. It didn't matter. She had a powerful feeling that Branch needed her, and nothing would stop her from going to him.

⚡

THE NEW GOGGLES hung around her neck. The sun hadn't risen yet and the streets crawled with night people. Myri rarely came out this time of day and never before by herself. The night people always did their nefarious business in the darkness, which was kind of weird, since there were no organized law enforcers… or laws. Some of the clans had tried to start patrols with volunteers. They typically didn't last long. Not many people were interested in risking their lives for others. And everybody stole from everybody, so no one wanted to enforce that. The old idea of "an eye for an eye" ruled the streets. Myri guessed that was why her dad did so well in the assassination business. Some people didn't want to get their hands dirty.

Myri ran through the streets. She didn't want to be distracted by anyone who would think her an easy target. She didn't have time to show them how wrong they were.

She reached the barricaded entry to Branch's clan's compound, an old high school, unsure exactly how to proceed. She'd never approached the entrance. Branch had always been out front waiting for her when she'd come during the day. He had no reason to think she'd be coming at this hour. Maybe she should just wait until daylight, then knock or something.

The sun peeked over the buildings on the east. Myri put her goggles on and tightened the strap around her head. She knew Branch would be up soon, working in his assigned garden. He preferred to work early in the day, when it was cooler and so he'd be done early enough to go do his own thing in the afternoon. She couldn't wait that long, though. She took a deep breath and stepped up to the doors, raising her hand to knock. She cocked her head to the side, listening. Faint even to her ears, she could hear someone yell for help… and it sounded like Branch. She listened for another couple of seconds. Other voices, threatening voices, were followed by sounds of a struggle.

Myri ran around to the side of the building, following the sounds. The top of a ladder stuck up a few inches above the inside of the tall wall. She glanced down at the ground where the ladder had been placed on this side and left marks in the dirt and gravel. They must have climbed up it on this side then pulled it over to climb down into the compound.

She adjusted the backpack so the straps hung over both shoulders instead of just one. She crouched then sprang up, grasping the edge of the twelve-foot wall. She pulled herself up then jumped to the ground on the other side, eyes scanning her surroundings before she even landed.

"Hey!" she yelled. A group of five, dressed all in black, including ski masks, spread out in one of the gardens. Two of them had Branch down on the ground, hitting and kicking him as he struggled to defend himself. "Hey! Get off of him!"

Myri covered the twenty yards between her and her friend in less than three seconds. She grabbed the first black-clad thug by the shirt and flung him ten yards behind her into one of his buddies that was digging something up from the garden. Myri turned and lifted the second attacker a couple of feet off the ground before body slamming her into the hard packed earth.

"Branch! Are you okay?" She knelt beside him and touched his shoulder.

Slowly, he uncurled from the fetal position. Blood dripped from his nose and one eye had already started to swell. "Myri? What…"

A flick of his eyes notified her that someone was coming up behind her. She jumped up to a crouching position and pivoted, sticking one foot out to sweep the legs out from under her would-be attacker.

Surprise registered on the large man's face as his feet flew into the air and he landed on his back with a whoosh of breath.

Myri stood and faced the aggressors, shielding Branch with her body. "You might want to gather your injured friends and get out of here while you can." Her voice shook, not from fear but from anger.

The teen boy nearest her looked at his three fallen comrades then narrowed his eyes at her. "How did you do that?"

"I'm stronger than I look." She stepped toward him.

"Yeah, well, I'm not scared of no little girl." He charged.

Myri met him with a flying double kick to the face. He dropped like a dead bug, out cold.

"What are you?" the big man on the ground said, still trying to catch his breath.

"I'm Myrikal."

A group of people burst out the back door of the compound, armed with everything from baseball bats to rakes and shovels. One woman even had a sawed-off shot gun.

"What's going on out here? Branch? You okay?" the woman in the lead asked.

Branch groaned as he pushed himself up to a sitting position, cradling his already hurt arm across his chest. "I will be. These guys in black attacked me and were trying to steal food. They trampled my garden."

"What about her?" She pointed her bat toward Myrikal.

"She's my friend. She saved me."

"You expect us to believe that scrawny girl did this to them?" another man asked, gesturing to the downed thugs.

Branch winced as he shrugged a shoulder. "Believe what you want. It's true."

The group of compound leaders encircled the intruders.

"Did she really do this to y'all?" an older man with a southern accent asked the large man Myri had leg-swept.

The man growled and narrowed his eyes at Myri. "Yeah. She did. She's a freak."

"Now that you guys have the thieves under control, is it okay if I check on Branch? Bandage his wounds and stuff?" Myri asked quietly.

"Uhh… yeah, sure, I guess." The lady with the bat looked around at her armed companions. No one seemed to have a problem with her decision.

Myri backed up then knelt beside Branch. "Where are you hurt?"

"Everywhere." He groaned and laid back down. "What are you doing here?"

She reached for his river creature-bitten arm. "I've been worrying about your arm all night. I wanted to come check on you." She dropped the backpack to the ground. "I brought some supplies."

Branch grasped her arm. "Don't get them out until the others leave," he whispered. "They'll try to take them."

"O…kay." She glanced at the crowd. The compounders were forcing the uninjured and less-injured thugs to carry the two unconscious ones. "Where are they taking them?"

"We have a place inside. Like a jail, I guess. They'll keep them locked up for a couple of days, try to scare them so they'll leave us alone and go after easier targets. Then let them go."

The group started filing into the building. "Want me to send Brenda out to check on you, Branch?" a man yelled.

"No. I'm fine."

The man raised an eyebrow and nodded before stepping through the door and closing it behind him.

"Let me see that arm." Myri held her hand out.

Branch stretched his arm toward her. Myri pushed his long sleeve up above his elbow and sucked in a breath at what she saw. His arm was swollen and red a couple of inches above the bite, all the way down to his fingertips. Pus and blood oozed from the puncture wounds. Myri lay her fingers on the red skin and frowned. "It's hot as the sun."

"Yeah," Branch said. "It's infected. I'm pretty sure I'm gonna' die."

Myri's frown deepened. "No. You aren't. I won't let that

happen." She unzipped her backpack and pulled out the water and clean cloths. "This might hurt." She poured the alcohol-water mixture on the puncture marks.

"Ow!" Branch tried to pull away, but she had a hold of his arm.

"I told you it might hurt."

"How do you know it hurts?" He scowled at her. "Nothing hurts you."

She dipped her head lower. He was right. She didn't know what pain felt like. Physical pain at least. "I've cleaned a lot of wounds for my dad. He always swears at me and stuff."

"I'm sorry, Myri. I didn't mean to snap at you. I promise not to swear at you."

She nodded without looking at him. She wiped the wounds with a clean cloth then repeated the procedure until the bottle was empty. Satisfied that it was as clean as it was going to get, she wrapped the gauze around it and secured it with tape. "I have a week's worth of penicillin here. You need to take one now and another one before you go to bed tonight. Then twice a day until they're gone."

His mouth fell open. He looked from the bottle she held and back to her face. "Where did you get penicillin? That stuff's like gold."

"It's one of the ways people pay my dad for… jobs he does. We have a ton of it."

"Don't go around telling people that. I've heard of people killing for this stuff."

Myri snort-laughed. The irony.

"Why is that funny?" Branch asked.

"It isn't." She picked up the other clean cloth she'd brought. "Now let me see what they did to your face."

"Dang it!" he said. "I just realized something. You saved my life again. Probably twice with the penicillin. I owe ya' another one.

I'm seriously never going to catch up at this rate. Myri-6, Branch-1."

⚡12⚡

The wounds on Branch's arm turned a corner after he'd taken the antibiotics for a couple of days. Myrikal impressed upon him the importance of finishing the course she'd given him. She put the fear into him when she told him his arm would have to be amputated if the infection came back.

It had been a few days since she'd last seen Branch. Russ kept her glued to his side more than usual, and she itched to get away and see her friend.

"What are we doing today?" she asked.

Russ rubbed his eyes then ran his hands through his messy hair. "I need to go meet with Roman about a job. Then we need to go pick up some supplies. We're running low on food. I'd like to find some of the fresh fruit and vegetables I've been hearing about."

Alarmed that he'd somehow found out about Branch's clan and their successful gardening, she asked, "Where did you hear that?"

"At the bar, where else?" He took a swig out of his flask and screwed the lid back on.

"Where are people getting it from?"

"I don't know. Some of the clans are apparently growing it. Go get ready We're leaving in five minutes."

He rarely took Myrikal with him when he met with Roman— the one and only liaison between prospective clients and Manhattan's best assassin. She figured he wanted to take her today so she could carry the supplies. Russ was in great shape for a man in his mid-forties, but more and more often, he made her do the heavy carrying. Why not? If you had access to a pack mule, you used it. It was the smart thing to do.

Myri sighed and trudged to her train car to grab her goggles and pull her hair back into a ponytail. Or a mule tail. She rolled her eyes at herself. *Dumb joke.*

⚡

THE KITTEN SWATTED at the feather Myrikal dangled in front of it. Myri smiled at its antics. Russ had been inside the "diner" for a while. Roman stumbled inside shortly after her dad. She leaned back against the brick wall and stared up at the cloudy sky. She smiled again when the kitten crawled into her lap and curled up into a purring ball of fur, worn out from its vicious attacks on the feather.

"Come on, let's go," Russ said.

She jerked, startling the kitten off her lap. It scurried into a pile of trash and disappeared.

"We're going to take a little detour before we go to Central Park. I have some recon to do for the next job." He headed off down the sidewalk.

Myri pushed to her feet and followed him. He'd never included her in "recon" before, and it scared her. She knew he'd been grooming her to join the "family business" her whole life, but she wasn't ready to participate. He'd told her he wouldn't give her her first job until she was fifteen. Hopefully he stuck to that. That gave her at least two more years to… to what? She wasn't sure. To conform to his heartlessness? To find a way out?

Lost in her thoughts, she almost bumped into Russ when he stopped walking. Her heart stuttered when she looked up. They'd stopped across the street from Branch's compound. Her father stood, examining it with intensity. Her fluttering heart nearly stopped when Branch came around the corner. He looked up and saw her and started to smile, raising a hand in her direction. She shook her head violently, whipping her ponytail back and forth like the winds of a hurricane. His smile dropped to a frown. He glanced at her father, then made an awkward pivot as if he'd meant to walk the other way the whole time.

"Russ." She swallowed. "What are we doing here?"

He stared down at her, eyes steely, then turned his head and watched Branch walk down the street. "You know that kid?"

Shoot. "No. I mean… I might have seen him around once or twice." She licked her suddenly dry lips. "He's not the… the target is he? I mean, he's just a kid…"

He focused his heartless gaze on her again. "Kids can be targets, too, Myrikal. They die just the same as adults." He narrowed his eyes. "Most of the time."

Instead of shrinking away from him as she usually did, she narrowed her eyes—imitating his look. She straightened her back and raised her chin. "Yeah. Some kids won't die, will they?"

His eyes widened almost imperceptibly. Was that a flicker of fear she saw there? He looked away from her abnormally unwavering stare. "C'mon. Let's go get some supplies."

She would not let her father kill Branch. No way.

⚡

MINUTES DRAGGED ON TO HOURS. Myrikal lay awake but feigning sleep in her train car. She lay still, listening for Russ. The quiet *swoosh* of his well-oiled door sliding open carried to her hypersensitive ears. She threw the thin blanket off and hurried to dress in the clothes Branch had given her. She'd cut the other sleeve off the hoodie to match the one she'd torn off to use for Branch's wound care, her scrawny arms hung bare. She counted to twenty slowly, hoping that was enough time for him to have turned the corner leading to the stairs. Shoving her hair into the hood, she cinched it down around her face and tied it under her chin. She didn't need to follow him. She knew where he was going and she knew she could get there before him. What she didn't know was how to get inside. Or how to find Branch once she figured it out.

Myri peered around the wall at the top of the stairwell. Her dad, long black trench coat flapping behind him, rounded the corner down the block. She took off running the other direction, turning down another block parallel to the one her dad strode down.

A single light waved in an upper window of the former high school turned compound. Myri pulled herself over the wall into the gardens and honed in on that window. That had to be him. Branch often stayed up late reading his comic books, and she'd just recently given him a candle and some matches. She'd been fast in getting there, but her dad couldn't be more than a few minutes behind her. Thankful for her slight frame, she climbed up the thick ivy vines growing up the brick face of the building.

Myri reached the third story window and peered inside. A candle flickered in the sectioned-off area of the former classroom. Branch's head tilted down, the top visible to Myri as he flipped through a comic book. She tapped on the cracked glass of the window. Branch jumped and his head flew up. He stared in the direction of the window. Myri realized he couldn't see her, hidden in the shadows.

Moving in slow motion, Branch laid the comic books aside and rolled off the side off the mattress. He crouched on the floor.

"Branch," Myri voiced in a loud whisper. "It's me, Myri."

Wary, he scooted over to the window, leaving the candle burning behind him. "What are you doing here? Are you okay?"

"I'm fine. You're not. You need to get out of here."

"Why? What's going on?" He struggled to open the window, pushing against the rotted wood of the sill.

Myri held to the vines with one hand and slid the window open with her other hand. She climbed through the open window and shielded her eyes from the flame of the candle. "I think you might be in danger. I'm positive *someone* here is in danger."

"What kind of danger? Should we wake everyone up?"

This was the only secret she'd kept from her friend. He'd asked multiple times what her father did, what he was training her to do. She'd always deflected his questions or just flat out refused to answer. She didn't want to tell him now. She drew in a deep breath and held it for several seconds before blowing it out through pursed lips. "Have you heard of Assassinator Anon…"

"The Assassinator? Of course I have. Everyone has. He's deadly."

Myri grabbed Branch's shoulders and stared into his eyes. "*He* is my dad." She let that sink in before continuing. "From what I can tell, someone contracted with him to *take care of* someone here. He's on his way."

Branch closed his gaping mouth and shook his head.

"Branch," Myri tightened her grip. "I think it might be you."

"Me? But… I'm just a kid. Why would someone…"

"You wouldn't be his first kid target."

"But why? What makes you think it's me?" His frown deepened.

"I don't know. I'm not even sure it's you. I just know it's someone here and we need to leave now!"

"And what? Just let him kill someone else in the clan? Myri—" He shrugged out of her grip and balled his hands into fists. "Can' you just stop him?"

Could she? Of course she *could*. The true question was *would* she? Would she be able to defy her father? Would the years o training and brainwashing and overlord-ship prevent her from doing the right thing? What *was* the right thing?

She heard his voice in her head, repeating his mantra he'c drilled into her her whole life.

People are evil.

We need to be the wolves.

We are *the wolves.*

Images flashed in her mind of all the horrible things he'd made her watch other people do. She slid to the floor and put her face in her hands. Did people deserve to die? Branch didn't deserve to die. Branch was good. He was her friend.

More mantras echoed in her head.

It's just a job.

Is the wolf bad who kills the baby deer for food?

People are evil.

Her dad's voice crashed off the inside of her skull like a boulder falling down a mine shaft.

"Myrikal," Branch pulled at her hands. "You can stop him. You have to stop him."

The terror-filled quiver in his voice bulldozed over the sound of her dad in her head. She wouldn't hurt Russ, but she *would* stop him. She grasped Branch's hands and lifted her head. "Okay."

She tensed the muscles in her legs and started to stand, only to be knocked to her butt by a blast that roared through the entire side of the building. Myrikal reached out, blindly searching for Branch, the brightness of the flames rendering her vision useless. "Branch?"

Cries of surprise, fear, and pain filled her ears from all corners of the large building. A second explosion detonated nearby. Myri cussed herself for not bringing her goggles as she groped around on the floor for her friend. Her hand collided with his bare foot. She felt her way up to his face and leaned in close with her ear next to his mouth. His breath brushed against her cheek and she released a frantic sob she'd been holding in.

"Branch?" Myri shook him gently. He didn't respond. The flames tore at the makeshift walls separating Branch's "room" from others. She lifted his much bigger body and flung him over her shoulder. The only way out now was through the window. Myri slid her free hand along the outside brick, feeling for the vines. Some had burned away and what remained wouldn't hold her weight alone, much less both of theirs.

She tried to shut out the screams as she squeezed through the window with her friend. She held tight to his flaccid body as she leaped to the ground three stories below. She let her knees absorb most of the jolt, trying to cushion the landing for Branch. She laid him on the ground and checked his breathing again. It seemed stronger and he moaned and moved his head away from the heat of the roaring fire.

"Branch?"

Still no coherent answer. Myri paused and listened. Worse than the screams and cries for help, now she heard only the sound of the crackling fire and crumbling building. A tear evaporated in the heat as soon as it spilled over. She lifted Branch back to her shoulder and ran. Her mind churned, a turmoil of scrambled thoughts, and she paid no attention to where she ran. The familiar form of the subway cars beneath the city loomed before her. Her feet had taken her home.

Branch stirred, moaning. Myri laid him on the small mattress she used as a bed. He opened his eyes and blinked several times. "Myri?"

She poured water on a cloth and dabbed at the red and partially blistered skin of his face. "Yes."

"What happened? Where am I?"

Myri clicked on a flashlight she'd set next to the bed so Branch could see. "You're at my place. Please don't talk for a minute. I need to go see if my dad's here. Understand?"

He nodded. Sudden realization lit up his eyes. "Your dad… he…"

"Shh!" Myri hissed, putting her finger to her lips. "I'll be right back."

Branch tried to push up to his elbows, but moaned and collapsed back down to the bed.

Myrikal snuck through to her dad's car. He wasn't there. He

hadn't returned from his stupid "job" yet. She made her way back to her room and knelt beside Branch. "He isn't back yet. He probably stopped at the bar to celebrate another job well done." She wiped a tear from her cheek.

"I don't remember exactly what happened." He looked up at her.

"Where are you hurt?" She picked up the wet cloth and returned to dabbing at his face and arms. A small cut oozed blood into his hair.

"Myrikal." He stopped her hand with his. "What happened?"

She set the cloth in her lap and looked down at her hands. "He blew it up. Burned it down. I got you out."

"What about the others?" He grunted as he pushed up to his elbows. "Myri. What happened to the others?"

All she could do was shake her head as the tears fell to her lap.

"Myri?" his voice rose, hysteria creeping in.

"Myrikal!" Russ's voice burst into the room a half-second before his body did.

She jumped to her feet and spun with her back to Branch. She spread her arms out in an inane attempt to hide him from her raging father. Not knowing what to say, she stayed silent.

"Who's that?" Russ's words slurred against his drunken tongue. He peered around Myrikal. "Is that the kid from that compound? The one you said you didn't know the other day?"

"He's hurt," she said. "I… I'm just cleaning his wounds for him." She side-stepped to block her father from getting closer to her friend.

"And what's he gonna' do for us?" He leaned toward her, the stench of his breath nearly knocking her off her feet. "We don't do things for free."

"He… he already paid. He gave me these clothes." She gestured to the hoodie and jeans she wore.

"The clothes I provide for you aren't good enough?" Anger lashed in his eyes and he stepped toward her.

She held her hands up. "They're great."

"Myrikal. Move." Russ tried to step around her, his narrowed eyes looking at Branch. "I need to finish the job I just got paid for doing."

Branch sat and pushed himself up against the wall.

"No." Myrikal raised her chin and kept her body between her dad and her friend.

Russ's eyes widened and his body wavered as he took a half-step back. "Are you going to stop me?"

"If I have to."

"Fine." He turned as if to go toward the door. Quicker than his drunkenness should have allowed, he grabbed the gun he always kept tucked into the back of his pants and brought it up, aimed at Branch's head.

As his trigger finger flinched, Myri moved to block the bullet and, without any forethought, shot electricity from her fingers straight into the barrel of the gun. Slow-motion to her eyes, the bullet and the spark met at the tip of the gun's barrel. A small explosion ripped the barrel to shredded metal, and shrapnel flew through the air. Russ swore and dropped the disfigured weapon. He cradled his bleeding gun hand against his chest.

"Come on, Branch. I'll walk you safely out," Myri said without taking her eyes off her father.

"If you leave, don't plan on coming back!" Russ yelled.

"I'll be back." She sighed. "You need that hand taken care of." *Besides, where else would I go?*

Russ stared at his daughter, but didn't reply.

Branch grabbed the flashlight and grunted as he struggled to stand. Myri reached to help him, but he jerked his arm away from her. She kept her gaze on her dad as she backed out the door behind the limping Branch.

She caught up to him and tried again to take his arm to help him walk, afraid he would pass out.

Branch pulled away from her. "Don't help me. You've done enough. Two more points for Myri," he said mockingly.

"Branch… I…" She raised a hand to touch his arm, then let it drop to her side. "I'm sorry."

The dim beam of the flashlight lit on a rat as it scuttled across the cracked concrete of the subterranean tunnel. Branch stopped and whipped around to meet her gaze, his bloody, tear-stained face a mask of hurt and anger. "I thought you were a superhero. Well, you're not. Superheroes save *everyone*, not just one stupid, chubby kid." He spun around and walked faster toward the stairs.

"I never said I was a superhero! I'm just a girl."

"Yeah. A girl who's training to be a cold-blooded killer like her father." The early morning daylight lit the stairs as he climbed out into the city.

"Wait, Branch." Myri stepped alongside him. "Where are you going to go?"

Handing her the flashlight, he said, "Does it even matter? Don't worry about it. Just go back to your murdering father. Make sure his hand is okay so he can murder more people. I'll survive. Or I won't. It doesn't matter."

The world closed in around her as her only friend walked away. The dim sunlight burned her eyes, but she didn't blink. She didn't breathe. She didn't go after him.

PART THREE
MYRIKAL, BRANCH, AND CENTRAL PARK

⚡13⚡

Central Park had been transformed. Or was being transformed. Myri sat atop the remains of a tall building, her legs dangling over the crumbling edge. The wall was still going up. That had been started only a few weeks ago, but the progress was amazing. She listened to the distant sounds of labor—pounding, sawing, men and women yelling over the din. The new clan was serious about their take-over of the park.

Myri sighed and shoved off the edge of the building, landing on the street fifteen stories down. She walked past the charred remains of Branch's old compound. The same gut-churning emptiness that had pierced her soul every time she thought of her former friend struck again. It had been almost two years. Her father hadn't let her out of his sight for the first six-months after he'd killed Branch's entire clan. The entire clan except Branch, the only one she'd been able to save.

Two things had stopped her from sneaking off to find him: fear that her dad would then be able to find him and finish the job she'd interrupted, and fear of Branch's rejection if she did find him. She didn't blame him for hating her, but hoped—against everything she knew in her heart to be true of this horrible world—that he would forgive her. So she'd spent the next six months looking for him covertly in the places she and her father had gone, hoping to just catch a glimpse of him. To know he was alive. But nothing. No sightings.

Russ eased up on her a little after that and she'd been able to search in earnest. She'd gone repeatedly to all the places they used to hang out and everywhere else she could think of that he might possibly go. Not a trace in two years.

She kicked a stone and watched it sail through a wall a block away. Not a trace. She hadn't been searching the last six months or so. At least, not intently searching. She always looked for him wherever she went. Always hoping to catch a glimpse of her friend if only to know that he'd survived.

Fifteen now, she'd grown out of the clothes Branch had given her. Had grown out of the ugly red unitards her dad insisted she wear. She looked down at the jeans and T-shirt she'd pilfered for herself. She'd discovered a lot of hidden treasures in the crumbled buildings no normal human dared or could enter.

Because their "home" in the subway cars had been "compromised" when she brought the injured Branch there, her dad insisted on moving. They still lived underground, just in a distant part of the city. She headed back that direction. Russ would be waiting for her.

⚡

"WHERE'VE YOU BEEN?" Russ asked in a carefully controlled tone.

His outward attitude had changed toward her since the Branch incident. She knew he still detested her, but he was wary now that she was getting older, now that she'd defied him once. He rarely spoke to her in the disrespectful way he always had before.

"Just out for a run." She dropped her goggles on the table. "They're almost finished with the wall around the park."

Russ shook his head. "That's ridiculous. Clans disgust me. What gives them the right to take over Central Park?" He smiled grimly. "Maybe we'll let them get all the hard work done, then you and I will take it from them."

"Like you took Branch's clan away from him?" Seeing the ruins of the compound again put her in a sour mood.

A flash of something—anger? fear? disgust?—sparked in his eyes. "Did you find him?"

"Do you think I'd tell you if I did?" Her dad usually steered clear of the subject of Branch.

Russ shrugged. "He's probably long dead, anyway."

"Yeah. Probably." Myrikal folded her arms and turned away from her father.

"Look," Russ said, "I don't want to fight with you. Let's go get some practice time in. I need your help with a job tonight."

She whipped her head around and stared at him.

"Don't worry," he said. "I just need you to be a lookout for me, alert me if someone's coming. You'll be away from the action."

He'd always told her she'd be ready to do jobs on her own when she was a around fifteen. She expected him to make the suggestion anytime, now that she was there. She took a deep breath to calm her rattled nerves. What did it matter? Helping him assassinate people was just as bad as doing it herself. He'd pounded it into her head her whole life that people were bad and not worth the guilt she felt. And… he was right. She'd seen nothing to prove him wrong in the last couple of years. This world sucked. Humans didn't care about each other. It was a do-whatever-you-needed-to-do-to-survive world. And Myrikal was a survivor if nothing else. "Whatever. Let's go, then."

She grabbed her goggles and pulled them over her head, letting them rest against her chest. The dim light of the flashlight her father needed to see with no longer bothered her sensitive eyes.

They trekked to the remains of Madison Square Garden, where her dad had told her a huge building had once stood where crowds of people went to watch sports games or concerts. It had been leveled in the 'quakes. Myrikal and Russ, mostly Myrikal, had cleared out an area hidden in the piles of rubble where they'd been going to practice.

"Okay." Russ stood atop a hill of bricks. "Let's practice with moving targets today." He flung a plastic disc into the air.

What used to take her several minutes—and an unhealthy build-up of anger, frustration, or fear—now occurred the instant she focused. Heat arose in her chest as the tingling sparks erupted from her fingertips. She flung her hands out and blasted the disc to smithereens only a couple of feet from where it had flown from Russ's right hand.

He stumbled backward, almost falling off the pile. "You're, uh… getting faster. Try not to take my hand off, please." He examined his scarred hand—scarred from his gun blowing up when he'd tried to shoot Branch.

"Sorry." She held onto the power, awaiting the next target. It came in the form of a dagger, thrown straight toward her face by her dad, using his left hand. Myrikal zapped it and it landed in a smoking heap of melted metal at Russ's feet.

"Okay, then." Russ looked down. "Remind me not to use my good weapons for practice anymore. But, then again, why worry about wasting them when I have a deadly, reusable, unbreakable weapon for a daughter?"

A weapon. Is that what she was?

For a short time, she'd believed she might be something more. She thought back to when Branch had shown her his comic books. *He'd* been convinced she was a superhero. Until she proved him wrong. "This really isn't challenging anymore. What else ya' got?"

"Nothing." He picked his way carefully down the pile of bricks. "Maybe we should rustle up a couple of river monsters for you to spar with."

She knew he was only half joking. "Been there, done that."

He stopped a few feet in front of her and studied her with his head tilted. "Well, I guess maybe it's time for the training to end."

A small sound of protest escaped her throat. What came after training? Playing in the real game. She didn't want to play in the real game. Did she? She forced the fearful, *pathetic* thoughts from her mind. It was just a job. Just a way to survive. They were the wolves. *She* was the wolf. She straightened her shoulders and stuck her chin in the air. "What now, then?"

A feral grin spread across his face. "Now, we wait for Roman to come through with another job."

⚡14⚡

A light rain drizzled from the low-lying clouds. Myri pulled her goggles off and let them hang around her neck. She still couldn't handle medium to bright light, but she'd slowly built up a tolerance to low light. She'd take her chances with the rare lightning strike. She could sense when it was building up in the clouds above, a powerful rush spread through her body just milliseconds before a bolt would strike. Just enough time for her to close her eyes. There had been no lightning with this meager storm, though.

She'd needed some fresh air. She and Russ would be going to the "diner" to meet with Roman later that evening. He'd come through with another job. This one would be hers.

She watched people as she walked the streets. Would one of these people be the one whose life she'd snuff out like the flame of a candle in less than twenty-four hours?

Most of the people didn't even look up as they passed. No one waved or smiled or even acknowledged her. As she observed those around her, she only saw negative interactions. One person accidentally bumping another and the bumped person reacting with a cuss word or obscene gesture. Cat-calls—of which she received many herself. Name calling and harassing of those less fortunate or different or crazy. Bullying. Nothing good happened in these streets. She concentrated on that instead of the queasiness in her stomach whenever she thought about taking a life. *Just think of them as monsters, like the one you killed to save Branch.*

Myrikal looked up, surprised to see she'd reached the edge of the large area of Central Park that was now walled-in. Why did one clan need so much room to themselves? She approached a small group of people working to reinforce the outer wall, intending to get some answers to her questions.

"Hey," she said.

They turned toward her. Her eyes zoomed in on one man in particular, crouched down, adding cement to the bricks at the bottom of the wall. Their eyes met and, after a slight hesitation, he jumped to his feet and stepped toward her. "Myri," he breathed.

She squinted her eyes, trying to reconcile this familiar but older face with the chubby boy she'd known as her only friend. "Branch?" She scanned his tall, muscular body before returning her gaze to his face.

He dropped the tool he'd been using and closed the distance between them. He embraced her, lifting her off her feet. "Myrikal! I… I can't believe it's you!" He set her down and held her at arms' length. "You've… uh… grown up a little." His eyes moved to take in her body. "Can't call you scrawny anymore."

"And, I can't call you chubby anymore." Myri started to smile but cut it short. "Where have you been? I looked all over for you."

He glanced at his companions then back at her. "Let's go for a walk."

"Okay…" A dozen different thoughts bounced around in Myri's head. Didn't he hate her? If he hated her, why did he hug her? Where had he been? Was he part of this new clan now? He'd grown up. How old was he now? Sixteen? He was cute. He'd hugged her. It felt good.

Myri shook her head to clear the jumbled thoughts.

"Are you okay?" Branch stared sideways at her.

"Uhh…" She hadn't been aware he'd been watching her as they walked away from the wall. She turned to face him full on, walking backwards. "Don't you hate me?" The words fell from her mouth like vomit.

A single drop of rain drizzled down the side of his face. He stopped and reached for her, his warm, calloused hand closed over hers. "No. Myri. I never hated you. I could never hate you." He paused and looked down at their clasped hands. "I forgave you almost the instant I turned to walk away from you that night."

"But… why?" Tears pushed at the backs of her eyes. "You were right to hate me."

"You didn't do anything wrong, Myrikal." He squeezed her hand. "I was angry and devastated and I took it out on you. You were… we were just kids. *You* didn't kill my clan."

"But my dad did. And I'm just like him." One tear pushed through and slid down her cheek.

"No…" Branch stepped toward her. "Myri, you haven't killed anyone, have you? Please tell me he hasn't made you start…"

"Not yet," she interrupted, "but I will." *Soon,* she thought. *Tonight.*

"Myri, look at me." He waited for her to comply before continuing. "You don't have to be what he wants you to be. You have other choices."

"What other choices? I'm not a superhero, Branch! You told me that yourself. I can't save people so I might as well do what I've been training for my entire life. People are all horrible anyway."

Branch frowned and spoke quietly. "Am I horrible, Myri?"

Her face twisted up. Confused thoughts invaded her mind. She'd spent the last two years hating herself and learning to hate everyone else in the world, too. Branch had left her and she deserved it. "No… no. Not you." She gripped his hand tighter and leaned in to whisper, "But I am." She pulled her hand away from his, spun around and pushed off into a fast run.

"Myri! Wait! Don't go! *Myrikal!*"

⚡

Russ almost had a smile on his face. "I got you something." He handed her a bag. "Tonight is the start of a great partnership. We'll work as a team just like your mother and I used to."

She stiffened. She held the bag limp in her hand, her lips slightly parted in surprise. He never talked about her mother.

"Open it, Myrikal. Consider it a late birthday present for your fifteenth birthday."

Frowning, she reached into the bag. A familiar cloth slid through her fingers. Lycra. He'd gotten her another unitard. She pulled it out and dropped the bag to the floor of the subway car. At least this one wasn't red. Not that it was much better. The long sleeved, full-length, body-hugging leotard was black with bright yellow bolts of lightning covering it front and back. She held it up to her five foot seven frame. "Umm… thanks? But I have clothes now."

"I know, and those are fine for everyday use. But I want you to stand out when we're doing jobs. I want people to see you coming and shake with fear. I want them to know they're about to be killed by Brannen and Brannen Assassination Associates, LLC. I want the witnesses to spread the word. It'll be your signature."

Whatever. She didn't really care. She'd be able to move around better in it, anyway. The flexible material was less restrictive. "Fine. Thanks. I'll go change."

"Wait, I have one more thing." He turned and grabbed something behind him and held it out to her.

She took the black wrestling-style boots from him and raised an eyebrow. She'd worn shoes off and on in her life, but she didn't need them, nothing could penetrate or injure her bare feet. "More of my signature?"

He nodded, a crooked grin causing the wrinkles at the corners of his eyes to deepen.

⚡

Myri stretched then jumped up and down, flexing her toes. The boots had thin, flexible soles that shifted well with her movements. Lacing them up was a pain, though. They came almost to her knees.

She stepped back into the shared subway car where her dad stood waiting. He nodded. "You ready? Did you decide how you're going to do it?"

She shrugged. "Electricity, probably." She'd been trying not to think about it. About anything. Images of Branch kept breaking through the carefully constructed barricade she'd been building in her mind her entire life, especially in the last couple of years.

She silently repeated her dad's mantra.

People are bad.

It's just a job.

Be the wolf.

Predator not prey.

"Let's go," she said, the silver streak in her hair glinting with the light from Russ's flashlight as she turned toward the door.

⚡15⚡

The End of Times bar teemed with occupants. Russ scowled as they stepped through the door. "What the hell? There are never more than a couple of people here." He pushed his way around a couple that stopped to stare at Myrikal.

Myrikal followed her father to the back, near the kitchen where he "persuaded" a man to move to a table across the room by showing him the loaded gun at his hip.

Russ said, "Sit at this booth behind me until you see Roman come in, then move over here with me."

She nodded and scooted into the seat. She lowered her head to her hands and tried to crush the brooding thoughts floating around inside. *You have other choices.* Branch's words kept invading her mind. *Do I?* Every time she thought about "other choices" her heart started racing. The beats pounded a rhythm inside her skull.

"*Ahem.*" Russ cleared his throat.

Myri looked up. Roman mumbled to himself as he made his way toward them. Myrikal slid out of the booth and sat across from her dad.

A waitress approached as soon as Roman was seated. Her mouth turned up in a grimace that was probably supposed to be a smile. "What can I get for you Mr. B?" She glanced askew at Myri. "And your… friend, here."

"Daughter. And just bring two of the usual." His eyes flicked to

Roman then back to the waitress. He stopped her with a hand on her arm as she turned to walk away. "What's with all the people here?"

The waif-like server shrugged. "They're from that new clan in Central Park. They actually pay with gold coins."

Russ scowled as he looked out on the crowd.

Myrikal had only come to these meetings a few times with her father, and she'd never actually gone inside the bar with him. The waitress nodded and scurried away, glancing nervously back at Roman when he yelled out, "Shut up! I need to concentrate!"

Balancing three whiskey glasses in her hands, the waitress served Russ first, then Myri, before warily setting the third glass in front of the crazy. "Let me know if you need anything else," she said to Russ.

Roman licked his lips and cracked his knuckles before reaching for the glass.

"No, Roman." Russ smiled at Myrikal like they were having conversation. "Not until you give me the information."

"Yeah… yeah. I got it, boss." He licked his lips again. "I got it."

"Focus, Roman. Who and where. That's all I need to know."

"Yeah… yeah. Okay." He pounded a fist into the side of his head a couple of times. "Name's Megan. Blonde hair. Twenty-five or so." He dug around in his jacket pocket then threw a crumpled paper on his table. "There. There's the where. And stuff. Other stuff." He reached for the whiskey and tossed it down his throat.

Myrikal stared at the glass of amber-colored liquid in front of her. The strong scent burned her nostrils and she pushed it away, wondering if maybe she should choke the vile stuff down. Wondering if it might help to numb her near apathetic emotion even further. Close the lid on the coffin where her concern for humanity still existed as just a spark of what it used to be. She shook her head. "Are we done here? I'd like to get this over with."

Russ cocked his head to the side. "There was a time I wondered if this day would ever come. I'm glad you got over your misgivings about the family business."

Stomach churning, Myri stood. She swiped the crumpled paper off Roman's table as she stormed toward the exit, not waiting to see if her dad followed.

Outside, she hid beneath the building's eave and straightened out the paper with her shaky hands. She noted the information then handed it to her dad as he walked out the door.

He glanced at it and shoved it in his pocket. "You ready?"

Afraid her voice would shake and reveal to him her frayed nerves, she just nodded.

"Follow me." Russ took off at a jog.

To keep her mind off the grisly task ahead, Myrikal counted the number of steps she took to reach the point of no return. Her mind still snuck in thoughts around the rote counting. Once she'd spilled innocent blood she could never turn back. Her father would say there was no such thing as innocent blood. Blood was just blood. People were just people. And people deserved to die if they were too weak to protect themselves. Myrikal pulled her goggles up and settled them over her eyes, tightening the cord behind her head. She didn't need them in the dark of night, but she wanted to hide her eyes from her dad, from the world.

Russ ducked into an alley next to a former fire station. Warn-down letters and a faded sign designated it as "Engine 6."

"Okay," he whispered as soon as Myri joined him. "The blonde girl named Megan is your target. What are you going to do if there are other people in there?"

They'd been over this multiple times. Myrikal sighed and rubbed her temples. "I leave them alive. You… *we* want to have witnesses to spread the word." Her mind split off into two different directions. One side focused on the job—what she planned to do, what she planned to say. The other, quieter side, whispered her father's mantras. *People are bad. We are the wolves. It's just a job. People are all bad.*

A weak cry followed by a loud bark reunited her mind into one, focused entity. She slid back out into the street, holding up a hand to her dad to quiet his coming protest. She crossed the street, made up of cracked asphalt and fallen debris, and snuck quietly up to the broken building the sound had come from.

Inside, a small girl cowered in a corner, tears streaked through the dirt covering her face. A large dog stood in front of her, protecting her frail body with his massive one. His lip curled into a snarl and low, guttural growls sounded in his throat. In front of the dog and the girl stood a boy, maybe ten-years-old, scrawny arms and torn clothes. Blood dripped from his nose and a cut over his eyebrow. His back to the girl, he faced a trio of aggressors twice his size. "Leave her alone." His voice quivered.

"We ain't gonna' hurt her," one of the men said. He sneered. "Promise."

"Yeah, yeah," a woman with crazed eyes said. "She'll *enjoy* her new home… and bring in lots a money and goods for us." Her voice cracked with wicked laughter.

A quiet whimper escaped the girl and she buried her face in the dog's thick fur.

The man stepped toward the boy, hands balled into fists. "Now outa' my way and call off that dog or I'll slit its throat and eat it for dinner."

The little boy stood his ground. His hands shook as he raised his arms as if to ward off the imminent blows.

"Stop!" Myri's firm voice carried over the whimpering girl and the growling dog, bringing everyone within earshot to stand still as statues.

"Who's there?" the third man, standing back a few feet from the other two adults, asked. He squinted and shoved a burning torch in Myri's direction.

"I'm Myrikal." She stepped into the circle of flickering light. "And I suggest you leave. Now."

All but the little girl turned toward her and stared. The first guy, the one closest to the boy, looked Myrikal up and down and licked his lips. "Well, well, well. What have we here?"

He took a step toward her and she put her hands on her hips. A breeze flew through the doorless entry where she stood, blowing her hair around her face and shoulders.

"You're what?" the man asked. "Fourteen? Fifteen? You'll bring a nice price on the market, too." He glanced at the little girl. "Not as nice as that one. My clients like 'em young."

"Shut. Up." Myri ground her teeth. "You get one chance to leave and I suggest you run."

The two men snickered, but the woman's eyes widened. The man near the boy started to speak, "If you think…"

Myrikal didn't let him finish. She leaped from five yards away and struck him in the jaw with her foot. His head whipped back and his feet lifted off the floor. He landed in a crumpled heap in front of his female companion.

Myri stood in a crouch between the nasty trio and the kids. She flipped her hair back. The quick movement enough to break through the shocked fog of the two still standing.

"We're leaving!" The female shrieked. "Can we…" She shot a quick glance at their fallen companion.

"No." Myri cut her off. "Leave him and go."

The two miscreants scrambled for the exit, the female looking back only once.

Myrikal knelt in front of the young boy. "You are very brave. What's your name?'

He sniffed and smeared the blood from his nose across his tattered sleeve. "Dal." He blinked back tears and his body trembled as the adrenaline storm subsided.

"And what's her name? Is she your sister?"

Another sniff. Dal shook his head. "I don't know her name. I just heard her cryin' and me and Lobo came to see what was goin' on."

"Lobo's the dog?"

He nodded.

"And you don't know this little girl?" Myri gestured to the small girl who peeked up over the dog's back with her dark brown eyes.

Dal shook his head and slowly slumped to the ground. He wrapped his arms around his bent knees. "I thought they were gonna' kill me. Or worse."

The dog whimpered, looking back and forth between the little girl, still holding tight to his coat, and the boy.

"Why don't you come over here with us, sweetheart," Myri said. "I think Lobo wants to come to his boy."

Lobo twisted his head around and licked the little girl's face. She smiled a little then pulled herself up to stand next to the big dog. Her clothes, though dirty, weren't ragged or worn looking. She shuffled over to stand beside the boy, looking up at Myri with her big eyes.

"Are you okay?" Myri asked.

The girl nodded. She looked up at the bigger boy then wrapped her arms around him in a quick embrace.

Dal blushed and patted her on the shoulder. "I'm glad you're okay."

"What's your name, sweetheart?" Myri asked.

The girl frowned and shook her head, motioning to her mouth.

"Can't you talk?" Dal asked.

Another shake of her head.

Myrikal and Dal looked at each other. "Do you have a family?" Myri asked.

The girl nodded with a smile.

"Can you take us to them?" Myri asked.

The girl nodded.

Myrikal turned to Dal. "What about you, Dal? Do you have a family?"

"Nah." He shrugged. "My dad got sick and died last year. Lobo and I just live on the streets."

"Myrikal," Russ yelled. "What are you doing?"

She turned to the open doorway and scowled. "I'm *helping*."

Russ stepped inside. "How many times…"

For the second time in as many minutes, Myrikal held a hand up to her dad, cutting off his lecture. "You kids wait here. I'll be right back." She smiled at the girl. "Dal and I will walk you home, make sure you're safe."

The girl smiled back and ran her hands through Lobo's soft fur.

Myrikal stood and spun to face her father. She caught the slight cringe in his shoulders as she approached at a quick clip. "You were wrong. We are not wolves. We are humans, and not all humans are evil." She gestured behind her. "That young boy and his dog hold more compassion in their little toes than you have in your entire body."

"Myrikal, listen…" Redness flushed his neck and rose up into his face.

"No, you listen." She stepped closer and pushed him back a step with one finger to his chest. "I'm done with you. I'm not going to follow in your footsteps." She leaned in and whispered near his ear. "And I *will* stop you from doing your *job* whenever and wherever possible."

Spittle flew from his bottom lip as he yelled, "You are my daughter! You have to do what I say! You… you have nowhere else to go."

Myrikal smiled. "Nice try, *Dad*. But I do have somewhere else to go."

He cringed at her use of the title he'd forbidden her to use her entire life. He opened his mouth to speak again, but Myri shoved him before any sound came out. She watched as he landed, sprawled on the asphalt half-way across the street.

"Leave now. Tonight's job has been cancelled." Her strong voice carried even though she didn't yell.

Moaning, Russ dragged himself to his feet. With one half-enraged, half-fearful look over his shoulder before heading off, he limped down the mostly deserted street, away from Engine 6. Myri watched until he was a safe distance away.

"Okay," Myrikal nodded at the little girl, "you lead the way."

She led them on a twisting path through the city to the outskirt of where most people lived. Even Myrikal had trouble keeping track of all the changes in direction.

The eastern horizon showed signs of lightening with the approaching dawn by the time the little girl stopped in front of a large wall of loose rocks interrupted by a steel gate. She pulled three times on a cord partially hidden in a crevasse. A distant bell chimed within the perimeter of the wall.

A middle-aged woman, flanked by two large men, hurried to the gate.

"Chansong!" The woman rushed forward, tears springing to her eyes as she reached to open the gate. "Where have you been?" She pried the gate open on its rusty hinges and knelt to receive the little girl into her embrace. The two men stood behind her, intent on not allowing the strangers to enter.

Dal looked down and shuffled back and forth.

Myri crouched down to talk to the woman. "We found her in the city. Is she your daughter?"

The woman grabbed Myri's hand and squeezed. "Yes, yes Thank you so much! She loves to wander around, but she'd never been out past dark before. She's always home before then. I was so worried."

"There were some people trying to take her." Myri stood and put her hands on Dal's shoulders. "Dal and his brave dog protected her."

Dal found his voice. "We tried, but Myrikal is the hero. You should have seen her bash that guy's head in with a flying kick!"

"Well, I thank you. All three of you."

"What clan is this?" Myri asked. "I didn't think there were any out this far."

"We're one of the repopulation clans. Women and couples who find themselves with child come here."

One of the burly men spoke up. "We protect them. Not many people are fertile since the 'quakes. It's important to ensure the human race continues." He shrugged. "Who knows, maybe someday we'll get back all that we've lost."

"What's your story, brave young man?" Chansong's mom asked Dal.

He shrugged, his previous shyness returning.

Myri answered for him. "His name is Dal. He's an orphan, living on the streets."

"Oh! That won't do!" Chansong's mom said. "That won't do at all! You can come live with us, Dal. You can be Chansong's big brother."

The tension flowed out of his shoulders where Myri still rested her hands, but returned when he looked at Lobo. "What about my dog?"

The big guy holding the gate open replied, "He's welcome, too. Dogs are great protectors and are usually pretty good at finding their own food."

"Okay then." Dal smiled, the dried blood on his face cracking. "I always wanted a little sister."

"And what about you… Myrikal? Do have somewhere to call home?" Chansong's mom asked.

"I do." At least she hoped she did.

They said their goodbyes and Myri watched the five of them—six, counting Lobo—walk away behind the big gate. She took a deep breath and tightened the goggles around her head, then headed out to find Branch.

16

E ven sitting out in the rain, back pressed against the newly
constructed wall in Central Park, Myrikal felt better than she
ever had. At least as far back as she could remember. She'd broken
through the barricade of apathy and anger Russ had been building
in her head and heart for her entire life. And she'd done it before
making the terrible mistake of killing an innocent person. Or a
not-so-innocent person.

Did it really matter? Unless she had to kill in order to save
someone's life, she wouldn't do it. She wouldn't kill people. It was
wrong, no matter what her dad said.

She could easily get into the new compound, but she didn't
want to start out with a bad first impression. She'd wait for Branch
to come out. Hopefully that would be sometime today instead of
days from now. Either way, she didn't care. She smiled as she
watched a couple of small birds building a nest in the top of the
tree whose branches kept most of the drizzling rain from hitting
her.

The rain grew heavier and the sky darker. She could only
remember one other time the rain fell in sheets like this, years ago. A
bolt of lightning lit up the sky, a boom of thunder following almost
immediately after. Myrikal's hair stood up at the roots and her skin
tingled, alive with electricity. Almost in a trance, Myri stood and

walked, then jogged, then ran toward a small clearing rimmed by the tallest trees. She stood in the middle, arms spread wide and face tilted up to the sky and called down the lightning to her. There was no other way to describe it. Her very being connected to the charges preparing to release. Her skin crackled in preparation. A primal roar built in her lungs and she released it to the sky just before the lightning struck—a bolt to each of her outstretched hands.

She drew the energy in, eyes shut tight, lungs full, and heart beating a rhythm matching the patter of rain about her. The split second the lightning joined with her seemed like an eternity. She stood, arms still flung wide, and her muscles strengthened, her mind grew more aware, her blood pumped fiercer through her veins. Pure ecstasy.

"Myri?" Branch's worried voice penetrated her trance. "Myrikal, are you okay?"

Blinking, Myri took a deep breath and relaxed her tense muscles, letting her arms drop to her sides. She smiled and focused her vision on Branch and his companions. "I'm more than okay for the first time in my life."

Mouth twisted to the side, Branch's brows drew together. "That's... good. What... uh... what are you doing here? And, what was that all about?" He gestured hesitantly at the cloud darkened sky.

"I..." Myri looked around at the small group that had gathered. "I came to see exactly what you meant when you said I have other choices'. And that?" She gestured the same way he did. "I'm not exactly sure. It was like instinct, and now I feel amazing and full of energy and light."

A cautious smile replaced the concern on his face. "Well, let's go somewhere and talk, then." He touched her arm, then jerked his hand away as a strong static-like shock passed between the two of them.

"Oh, sorry!" Myri frowned. "Are you okay?"

"I'm fine. Just a little *shocked* to see you." He wiggled his eyebrows.

"Ha, ha." She rolled her eyes.

Branch looked back over his shoulder at the gathered crowd. "You guys go ahead and get started without me. I'll be back in a while." He cautiously took Myrikal's arm, minus the shock this time, and led her away from the group.

They walked for a few minutes, ending in an area recently cleared of brush and debris. To Myrikal's surprise, a newly constructed picnic table—the likes of which she'd only ever seen in pictures or as broken pieces of jagged wood that had been chopped to bits to be used as firewood – waited there. "Where did this come from?" She looked around, sure she'd been in this area before.

"The clan built it. Hopefully it'll last longer than the last one. Trying to keep people from destroying things outside the wall has proven to be difficult."

"That doesn't surprise me one bit."

"So," Branch sat on the rain soaked bench, "what's going on with you?"

Myri, too hyped-up to sit, stood in front of him. "I didn't do it. I didn't kill anyone." She frowned. "I almost did. I was going to, but something happened that stopped me just moments before…"

"What happened? What stopped you?" Branch asked.

"I helped someone. Saved someone. But," she flung her leg over the bench and sat facing him, her legs bouncing up and down. "I don't think that's what stopped me—at least not completely. What stopped me was that *someone else* was trying to help first. He was getting his butt kicked, but he was still trying. Him and his dog." She shook her head as the recent event played in her head. "He didn't have a chance, didn't even know the little girl, but it didn't stop him from trying."

"That's great, Myri. But why did that stop you?"

She spread her hands wide. "Because! Don't you see? People

aren't all bad, they are worth saving. My dad was wrong. It gave me the push I needed to break away from him."

"Well," a wry smile touched his lips, "I think someone tried to tell you that."

Myri leaned forward and threw her arms around Branch. "I know. You are a big part of this, too. I kept thinking about what you said yesterday."

Face flushed with a combination of embarrassment and excitement, she pulled away and jumped to her feet again, splashing water from a puddle onto Branch's legs.

Laughing, Branch said, "I've never seen you quite this animated. I like it."

"I feel like I've been living in a bank of fog and I've just found my way out." She sat down again. "I know this world is still a mess. It's just not nearly as bad as my dad brainwashed me into believing."

Branch nodded. "So, what's the plan, now?"

"I'm not exactly sure. Tell me about your clan? And, while you're at it, tell me where you disappeared to the last couple of years."

His eyes lit up and he leaned forward. "After… uh… my old clan was killed. I tried to find you, but you'd already evacuated your train cars. So I left the city for a while. I just wandered around, nearly starving, not caring."

"That sounds pleasant," Myri interrupted.

"Yeah, it wasn't great. But then I found Cascus. Or he found me."

"Who's Cascus?"

Branch drummed his fingers on the table top. "He's the leader of The Clan of the People, the COP. I was his first associate. We kind of built it up together."

"Clan of the People, huh. What's the focus of this clan?"

"The main purpose is to rescue people."

"Rescue them from what?" Myri asked.

He shrugged. "Anything. Themselves, abusive situations, other clans, living on the streets. We want to return the world to what it was like before the 'quakes, only better. Cascus has a great vision, and he's making it happen." Branch gestured at the picnic table.

Suspicion crept up in Myri's mind. "This picnic table is great and all, but it isn't exactly world changing."

Undeterred, Branch continued. "It's just a small part of his plan. He says that people forgot what it was like to make things and how good it feels to take pride in our surroundings. Myri," he grabbed her hand, "you should see what we've done inside that wall!"

Yeah, the wall. "How many people are in your clan? That wall went up awfully fast."

Branch looked away and dropped her hand. "Cascus has asked us to keep some details within the clan." He paused. "But I trust you, so I'll just say more than thirty but less than a hundred."

She rolled her eyes. "Why keep secrets?"

"It's for our protection. He says that the less outsiders know about us, the better. He's afraid that some of the people we've rescued would be in danger if their prior acquaintances knew enough about us."

Myri nodded slowly. "I guess that makes some sense. My dad's paranoia made for some pretty strict safety rules growing up."

"Any more questions?" he asked.

"You said the *main* purpose of the clan is to rescue people. What are the other purposes?"

He swept his hand back toward the compound. "Rebuilding. Starting the cleanup that should have happened a couple of decades ago. It's far past time to start *living* again instead of just existing as we have been. Cascus gives us jobs with a purpose."

"What kinds of jobs?" Myri thought about the "job" her dad had raised her to do. Not all jobs were created equal.

Branch sighed. "It'll be easier for me to show you. Let me g make sure Cascus is okay with me showing you around." He stood. "I'll be right back."

Running her hand along the top of the table, Myri bent to examine it closer. The boards were new. She inhaled deeply, the aroma of fresh cut wood making its presence known. They'd used power tools to construct it. How else could they have cut the boards so even? She straightened up. Myri hoped Branch would gain permission for her to go inside the walls. Otherwise, she'd have to go in without permission. She needed to see what was going on in there.

"Right back" ended up being quite a bit longer than the words implied. Myrikal had time to pull her wild hair back into a braid, the silver streak weaving in and out like a sparkling ribbon. And to wear down the ground around the picnic table with her constant movement.

The soft crunch of Branch's feet on the vegetation alerted her of his pending return long before she caught sight of him on the curving trail.

"Good news, Myrikal!" he said as he bounded into the clearing. "Cascus says you're welcome to tour our compound. He's hoping we can talk you into staying a while, maybe even join us."

His giant smile revealed a dimple in his left cheek that she'd never noticed before. She smiled back, but it soon turned to a thoughtful frown. Her hope, when coming here in the middle of the night, had been that she'd be welcomed. That she'd find a new home here with her only friend. Doubts crept in. "He made that offer without even meeting me? Does he let everyone in like that?" There were definitely people she'd want to keep out of a clan whose purpose was to regrow civilization. People like her dad.

"No, of course not." He furrowed his brows. "I may have told him about you before." He looked down, digging at the ground with his foot. "In fact, I may have talked to him a lot about you in the beginning, when it was just him and me."

"What did you tell him?"

"Almost everything." Branch glanced up and met her eyes for a split second before returning his gaze to the ground. "Everything except the one thing I promised you I would never tell anyone."

Myrikal thought about all the things Branch knew about her, sure it was her one weakness he had kept to himself. "He knows that my dad killed your entire clan and I couldn't stop him? He knows I was supposed to be an assassin?"

Branch nodded. "You were just a kid when your dad set off that explosion. You saved *me*. Cascus understands that you have no control over who your parents are or how you were raised. What matters is who you are now and the choices you've made."

"Did he see… does he know about what happened with the lightning earlier?"

"Yeah, he knows. He didn't see it, but news of impossible feats travels fast."

"And that doesn't scare him?" Myri asked.

"Not at all. He's fascinated with you." Branch jerked his head back toward the compound. "On that note, let's go see what he's built here, we shouldn't keep him waiting."

The exhilaration she'd felt after harnessing the power of the lightning, faded to an almost imperceptible pulsation. Why shouldn't they keep him waiting? Was she jumping from one tyrannical situation to another? She really didn't want another person telling her what to do and think and feel. She'd just freed herself from Russ and she wanted to *stay* free. She hesitated as Branch started walking.

Branch stopped and looked over his shoulder at her. "What's wrong?"

She sighed. "This is all happening too fast, I think."

He walked back to where she stood and draped an arm around her shoulders. "We don't have to go tour the compound right now if you don't want to. I thought you wanted to see it. I'm sorry."

Myri rested her head on his shoulder. "No, I'm sorry. I'm just little nervous. I haven't exactly interacted with many people in my life."

"Yeah, I never really thought about that. I've always been a talker. It's gotten me in trouble a few times." He squeezed her shoulders and laid his cheek on her head. "It's your call, Myri. You tell me what you want to do."

"What if I say I want just the two of us to go live somewhere?" Myrikal whispered.

Branch's muscles tensed and he held his breath for several heartbeats. He finally exhaled. "I'd do that if you really want to, but I really want you to give the COP a chance." He moved to stand in front of her and took her by the upper arms. "I know you aren't used to being around people, Myri. But you can get used to it. Heck, you might even decide you like it." He smiled.

That mischievous smile brought back a flood of memories of the times she'd been able to sneak away from Russ to go hang out with Branch when they were younger. Before her murderous dad had ruined everything. "If it'll make you happy, I'll give it a try. Just don't leave me alone with anyone."

"It's a deal. Ready?"

Myrikal swallowed and nodded. A little bit of her earlier excitement at the new adventure and freedom started to return, dampening her apprehension. If this turned out to not be her "thing", she could set out on her own and Branch would come with her. That's all she needed to think about.

A rush of warmth flooded up her arm as her best friend—her only friend—grabbed her hand and walked toward his home.

⚡

THE THUNDERSTORM BLEW past and Myri stood with Branch on the cusp of several large fields, each showing signs of new plant growth. "How long have you guys been working on this?" She'd only noticed the wall going up a few weeks prior, but the work that had been done there had to have taken longer than that.

"A couple of months." He looked over the fields, a gleam of pride in his eyes. "It's amazing how fast things get done when you have a large group working together."

"But this whole area is transformed. It's unrecognizable from the park I've always known."

"In a better way, I hope?" Branch glanced down at her.

"Oh, yes. It looks like the pictures I've seen of what the earth looked like before the 'quakes."

Beaming, Branch nodded. "We started by clearing out all the dead trees and bushes. We cut and piled the wood to use for fires and other projects. We tore down the living trees and dug up the ground here so we could plant food." He nodded to the right. "Cascus even designed a greenhouse for us to grow stuff in during the colder months."

"What's a greenhouse?" Myrikal wrinkled her nose.

"I'll show you when we tour that side of the compound. It's a building with special plastic covering it to keep the warmth in so the plants will grow. Cascus knows all kinds of things about… well, about everything, really."

"Too bad he was called away before I could meet him," Myr said, not at all thinking it was too bad.

"You'll get a chance to meet him soon, I'm sure."

Knowing how much Branch loved growing things and talking about growing things, Myri said, "Tell me about what you're growing here. I assume you've had a big hand in this part of the creation—or, re-creation—of how things were."

"Come on, I'll show you." He grabbed her hand and pulled her closer to the fields full of neat rows of growing vegetation.

No fruit or vegetables blossomed from the budding greenery yet, but every row had something peaking up from the rich soil. Myrikal drew in a deep breath, the scent of fresh turned earth and budding plants a new and pleasant odor.

"I think I told you once about which plants grow better in dim light. That's all we've planted here for now, but Cascus has a plan to create enough light to grow some of the other stuff…"

"What…"

"Don't ask. He hasn't even told *me* his plan, just that he's working on one."

Branch showed her the rows of blackberry and raspberry bushes, and strawberry and rhubarb plants. Several rows of tiny trees, just breaking through the ground, were labeled as "cherry" and "pear." The large field next to the bushes contained lettuce, radishes, carrots, potatoes, spinach, beets, cabbage, cauliflower, celery, and peas. Myrikal had only a vague idea of what most of the vegetables were, and hadn't tasted any of them fresh from the ground. Except for the strawberries Branch had given her to celebrate her thirteenth birthday.

"This really is amazing." Myri touched his arm. "And those little houses you're all building…"

"You wanna' go see mine? I used both logs and rocks to build it." He beamed. "I wanted it to be all new, so I didn't use any of the reclaimed materials."

"Of course I want to see it." She'd been entranced by the layout of actual dirt roads between the tiny houses, like a real neighborhood. The idea of everyone not just having their own place to call home, but building that place from scratch instead of just claiming a spot in some old building, exhilarated her.

Branch's steps sped up. "You can stay with me while we build you your own house. *If* you decide to stay, that is."

She'd been absolutely sure she wouldn't want to join his clan when they'd still been standing on the other side of the wall. Now, after seeing everything they'd been able to build in the short time they'd been there, after seeing the cute little houses… "I'm still not a hundred percent sure, but I think I'd like to give it a try. Maybe."

"Haha," he laughed. "Way to commit, Myri." He grabbed her hand and turned down a little dirt road.

"How big is this place? The compound? It looks a lot bigger than I thought Central Park was."

They stopped in front of a small house that smelled of fresh cut trees.

"The park itself is about two-and-a-half miles long and a half mile wide. We're using about two-thirds of that. Cascus wanted to leave a little bit outside the walls for the people of Manhattan." Branch let go of her hand and reached to open the door.

"And you all are cleaning up out there, too?" She remembered the newly constructed picnic table.

Branch nodded. "It's important to Cascus that we show benevolence to everyone."

"Benevolence?"

"Yeah." He shrugged. "It means kindness, basically. He says it's the only way to rebuild and win people over without violence. Show them kindness, show them what stability looks and feels like, and they'll want to join us."

"That's what he wants? More people to join you?"

The whisper of wood on wood wafted in the air as he pushed the door open and gestured for Myri to go inside. "Yes. That's what he wants. Rebuild, protect, and reinvent humanity. It's a lofty goal."

Something he'd said scraped at the edges of her mind—"without violence." She lost her train of thought when she stepped through the doorway. Branch's little house was amazing. Just what she imagined homes before the 'quakes looked like, before all the death and destruction. Before people stopped caring about anything but where their next meal would come from. Before the word "home" was lost to the need to find shelter anywhere possible.

Two small windows allowed the scant light from the shadowed sun to shine inside. Two *unbroken*, clean windows. It took her a minute to figure out what was different about the smell, besides the newness of everything. No dust. No mold. No mouse or rat drop-pings. Myrikal closed her eyes and inhaled deeply.

"What do you think?" Branch interrupted her thoughts.

Eyes sparkling, she answered, "It's amazing."

A huge smile cut across his face, revealing the dimple in his cheek. "Wait 'til you see the rest of it. Come on."

He grabbed her hand and led her further inside. "I found this couch and that chair," he pointed to the furniture, "in an aban-doned office building. I stripped them down to the bare bones and then re-upholstered them. There's all kinds of unused material out there because nobody has the desire to make anything new."

"Or they just don't know how." Myri marveled at the job he'd done. "How did you figure out how to do all this?" She made a wide, sweeping gesture to take in the entire house.

Branch shrugged. "A little bit from books, but mostly from Cascus. He seems to know everything." He pulled her into the small kitchen area. "Like this," he pointed at the sink. "Before we even started building, he had us lay down pipes so we could have running water."

"Where does the water come from?" She wrinkled her nose, thinking about the dirty, slimy water in the rivers and ponds nearby.

"We built a water tower. With a filtration system." He turned the faucet on and clear water flowed from it. "We don't even have to boil it before drinking it."

She'd never had to do that anyway because she didn't get sick, but her father had to. "Wow. Where did you say Cascus is from?"

"I didn't." He looked away from her. "He says he doesn't remember. He only remembers the 'quakes and the sickness after-ward, nothing before that."

"Do you believe him?"

A flash of something—anger maybe? or defensiveness?—lit up his eyes for a brief moment. "Of course I do. Why wouldn't I? Why would he lie about that?"

"Chill, dude." Myri smiled. "It just seems odd, is all."

He raised an eyebrow at her and his mouth twitched as if he was trying not to laugh. "*Chill dude?*"

Myri shrugged. "I heard it on the street. It seemed fitting for the situation."

A pounding on the door limited his retort to a rolling of the eyes. "Come in," he said.

"Hey, Morgan." The blonde girl, maybe a little older than Myrikal, looked her up and down with a quick glance before turning her full attention on Branch. "The boss wants to see you." She flicked her eyes at Myrikal again. "Alone."

⚡17⚡

Morgan? Myrikal thought back to when they'd first met. Was that Branch's real name? Myri stole a quick peek at the girl. Was that makeup she was wearing?

"Hey, Myri," Branch said. "I'll be back in a few. I know I said I wouldn't leave you alone with anyone, but maybe Alyssa can finish showing you around and I'll meet you back here?"

Myri nodded. "Yeah, okay. See you then." What should she do? Should she smile at the girl? Introduce herself? Her awkwardness had only gotten worse in Branch's long absence from her life.

The girl solved Myri's dilemma as she yelled at Branch's back as he hurried out the door, "Way to introduce me to your friend!" She turned to Myri and rolled her eyes, half-smiling. "I'm Alyssa. And, you must be Myrikal. Morgan talks about you all the time."

"He… he does?" Myri's face flushed when Alyssa's eyes flicked quickly down at her flashy unitard. She'd never thought much about what she wore before, nobody on the outside seemed to care or pay any attention to the skin-tight outfits her dad had always insisted she wear. But Alyssa had on normal clothes. And she looked cute. Myri looked down at the lightning-splayed, black spandex and crossed her arms over her chest.

"The goggles I get. Morgan told me your eyes are sensitive. But what's with the lightning-queen get-up?" Alyssa asked.

"Oh, well… it's… my dad always…" Myri sighed. "Yeah, I need to get some new clothes."

Alyssa laughed—not a laugh that made Myri cringe with embarrassment, but one that made her want to join in. "Don't worry about it, kid. You actually pull it off quite well. My short, stubby stature would never allow me to look *that* good in that thing. But, if you want, I can show you where you can get some new garb. You can trade some work for it."

"That'd be great." Myri relaxed her crossed arms a little.

Holding the door open, Alyssa asked, "What has he already shown you and what do you want to see next?"

"He showed me the central square and the gardens. I'd like to see more of how you're constructing the buildings and furniture. I can't believe how fast this has all taken shape." She stepped out onto the porch and cocked her head to the side. "Are those *power tools* I hear?"

"Yes. The Boss is a genius. He invented these batteries we use for our tools. He said he'll be able to make them work to power our houses, too, but he wants us to get more of the infrastructure built before we move on to that."

"Where did you get the tools?" They walked down the gravelly road as they talked.

"Oh, they're all over the place. Abandoned because no one's been able to use them for so many years."

The "batteries" looked like something a mad-scientist slapped together from spare parts. Larger than Myri had expected, they looked nothing like the batteries she'd seen and used. They were housed in a special building Alyssa called the "power house."

"We bring the tools back here at the end of the day to be recharged for the next day's work," Alyssa explained.

The roots of Myrikal's hair tingled and her nerves pulsed with energy in rhythm with the pulsating green liquid flowing through clear tubes atop the "batteries." It pulled at her, wanting to drink of her energy. It felt *alive*. "Do you feel that?" she whispered rubbing her hands up and down her arms to try to rid herself of the sensation of bugs crawling under her skin.

"Feel what?" Alyssa scrunched her eyebrows together.

Realizing that her weirdness was showing again, Myri shook her head and tried to smile. "Nothing. Where to now?" She backed out of the building, relieved that the pull on her nerves subsided.

Alyssa stepped up beside her. "Nothing, huh? It didn't seem like nothing from the look on your face."

Not knowing how much the girl knew about her special *abilities*, she said, "I don't know, maybe I'm just not used to being around powered up batteries."

Alyssa looked sideways at her for a few seconds before responding. "It probably has something to do with your affinity to getting electrocuted with lightning and coming out of it unscathed."

Myri sighed. "You saw that, huh?"

"Yep. I saw that."

Feeling the need to explain the unexplainable, Myri said, "I've never done that before. It just kind of… I don't know… called to me, I guess."

Alyssa shrugged. "You're a strange one, that's for sure. But *normal* stopped existing when the 'quakes hit. So, whatever. It's cool."

"Really? You aren't freaked out about it? About me?"

"Nah. Your special abilities could come in handy with The Boss's plans. We all have a part to play in this new world."

"What plans?"

Alyssa waved to a group of people putting up a fence. "I'll leave that to him to tell you." She pointed at the grassy area inside the unfinished fence. "We're going to try to catch some wild pigs and goats. Cascus said he knows where some are about a day's travel from here."

"What for?" Myri watched the people work in teams to pound fence posts into the ground.

"Food, of course. Pigs are good to eat and you can milk goats and use it to make all kinds of stuff."

"I guess I knew that. I mean, I've read about farms and stuff." She turned to Alyssa. "This guy really does want to make things like they used to be, huh?"

"Better, Myrikal. He wants to make them *better* than they used to be."

"Why? I mean, what's his motive? What does he get out of it?" Her dad's lifelong teachings still crowded her thoughts.

"His motive is to create a better place to live. For himself. For all of us."

Myri frowned, wrinkling her forehead. It all sounded great. Heck, it all *looked* great, but… something nagged at her intuition. Not in a strong way, but a gentle tickling, like the fleck of a booger stuck to a nose hair at the outer rim of her nostril. Myri closed her eyes, giving herself a mental shake. *It's just Russ making noise inside my head. I left him behind yesterday. He's in the past and this is my future.* "Let's go see if Branch is back yet."

"Branch?" Alyssa raised her brows.

"Uh… I mean Morgan."

"Yeah, well, you'll have to tell me the story behind the *Branch* thing." Her eyes sparkled playfully as they headed back toward Branch's house.

"I think I'll leave that to him. It's his story to tell, not mine."

Alyssa shrugged. "Whatever. I admire your loyalty to him even though I'd really like to hear the scoop. You know, find out some embarrassing tidbits about his past."

Myri tried to keep from smiling as she thought about the first time she'd met Branch. That was his story to tell, too.

Waving from his porch, Branch stepped toward them, a smile on his face. "Perfect timing! I just got here a few minutes ago." He turned to Myri. "Did you get a chance to see everything you wanted to? What do you think?"

"You all have done some pretty amazing things here in such

short amount of time. How did your meeting go?" What she really wanted to know was what the meeting was about, but she didn't want to pry too much.

"It was good. He wants to meet you."

"Now?" She glanced down at her flashy unitard.

Catching on to Myri's thoughts, Alyssa said, "Oh, crap. We forgot to go to the clothing storehouse. Can we hurry and do that before Myrikal goes to meet the boss?"

A tiny flicker of worry flashed across Branch's face. "I guess so, if we hurry. He's expecting us back soon."

Myri straightened her shoulders. "No. It's fine. I should go meet him and make sure he's okay with me trading work for clothing before I just go barging in the storehouse." She chewed on her bottom lip for a second. "Thanks, though, Alyssa. Will you be around later to help me pick out some clothes?"

Alyssa winked. "You bet I will. My fashion sense combined with your rockin' body cannot end any way but amazing."

A flush spread up Myrikal's neck and face. She looked down, her mouth twitching into a weird little smile. "Thanks. I'll see you in a bit, then?"

"Yep." Alyssa turned to Branch. "See you in a bit, too… Branch."

His eyes widened a little and he glanced at Myri. She shrugged. "You didn't tell me to keep that a secret."

Branch laughed and waved as Alyssa walked away. "It's okay, I'll just have to think of a really mind-blowing story to go with it." He grabbed Myri's arm and stopped. "You didn't reveal the truth to her, did you?" The fake look of horror he plastered on his face made her laugh.

"No, *Morgan*, I didn't spill your dirty little secrets." The heat of his touch through the tight sleeve of her outfit made her lean toward him slightly. She tore her gaze away from his. "We should probably get to our meeting."

"Yeah." He cleared his throat and dropped his hand from he arm. "We should. Follow me."

Together again, it seemed to Myrikal that they'd never bee apart. The ease with which they fell back into their friendly bante relieved her battered soul. His appearance, however, was definitel *not* the same. The slightly pudgy kid she'd known had grown into tall, muscular—dare she think, *handsome?*—teenager. And that wa different. The innocent touch of yesteryear now caused a no unpleasant sensation wherever his skin met hers. It freaked her ou a little.

Maybe it freaked him out a little, too. They walked in silence t the center of the compound where the largest of the new building stood. When she'd seen it from afar, she hadn't noticed the diffe ence in building materials. She reached out a hand and brushe her fingers across the odd matter. The same sick feeling she'd expe rienced in the power house returned, only to a much lesser degre Instead of the sensation of bugs crawling under her flesh, this fe more like a light breeze lifting the tiny hairs on her skin. Still, gave her the creeps. "What is this?"

Branch shrugged. "I'm not sure. Cascus found it and brought here. He had enough for this building and the power house."

"Does he live in this building?"

"Yes. Downstairs. The main floor is for meetings an gatherings."

The door swung open and Myrikal stepped back.

"Come in, Morgan and Myrikal. Welcome to the Centr Building."

Myrikal started to think that Cascus's long flowing robe was strange choice of wardrobe—then she remembered what she wa wearing. She had no room to judge. She squinted, unable to see h face clearly. She tried to keep from grimacing as a strange od wafted from the robed man. She'd never experienced nausea in he life, but the way her stomach rolled now at the smell, she thoug she might finally know what it felt like to be ill.

"Have a seat, both of you," he said.

They sat on a small couch across a coffee table from Cascus. Branch, eyes never leaving his "boss," introduced Myrikal. "Cascus, this is my friend, Myrikal, that I've told you so much about."

Cascus nodded. "It is a pleasure to meet you, my dear. I'm very happy for Morgan that you've finally found each other again."

Myrikal swallowed down a wave of unease. "It's a pleasure to meet you as well, sir."

"Please, there's no need to call me 'sir.' You can call me Cascus or Boss—as many of the folks here call me as a term of endearment. We are all equal here, though. There is no boss. I apologize that I must get right down to business for lack of more time." He leaned forward. "What can we do to convince you to join us, Myrikal?"

Why couldn't she see his face clearly? She moved her gaze to his hands, the only other part of him that was visible beneath the robes. She blinked her eyes and squinted. She couldn't quite figure it out, but something was off with her sight. Branch nudged her with an elbow. Right. She should respond to Cascus's question. "Well, this way of living is not something I'm even remotely used to. It would take some adjustment. What would be expected of me in return for joining your clan?"

He steepled his fingers together—at least that's what she thought he did, it seemed like her vision cleared for a brief moment before fritzing out on her again.

"We would expect the same of you as of everyone else," he said. "You would be given a main job within the clan as well as being assigned other duties as needed. With plenty of free time in between. We strive for happiness here and I believe everyone needs to feel needed but also to have fun. Those are the things this world has been missing for the last twenty-five years or so."

Myri shook her head, trying to clear her vision. She really wanted to cover her nose with her hands or a thick cloth. She'd never experienced an odor like this before.

"Do you disagree with something I said, dear?" Cascus asked. Branch's leg bounced up and down beside her.

"Oh, no. No, not at all. What kind of job do you foresee me doing?" she asked.

She thought he smiled. "We just so happen to be in the midst of building a special team in which your unique talents will be a huge asset." He paused. "Morgan is a member of this team, as well."

"What is the task this team will be doing?" Myri asked.

"We just so happen to be holding our first meeting tomorrow to discuss that." He stood in a fluid motion and Myri's vision blurred further, it looked like two forms separated for a split second and then rejoined as he stood. "I'm sorry for the brief time I'm able to spend with you today, but I must be going. I have a prior engagement, as I stated earlier. I'm sure Morgan can answer any further questions you have. I hope to see you at the meeting in the morning."

Cascus swept out of the room, down a semi-hidden staircase in the back corner. Myrikal stared after him. She gasped, as, for the briefest of seconds, he transformed into a distinctly non-human form. Writhing beneath his blurred skin was a tangled network of the same pulsating green liquid she'd seen in the "batteries." She stared around the room, noting that nothing else in her line of sight was blurred or difficult to make out. Her vision, when looking at anything but Cascus, was perfect, as usual.

18

Alyssa's little house was a bit smaller than Branch's and the furniture wasn't nearly as nice. She had obviously scavenged it from within the city too, but hadn't done anything to improve it above cleaning it off a little. Myri took her up on her offer to stay here, worried that staying with Branch would be awkward. Myri had trouble sleeping, but it didn't have anything to do with the furniture. She was used to sleeping on old, dusty, torn couches.

Waking nightmares plagued her for the first time in her life. She couldn't remember anything concrete in the dreams, just vague images. Cracks in the earth, oozing coils of green gel-like substance, like something crawling from within the depths of the chasm. Sometime, hours before dawn, Myrikal gave up on sleeping. She got up and dressed in the new jeans and shirt Alyssa and Branch had helped her procure after the strange meeting with Cascus. She put them on over her unitard since she didn't know how long she'd be staying with Alyssa and didn't want to presume she could just store her stuff there.

Myri hadn't said anything to Branch about the problems she'd had with her ability to see Cascus clearly or the odor he obviously didn't smell. She needed time to think about what it could mean. She wanted to see if it recurred. Maybe it was just a one-time aberration. Maybe it had to do with the huge jolt of electricity she'd stolen from the sky earlier in the day. Maybe that's what had caused the strange dreams as she struggled to sleep.

Shaking the thoughts from her head, she quietly opened the door and slipped outside. She needed some fresh air before the meeting, still hours away. She wandered around the inside perimeter of the compound, noting a gated exit/entrance on each side of the rectangular structure. Two guards were posted at each gate, none of them seemed too concerned that she was wandering around in the darkness of pre-dawn.

She stopped in front of the two guards stationed at the entrance she'd come through the day before. A male and a female stood watch, crossbows strung across their shoulders.

"Hi. I'm Myri. Can I ask you something?"

"Sure." The male guard smiled.

"What, exactly, are you guarding against?"

"Intruders," he said. "When we first started to get things set up in here, we had a lot of outsiders trying to steal from us."

"So…" Myri looked at the female, "you aren't here to keep people *inside*. You're here to keep people out?"

The guard nodded. "Yes. That's right. The people that live here are welcome to come and go as we please."

"And visitors are welcome, as long as they're cleared through the proper channels first," added the man.

Good to know they weren't trying to keep people in. Not that that would be an issue for Myrikal. She could get outside the wall without any problem. "Well, if an older man named Russ tries to enter, don't let him. You guys have a good night."

"You too," the guards answered.

Myri re-oriented herself to this newly revamped place. She wanted to see if the tree where she'd first seen Branch was still standing.

It was. She didn't know why, but knowing it was still there gave her a great feeling of comfort. It had been tall the day Branch had been tied to a limb high up the tree, but it had grown even taller in the intervening years. The memory of their first meeting came flooding back, and, on a whim, Myrikal climbed up, smiling like a maniac the entire time.

Resting in the fork of two large branches atop the tree, she felt a sense of peace for the first time since entering the compound. She would stay for a while. Give it a try. The people there seemed to be happy. Much happier than those she'd met on the outside. Less frightened. Myri could leave anytime she wanted if things didn't work out.

From her comfortable perch high in the air, Myri gazed out upon the city beyond the walls of the compound. The chill air didn't bother her, but she noted numerous fires out in the streets, where people without shelter tried to stay warm. Cascus was right about one thing—it was time to move on in this world. Time to build anew instead of living in the ruins of the past. She smiled. That was good advice about her life as well. She wasn't sure if she trusted the Boss or not—more *not* at this point—but she trusted Branch. And this was as good a place as any to begin rebuilding.

She settled her goggles over her eyes as the dull orange glow of the rising sun tried to break through the thick clouds in the east. Even though it irritated her eyes, she thought she'd love to one day see the full effects of the sun, bright and yellow, without the constant cover of gray clouds. She wondered if other areas of the world were free of them, at least part of the time. She smiled again, knowing she could find out someday. An expedition sounded like a grand idea.

Someday.

⚡

THE MEETING TOOK place in the Central Building where she'd met Cascus the day before. Her outing had settled her nerves and she actually looked forward to finding out about the secret project Cascus wanted her to join in on. Alyssa seemed a little put out that she wasn't invited to be part of this group. She had a slight pout on her lips as she waved goodbye to Myri and Branch.

When Cascus entered the large room to stand at the head of the long table, Myri stiffened. The calm from her earlier walk dissipated as his skin seemed to undulate before her, fading in and out of clarity. This time, she heard it in his voice, too. There was the voice she thought he wanted her to hear—the one she was sure everyone else heard—and a deeper, alien voice superimposed on top of it every once in a while. She hadn't noticed that the day before.

Branch touched her arm and leaned in to whisper in her ear. "Calm down. You're going to break the table."

Myri looked down, only then realizing she gripped the edge of the table so hard her fingers left indentations in the wood. She pulled her hands down into her lap, hidden beneath the table, and tried to concentrate on what Cascus was saying.

"I'm glad you all could make it to our first meeting of the Defense Coalition." Myri kept her eyes downcast but had a feeling he was looking right at her. "I know you're all bursting with curiosity to know the responsibilities of this new group. First off, will expect you all to keep most of our activities a secret."

This didn't seem to surprise Branch, but the others at the table reacted with varying degrees of surprise, from raised eyebrows to choked gasp.

"I know," Cascus lowered his hands in front of him in placating manner, "we try to be a very open compound when comes to letting everyone know what's going on. However, th group will be doing some things inside of the compound as well a outside that, though not nefarious in any way, might be a b concerning to those who aren't in the know."

He paused to let his words sink in before continuing. "If this something that is going to be difficult for you, or that you strong disagree with, you are free to decline my offer to take part. You wi have to decide now, however, because once we get started, it's imperative that you stay involved."

Myri glanced around at the eight other individuals seated at the table. Even though she sat as far away from him as she could, Cascus's scent burned her nostrils. She pressed her hand against her stomach to try to squelch the unease there. No one so much as stirred at his offer to decline.

Cascus nodded, a dim smile on his blurry face. "Ahh. I thought I chose correctly for this team." He pulled his chair out and sat before continuing. "As you've probably garnered from the name of this team—The Defense Coalition—your duties will center around defending our compound. I expect for these duties to expand, hopefully quickly, to outside our walls. Remember that our end goal is to make the whole world a better place, starting here."

A man in his early twenties sitting next to Branch, raised his hand. Cascus nodded at him and he spoke, "We already have people guarding the entrances on a rotating basis. What will be different about this group?"

"Good question, Connor. The difference is that you will not be merely guarding against intruders. You will be actively seeking out trouble-makers. We've been lucky so far that few in our little community have revealed themselves to be prone to making trouble. But the possibility is there. You all will watch and listen and stop problems before they arise. And soon, you will take your special skills to the streets of Manhattan. It is my goal to be rid of any and all miscreants here and in the city," he paused and blew out a rancid breath, "and eventually, the world."

Myri winced as the fetid odor wafted toward her. She glanced around at the others. None of them seemed to notice. Did they really not smell it? Before she could stop herself, she blurted out, "Who gets to decide who is being a miscreant? Or what is considered 'making trouble'?"

The alien voice that only she could hear, apparently, growled low and menacingly just beneath the normal voice. "Good question, Myrikal."

She almost didn't hear his response as she squinted, trying to decipher his facial expression. The human face—which she was rapidly coming to think of as the façade—showed a benevolent smile. But the creature inside turned from flowing green to bubbling red. The image beneath waxed and waned, the human face winning out in the fight to stay out front most of the time.

"… decide on a code of conduct together. We'll start today." Cascus turned his full attention on Branch. "I need to go lie down now, I'm feeling a little under the weather. Morgan, would you please take over this meeting and let the team know the things we discussed last night?" He threw one last double-edged look at Myrikal before turning to glide off to the stairs.

"Okay!" Branch leaned forward excitedly. "Let's get started with the Code of Conduct."

Myrikal pushed back her chair and stood. "I don't feel... worthy, I guess... to decide what conduct is acceptable and what isn't, having recently come from my strange family situation. You guys carry on. Bran... *Morgan* can fill me in later."

Branch frowned. "Come on, Myri. Your input is important. And there's another assignment Cascus wanted me to talk to you about."

"What's that?" Myri glanced to where Cascus had disappeared down the stairs, distracted and only half listening.

"We need you to teach us self-defense. Like your dad taught you."

"Yeah, okay. I can do that. Just let me know when and where." She rubbed her stomach, the sick feeling dissipating now that Cascus had left. She turned and walked briskly from the room, careful not to touch the walls of the building as she pushed through the front door. Whatever material they were made out of gave her the same queasy feeling that plagued her when Cascus was nearby. And she needed to figure out why.

⚡19⚡

The strong wind moved the branches of the tree around her. The one she sat on swayed with each gust. The clouds to the west darkened worse than the ones overhead and lightning periodically flashed within them. Myrikal went straight to the tree after leaving the meeting. She had a lot to think about. First and foremost, should she tell Branch about what she saw and smelled when his apparent surrogate father came near?

She curled into a ball, resting her head and arms on her bent knees, her butt nestled in the fork of the two big branches. All she wanted was a new life, away from her killer father, and with her childhood friend. Things had turned complicated much quicker than she'd ever dreamed. Was it too much to believe that leaving her dad would simplify her life? Make her happier? Give her the freedom she'd been craving? Had she just crawled out of the jaws of a lion to be swallowed up in the mouth of a volcano?

Could she just leave? Change her mind and set out on her own? Of course she *could*. But she knew she wouldn't leave Branch. At least not until she figured out what was up with Cascus. The weirdness with him was so far beyond anything she'd ever experienced. She had no idea where to even begin. She didn't know if she should even bring it up to Branch. He seemed so enthralled by the "man" who'd taken the young, lost boy under his wing. She'd have to be careful with Branch. Subtle. Maybe she would have better luck with Alyssa. Myri's interactions with her so far had shown the older girl to be blunt and open to questions. Myri nodded to herself. Yeah. She'd start by finding out what Alyssa knew.

She jumped from the top of the tree, landing with slightly bent knees on the grass-covered ground below, wondering if Branch was still meeting with the "team." She turned her face to the clouds as they opened up and huge droplets of cold rain splashed into her. She headed for Alyssa's, determined to get some answers from her without her realizing she'd even been questioned.

⚡

ALYSSA ANSWERED the door and gestured for Myri to enter and have a seat on the ragged chair in her small living area. "You're soaking wet." She threw Myri a towel. "How was the top secret meeting?"

Myri shrugged, wiping rain from her face and hair. "Okay, guess. I left before it was over."

Raising an eyebrow, Alyssa asked, "Why?"

"I was feeling a little restless. I'm not used to being around a lot of people. Branch is going to fill me in later."

"Were there a lot of people there?"

Wait. I'm the one who's supposed to be asking questions. "Not really, guess. But more than one other person is 'a lot' to me." Without giving it too much thought, Myri decided to dive right in. "Cascu is a *unique* individual, don't you think?"

"Well, yeah," Alyssa answered. "I mean, he's really the first person—at least in our area—who's stepped up to make some real changes for the better. So if that makes him unique, I guess he is." She cocked her head to the side and narrowed her eyes. "Why? What do you think of him?"

Tread carefully here, Myrikal. "He seems very benevolent. Almost like he's, I don't know, *otherworldly* or something."

Alyssa frowned and narrowed her eyes even further, until they were just two slits in her face. "What do you mean by 'otherworldly'?"

Back-pedaling, Myrikal said, "Nothing. Like I said, I'm not used to being around people so it must just be me."

"Does he give you a weird vibe or something?"

"Um… no… maybe a little. Does he give you a weird vibe?"

A bit too defensively, Alyssa snapped, "No! He saved me from the streets."

Did Myrikal detect a little waver in her resolve to defend Cascus? She nodded slowly to give herself time to form her next question carefully. "Okay. I'm not saying he isn't a good person, he's obviously doing some great things here. I was just wondering if you ever… I don't know…. questioned his motives. You know, at first."

Alyssa sighed, leaned toward Myri and spoke in a low voice. "Maybe a little, at first, I may have gotten a creepy vibe from him. But I chalk that up to me just being paranoid. I didn't believe he could pull it off when he first told me about his grand plans." She spread her arms out in a gesture that took in their surroundings. "I was wrong."

The look she gave Myrikal told her she thought Myri was wrong, too. What she really wanted to ask her is what he *looked* like to her. She wanted to know if anyone else saw the strange images she did when she looked at him. Smelled the odor. Felt the queasiness.

Alyssa laughed, a nervous kind of chuckle. Still speaking in a near-whisper, she said, "The funny thing is, when he asked me if I wanted to start a new life—told me he'd give me beneficial work to do, make my life mean something—I thought he was a pimp." She laughed nervously again and looked down at her hands. "I thought he was asking me if I wanted to be a hooker. Like anyone would pay to hook up with this." She flipped her hands from her head down to her sides before leaning back on the couch.

"I guess that explains why you got a creepy vibe from him." Myri smiled. Alyssa was a dead end. Either she didn't see Cascus's altered form beneath his outer façade, or she did and was too loyal or too scared to divulge that information. "And you're adorable. I'm sure there are loads of guys who would want to hook up with you." Myri felt a rush of heat color her skin. "I mean, normal guys, not… not guys wanting hookers. Not that they wouldn't pay to… I'm just going to shut up now."

Alyssa laughed for real this time. "You aren't very good at giving compliments, are you?" She patted Myri on the knee. "It's okay. I got what you meant. Thanks."

"I'm not very good at conversations in general."

Alyssa stood. "You hungry? It's almost lunchtime. I was just going to eat and then head off to finish today's assigned job."

Myri most definitely did not feel hungry, her stomach still unsettled from earlier. "What's your job today?"

"Helping a new couple build their house."

"How long does it usually take to build one of these houses?"

"One week. Cascus has it down to a science. The exact amount of material, people, hours and days. We work together like an ant colony."

Myri quirked her mouth into a wry smile. "Like mindless drones?"

Rolling her eyes, Alyssa punched Myri's arm. "Do I look like a mindless drone to you?"

"No. Not at all."

"Good answer." She grabbed a chunk of bread and a handful of berries and ate them as she walked toward the door. "You coming with me? Or have you already been assigned a job of your own?"

Had she been assigned a job? She wasn't exactly sure. "I need to go see if Branch—Morgan," she corrected herself, "is back from the meeting yet. I guess I should have him fill me in."

"Okay." Alyssa opened the door and stood to the side to let Myrikal step out into the rain first. "I'll see you later, then?"

"Yeah. For sure."

"And, Myrikal," she said, closing the door behind her. "Try not to call down any lightning while you're inside the compound. I don't think the rest of us would fare as well as you do with electrocution."

Heat rushed to Myri's face again. "Yeah… I really wish people wouldn't have seen that."

$$\lightning$$

Branch wasn't at his house yet. Myri waited on the porch, watching the rain drip off the eave in soggy sheets. She perked up at the sound of his footsteps trudging through the mud and went out into the rain to meet him before he reached his house. "How did the rest of the meeting go? Sorry I didn't stick around."

"Yeah, what's the deal with that? You were sure in a hurry to get out of there." A slight scowl remained on his brow.

She knew she wasn't a good liar, so she'd have to tell the truth without telling the whole truth. At least, not yet. "I was feeling out of sorts. You know it was just a couple of nights ago that I was planning to kill someone I'd never even met. I really don't feel like I'm worthy to make rules for others to follow."

The harsh lines in his forehead softened and he reached for her hand. "I'm sorry. I didn't even think about that. I'm just so excited you're here with me, I keep forgetting how little time you've had away from Assassin Dad."

She squeezed his hand, glad he'd bought her half-true excuse. "Should we go inside and get out of this rain and you can tell me what you guys decided?"

He nodded and, still holding her hand, walked the short

distance to his little house. Once inside, he grabbed two towels and threw one to Myrikal before drying himself off with the other. "We came up with a list of serious offenses, those that we felt should get someone expelled from the compound. One of the other team members is a Bible freak, so he insisted that we style it like the Ten Commandments."

Myri raised an eyebrow. She'd heard of the Bible, of course there were often crazies that stood in the streets yelling about the end of times until they had no voice left. As far as she was concerned, the end of times had already happened—ten years or so before she'd been born. "The Ten Commandments?"

"Yeah, like No Killing, No Stealing, No Adultery. Stuff like that."

"Shouldn't you tell me all of them, since I'll be helping to enforce them?"

Branch shrugged. "Cascus actually has a different role for you to play, still as part of the team, just more attuned to your special abilities."

She didn't like the sound of that. "Like what?"

"Well, besides teaching the rest of us how to defend ourselves in this first phase of the Defense Coalition he wants you to just show your presence. And maybe show off your powers once in a while." He rushed to finish before she could interrupt. "Because it's very important to Cascus—and the rest of us—that the team have very little work to do. At least within the compound. He figured that an added incentive for people to behave, like knowing you can zap them into smithereens if they don't, can't be a bad thing. Does that make sense?"

Myrikal's foot bounced up and down on the wood floor as familiar feelings tore up her insides. This felt a lot like what her dad had wanted to use her for. *I want you to stand out. I want people to see you and start shaking with fear, knowing they might be next to die.* She shook her head. "Branch, I won't..."

He interrupted before she could finish. "He... we don't want you to kill anyone, Myri. But it can't hurt for people to know that you easily *could* if necessary, you know?"

She crossed her arms, her foot bouncing even faster now.

"It's about bringing back law and order to this world," Branch said. "Some people will follow the rules of humanity just because they're good people, like you and me." He smiled. "But there are people out there who only follow the rules when they're afraid of the consequences, like your father. He's never had any consequences because there hasn't been anyone enforcing any laws or rules or human decency in a very long time. Cascus thinks it's time to change that. He believes in something he calls *Ex Talionis*. It's the law of retaliation, where the punishment is like the offense in kind and degree. Law and order, Myri."

Thoughts of Branch's former clan, screaming as their building went up in flames, filled her head. All those innocent people. Children. And her dad was responsible for far more deaths than that. That was just the horror she'd witnessed at his hands. What if she could help stop him? And others like him? She didn't completely agree with this *Ex talionis*. Did killing killers just make *you* a killer? But could she, by her presence alone, stop others from doing it?

Branch stayed silent while thoughts raced around inside her head like a school of herring. He now leaned forward and searched her goggled eyes. "Myrikal, what are you thinking?"

A short, non-humorous laugh barked from her throat. "Too many scattered things to put into words that would make any sense."

"Summarize then."

She took a deep breath and loosened the grip of her crossed arms across her chest. "I won't kill anyone. Not for you or anyone. Unless it's the only way to save another life, I guess. But I see how this plan can be a benefit to building a better world and I'm willing to give it a try." She remembered something Branch had said earlier. "You said 'first phase,' how many phases are there to this plan, and what are they?"

Branch relaxed the tenseness in his shoulders and leaned back in his chair. "Just two, really. The next phase involves going outside of our little community and trying to establish some order in the rest of Manhattan. And someday, beyond."

"That's a pretty ambitious plan." The writhing, green, living fluid beneath Cascus's human veneer popped into her head.

"Cascus is a pretty ambitious man," Branch said with a proud smile.

Is he a man? What else could he be? Myri closed her eyes and leaned her head back on the couch. Maybe the problem wasn' Cascus. Maybe it was her. Like an allergic reaction or something. Could she even *be* allergic to something? She had no idea.

Branch leaned forward and took her hand. "And with you on our side, I think we just might be able to pull it off."

She smiled as his touch warmed her skin, but still, she shook her head. "I'm not a superhero, remember?"

Those were some of the last words he'd said to her before he'd disappeared from her life a couple of years ago. He winced and let go of her hand, standing. He turned away from her and paced the short length of his small living area. "I was wrong to have said that, Myri. I was an angry, dumb kid." He spun around and faced her. "I was wrong, Myrikal. You *are* just like a superhero. You have amazing powers and strength and, most important, you are a really good person."

It was her turn to wince. She certainly didn't think of herself as a good person. She'd almost killed someone just because Rus wanted her to. She'd almost gone ahead with his plans for her to join the family business. A *good person* wouldn't have even considered it. Plus, her dad's teachings had molded her, hadn't they? She'd learned to be paranoid and to not trust people. She thought about voicing some of these thoughts out loud, but Branch interrupted them.

"Look, I know you just got out from under your dad's rule and you're still trying to figure things out. The fact that you le him is proof that you're a good person." He sat next to her, turned slightly to face her. "You don't have to decide anything right now. Just observe us for a while if you want, see if what we do is something you can agree with. You can teach us self-defense and we can build you your own house. How does that sound?"

The earnestness in his eyes tickled a smile onto her lips. "That sounds like a good compromise. When do we start? And can I choose where I want my house?"

Branch smiled, his dark eyes sparkling. "We can start the training this afternoon. I'd like to train at least twice a day for a while, until the team has the basics down. And as for where you build your house… did you have a place in mind already?"

"I do," she said with a mischievous smile.

He cocked an eyebrow. "Well, you just need to submit your request to the compound planning team and they have to approve it. Where are you thinking you want to build?"

"Our tree." The words left her mouth before her mind had a chance to stop her. Too bad her "powers" didn't include the disabling of her blush producer.

Branch laughed. "The tree where we first met? It must hold better memories for you than it does for me. Not that meeting you isn't one of the best things to ever happen to me. It was just the activities directly before that I'd like to forget."

Myri laughed, remembering younger, chubby Branch trying to talk his way out of further humiliation at the hands of the bullies who'd tied him to a limb high up in that tree. "And I want to build my house *in* the branches of the tree. Up high."

"Really? How come?"

Her expression turned thoughtful. "I feel like I need to be alone, but I also want to be with people. Having a tree-house will give me privacy when I need it. Plus, I can see out into the city from up there."

"That's going to be harder to build."

"I'll do all the heavy lifting and most of the work. I just need someone to show me how."

He gave a quick chuckle and shook his head. "Of course you will. And I'll make sure the team approves your request. If anyone deserves to be up where she can keep an eye on things, it's you, Myri."

20

The self-defense training sessions started out a bit shaky. Only one of the participants had even the first clue how to block a punch. Or throw a punch. Or deliver a kick. Or take someone down. She started with the basics—stuff her dad had taught her when she was a toddler. Ya, the team member with martial arts experience, was a huge help.

The building of the tree house went much smoother. The planning team approved her request with the stipulation that no one else would be approved to build up in a tree. With her strength, Branch's remarkable skill at building things, and Alyssa's occasional suggestions, her house was finished in less than a week. Alyssa insisted they furnish Myri's house almost the second it was deemed complete. "The sooner you have furniture, the sooner I can get you out of my house. The static electricity you create is enough to drive me crazy," she teased.

So, between training sessions, Branch's Defense Coalition shifts, and Alyssa's assigned jobs, the three of them went out into the city to scavenge for furniture. And since Myri could get into places no one else could and didn't have to worry about being crushed to death by falling debris, she was able to get some pretty nice stuff. The collapsed mattress store hid the best treasure.

After an evening training session and dinner with Branch and

Alyssa, Myri climbed up to her very own home and lay down t
sleep on her own, never-before-used mattress for the first time ever

⚡

MYRI AND BRANCH worked side-by-side harvesting the ripe frui
and vegetables from the garden. The Defense Coalition had bee
patrolling for several weeks and the team members showed som
real progress in the training sessions.

The two of them pushed fully loaded wheelbarrows toward th
storehouse where the food would be divvied out to eat fresh as we
as to be canned for use during the colder, non-growing season.

"So," Branch said. "You've been observing DefCo—that's wha
we've been calling the Defense Coalition—for a while now. Wha
do you think?"

The team really hadn't seen much action. The people that ha
been allowed into the COP were pretty obedient and just happy t
be there. Minor infractions had been dealt with quickly and fair
from what she'd seen. Unless there were things going on that sh
wasn't aware of—and she doubted that, she'd been keeping a ver
close eye on things—she felt that, so far, the Defense Coalition ha
been a positive addition to the compound. "I think you all ar
doing a great job."

"Does that mean you're ready to officially join us?"

She couldn't think of a reason not to. "Yes. I think I'm ready."

Branch dropped the handles to his wheelbarrow and pumped
fist in the air. "Yes! Cascus will be so happy!"

The smile on Myri's face faded at the mention of the cla
leader. She hadn't seen him since the first DefCo team meetin
Not for lack of trying. She'd been wanting to at least catch
glimpse of him, to see if the weird visual disturbances and sic
ening odor returned. She'd been trying to convince herself that th
two times it had happened before were just a fluke. A residual effe

of the lightning. She had a sneaking suspicion he was avoiding her. "When do I start and what will I be doing?"

"Let's drop these off at the storehouse and then go to my place and discuss it."

"Or we could go to my place and discuss it." She loved that she could say that. That she had a "place" to call her own.

"Okay, let's do that, then," Branch said. "I'll make you a salad."

"A salad?" Wasn't that just a bunch of green stuff?

"Yeah, don't look so worried. It'll be delicious. I just need to grab something from my house first."

Branch filled a bag with fruits and vegetables and they left the rest of the day's harvest in the capable hands of the storehouse workers. They stopped at his house and he ran in to grab his secret ingredient. He had an extra spring in his step as they walked to Myri's tree.

He talked as he stood in her small kitchen area, cleaning the salad ingredients with water running through a faucet from a storage tank she'd placed on the roof. "We'll be ready soon, I think, to take DefCo out into the city."

"How soon?" Myri asked.

He tore leaves of lettuce into bite-sized pieces. "Within the next couple of weeks, we'll take to the streets outside. That's when your powers will really be needed. Until then, Cascus wants you to be seen inside the compound."

"I have been seen inside the compound." She wrinkled her nose as he added different berries to the green-leaf mixture.

"Not just *seen*, Myri. You need to show off your abilities, like we discussed before. People know about DefCo now and they know that our main objective is to keep the peace by enforcing the Code of Conduct. Now, we'd like them to see you as part of our team. And see your powers."

Myri nodded, her brow creased. "So they'll think twice about fighting back against your authority, knowing what I can do and that I'm part of the team."

"Yes." He pushed a bowl toward her and picked up the other one, stabbing the contents with a fork. "Cascus wants to reinforce the idea that you're part of the team in other ways as well. I mean, everyone already knows you're helping us learn martial arts, but that doesn't necessarily translate into them knowing you're on the team. Cascus says that a visual reminder is important."

"What kind of visual reminder?" Myri took a bite of the salad. It actually tasted much better than she thought it would. "What did you put on this salad?"

He smiled as he chewed. "My homemade raspberry vinaigrette. Do you like it?"

"It's delicious." She swallowed and stabbed her fork into a big piece of strawberry. "So the 'visual reminder'?"

"Uniforms. Cascus had uniforms made for the team. They have a lightning bolt on the chest and right sleeve that matches the ones on your outfit. The one you had on the day you came here."

"He wants me to wear that thing?" So much for blending in. She'd really been enjoying that for the first time in her life.

"Yes, at least when you're out in the compound and especially out in the city."

"The boots, too?" She looked down at the casual shoes Alyssa had helped her pick out. She liked them. A lot.

"Yeah. Boots, too."

"I think I would have just lost my appetite if this wasn't so good." She shoved another bite in her mouth.

Branch smiled. "Ahh, come on. It'll be awesome."

Awesome? Or a little too much like living with her dad? Her paranoia melted a little as she caught sight of his dimple. "Okay. Let's be awesome then. Should we start today?"

"Yes. Let's start today." He shoved another bite in his smiling face.

Myri sighed and gazed wistfully at her jeans and cute shoes one more time.

$$\lightning$$

THE SMELL of the fresh cut wood used to build her treetop house filled her senses as Myrikal drew in a deep breath then stepped from the small platform built onto the porch. She dropped to the ground, some twenty-five feet below, and landed with hardly a sound, bending her knees to lessen the impact. A chicken, most likely escaped from the livestock area of the compound, squawked and flapped its flightless wings as it scrambled away, startled by Myri's sudden appearance.

Myri smiled, watching the tail feathers disappear into the tall grass. She walked at a leisurely pace, observing the activity all around her. The clouds, thin and scattered this afternoon, allowed the sun a rare, if dappled, appearance. The people soaked it in, their spirits lifted and their energy levels boosted. There was always a lot of activity in the compound, but it wasn't always done with this much enthusiasm. Even though sunlight messed with her eyesight and the cold had no effect on her at all, Myri still had an extra peppiness in her step as the warm rays found their way to her back.

Branch and the other DefCo team members stood in a loose circle in the Central Square in front of Cascus's dwelling. Branch looked up and smiled. "Myrikal, you look great."

The others stopped their conversations and straightened their shoulders at her arrival. Myri eyed their uniforms. They weren't so bad, at least they looked like normal clothes. She looked down at her flashy unitard and rejected a wince that tried to streak across her face. Why couldn't she just wear what they were wearing? She knew why. She had to stand out. That's what her dad wanted and that's what Cascus wanted. Is that what she wanted? Definitely not.

"Well?" Branch interrupted her thoughts. "What do you think?

We look all official and stuff, huh?"

Myri nodded. "Yeah, *you* do."

Either he chose to ignore her emphasis on the word *you*, or he didn't notice it. "Let's get started. We'll break up into pairs and check on the border guards first." He glanced at Myri. "You're with me and we'll take the north quadrant. Connor and Donna, east. Ya and Bryan, west—"

"I thought for sure you'd give me east," Ya broke in. "You know, 'cause I'm Asian."

Everyone stared blankly at him.

The older man—Myri guessed late forties or early fifties—spread his hands out and raised his eyebrows. "Because Asia is considered an eastern continent? Does no one look at a globe anymore?"

Branch shook his head and continued. "Aaron and Miguel, south. And, Vicky and Sandeep, central. And, remember, if you need Myrikal's help, shoot a flare into the air."

"You have flares?" Myrikal asked.

"Yes, we do." Branch pulled a metal tube from his belt, twice as big around as a pen, and showed it to her. "Cascus helped us design them. They are single use only and shoot sparks into the air along with a loud *bang*."

She squinted at the object in his hand. "How do they work?"

Branch flipped the tube sideways and pointed to a button near his thumb. "You flip the cover and push the button, the spring releases and hits a firing pin into a cartridge with gun powder in it and that ignites some chemicals and shoots it up into the air."

"Yeah," Donna pushed Connor's shoulder. "As long as you aim it towards the sky, huh, Connor?"

Connor's skin flushed red, but he smiled. "I didn't know it had a cartridge in it."

Donna turned to Myri. "Missed me by an inch. Singed the hair on my arm." She pulled her sleeve up to show Myri the patch of singed hair.

Myri smiled briefly then spoke with a serious tone. "My father always taught me to treat every gun as if it were loaded. Sounds like a good idea with these flares, too."

"Yeah." Connor nodded. "I definitely will from now on."

"Okay," Branch said. "Let's get going. We'll meet back here in one hour."

The sky darkened a bit and Myri glanced up at a large cloud now passing in front of the sun as she and Branch walked toward the front entrance. The sunlight had been nice while it lasted. "This really isn't going to take a whole hour. I mean, this place is big for a compound, but it isn't that big."

"I know. We want DefCo to be seen *and* interact with people. We'll take our time and talk with people on our rounds," Branch said.

Great, Myri thought. *Interacting with people is definitely not one of my strong suits.*

They continued walking to the main entrance where two "guards" leaned against the cinderblock wall on opposite sides of the opening.

"Hey, Morgan," the male guard stood straight. "What's up?"

"Hi, Gill." Morgan reached out to give Gill a fist-bump. "We're just doing rounds. How have things been at the main gate today?"

"Pretty uneventful."

"Yeah." The female "guard" stepped closer. "Except for that weird guy that came poking around about an hour ago."

"Oh?" Branch's voice rose in interest. "What did he want?"

"I'm not exactly sure," the girl said. "That's what made it so strange. I asked him what business he had here and he said, 'Uhh, none.' He kept asking us how many entrances we have. He didn't look either of us in the eye the whole time, just kept peering around us, looking into the compound."

"Was he a crazy?" Myrikal asked.

Gill shook his head. "I don't think so. After asking us for the third or fourth time about the other entrances I told him to leave."

"Did he give you any problems?" Branch asked.

"No. It was weird. He just grinned, gave a little salute, and turned and walked away."

A distant *bang* interrupted. Myrikal whirled around and spotted a flare erupting above the trees.

"That's coming from the west where Ya and Bryan went," Branch said. "Let's go."

Myri didn't wait for his command, she took off ahead of him.

"Don't worry about me," he yelled sarcastically as he ran. "I'll catch up!"

She smiled and put on an extra burst of speed. Branch could run almost as fast as her, but he'd never catch up with the head start she'd gotten.

Myrikal entered the clearing around the west gate and took in the scene with rapid-fire awareness. Ya, surrounded by three assailants—one of which was crumpled on the ground, bleeding from a head wound—held his own. He'd had extensive martial art training before Myrikal's quick defensive lessons. Bryan lay on the ground, struggling for control of a large knife held by the man straddling his chest.

From ten yards away, Myri left the ground, leaping toward his attacker. Her foot made contact with his head, pushing him off Bryan. Myri rolled once and jumped to her feet. The attacker rolled several times, limbs flailing, before coming to rest in a heap.

A quick glance at Ya showed her that he had things under control for the moment. She rushed to the guards, each held by gatecrasher with a knife. She jumped over them, spinning in the air, to land behind them. Grabbing the assailants each from behind by the collar of their T-shirts, she yanked them away from the guards, smashed them into each other with a bone-cracking *crunch* and dropped them to the ground. She retrieved the knives and threw them, end-over-end, at the nearest tree, embedding the blades into the trunk.

Ya incapacitated all but one of his opponents with whom he

was locked in a close battle. Myri hesitated, not wanting to interfere if Ya could handle it on his own. She rushed in when the assailant gained the upper hand, locking Ya in a tight choke hold. She pulled his arm from around Ya's neck and twisted it behind his back. She cringed at the sound of his shoulder joint tearing away from the cartilage and ligaments holding it in place. And again, when it *popped* as it dislocated completely. She hadn't meant to use such force. She'd only wanted to restrain, not injure.

The now captive intruder screamed. Myri released her hold on him as his knees buckled and he fell to the ground, reaching for his dangling arm.

"Wow. Nice job."

Myri spun toward the oddly familiar voice, hands outstretched in front of her, and froze. Some sort of recognition flitted across her adrenalin-hyped mind as she narrowed her eyes at the grungy man who held a gun to Branch's head.

"Don't move a muscle hero-girl, or I'll put a large caliber bullet through his head." He waved the gun in her direction.

"Okay." She released a flash of lightning from her fingertips straight into the man's shoulder of the arm with which he held the gun.

His body convulsed and he pulled the trigger as he fell. The bullet slammed into Myri's chest with such force that she stumbled backwards, but kept her feet. Branch bent at the waist and clapped his hands over his ears, too late to prevent any temporary damage to his eardrum from the close proximity of the blasting gun.

Myri ran to Branch's side while Bryan and Ya, with the help of the two gate guards, tied the intruders' hands behind their backs. "Are you okay? Did you get hit?"

"I'm fine." He straightened up. "I just can't hear very well—except for the ringing in my ears." He scowled. "Gah!"

"What?"

"I just realized the score is now nine to one. I'm never going to catch up."

Myri laughed. "I can't believe you remember 'the score'." She bent down to examine the man at their feet. He groaned and his eyes fluttered open. Myri leaned closer. "Huh. I knew I recognized this loser."

"You know him?" Branch asked.

"Only as much as I've seen him before. He was one of the ones trying to take that little girl I told you about the day I finally left my dad." She looked around at the others, her eyes landing on a crying female, blood running from her obviously broken nose. "And that one," she pointed, "was with him."

The man at Myri's feet tried to scoot backwards by pushing against the gravel. Myri stepped on his chest, exerting just enough pressure to keep him from moving.

"You killed Mark." His voice quavered.

"Was that the guy that was with you when you were trying to kidnap that little girl?" Myri's voice did not quaver.

"We… you…" He tucked his chin to his chest to look at her foot still resting there. "I can't breathe."

"You're breathing just fine." Myri eased up on the pressure a fraction. "I didn't mean to kill your friend. He should have backed off when I told him to."

Branch knelt down and looked up at Myrikal. "Let's get his hands tied behind his back and take these jerks to Cascus."

Myri started to move her foot then stopped and tilted her head to the side. "What's Cascus going to do with them?"

Branch stopped trying to roll the guy over—an impossible feat with Myri's foot still pressed against him—and looked up her. "He's going to keep them locked up until we can hold a trial in a couple of days."

"A trial?"

"Yes. A trial. Like they used to do before the 'quakes."

"Okay. I guess." Myrikal slid her foot off the guy in slow motion. The hair at the back of her neck prickled a little at the thought of Cascus.

As they gathered up the prisoners, the new guards arrived to relieve the two that had been attacked. It was slow walking with the injured prisoners limping and moaning, surrounded by the four DefCo team members, the now off-duty guards straggling behind.

"That was really amazing, Myrikal," Ya said.

"You were pretty amazing, Ya." She smiled at the older man. "Tell me again why I had to teach you all defensive fighting? You should have been the teacher."

"I have a few decades of training on you, young lady. But I can't come close to matching your instincts."

"We make a great team." Myri looked from Ya to Bryan and then to Branch. "All of us."

Cascus stood outside the doors of the Central Building, a wide grin on his face. On his outside, human face anyway. Flashes of green writhed beneath his facial façade. Myri's stomach lurched as the putrid odor emanating from the *man* dressed in robes hit her nostrils. She swallowed, determined not to show outwardly the effects he had on her on the inside.

"What do we have here?" Cascus asked. "I saw the flare and wondered if it was just a false alarm or the real thing. I see it was the real thing."

Branch climbed the stairs leading up to the compound's leader, a proud smile on his face. Under his breath, but still hearable by Myri, he said, "I told you Myrikal was amazing." Louder, so everyone could hear, he continued. "This gang tried to force their way into the compound. Luckily, Bryan and Ya were rounding on the west gate at the time and were able to set off a flare and assist the assigned guards in keeping them *occupied* until Myrikal and I could get there to help."

"I see." Cascus narrowed his eyes and frowned at the prisoners. "Well, bring them in and we'll lock them up. I'll question them after they've had a while to sit in solitude and think about their actions. I'll set a trial date after I've questioned them."

Cascus opened the doors and motioned for the crew to go

inside. He stopped the straggling guards and said, "I'll need to speak with you two before you go, too."

Branch herded the seven prisoners up the stairs, followed by Myrikal, Bryan, and Ya. The gate-guards stayed behind to talk to Cascus.

The stairs ended on a small landing with a hallway that stretched both directions. The long hallway consisted of doors every five or six feet on either side. The doors appeared to be made out of the same odd material as the outside of the building. Myrikal brushed one of them with her fingertips. The tiny hairs on her arm stood at attention. She jerked her hand away. This material, whatever it was, gave her the creeps.

Branch slid a steel bar back on the outside of the first door, unlocking it. Myri glanced in while he untied the hands of the guy with the dislocated shoulder, then stepped back as he shoved him inside. The room, no bigger than six feet square, contained only a thin mattress laying directly on the bare floor and a bucket, she assumed, for going to the bathroom in. Branch shut the door and slid the bolt to lock it. The man inside cussed loudly, yelling something about being claustrophobic.

"What are you gonna' do to us?" the guy who'd held the gun to Branch's head asked. His hair stood straight up, giving him a wild appearance.

The other captives looked at Branch, wondering, Myri was sure, the same thing.

"You'll be questioned and then face trial." Branch opened the next door and turned the gun-wielder to untie his hands.

"Trial?" The guy looked over his shoulder at Branch. "There ain't no *trials* anymore."

"There are here. We're starting over, dude. Cascus is going to make sure we do things right this time." Branch pushed him into the small cell and slammed the door behind him, bolting it shut.

The other prisoners remained silent as he repeated the process with each of them.

⚡21⚡

DefCo's official first day of rounds ended up netting one more rule-breaker. Connor and Donna hadn't needed Myrikal's help with this one. They led their prisoner up to the Central Building as Myri and Branch exited. The boy couldn't have been more than eleven or twelve years old, eyes wide and frightened.

"What do you have here?" Branch asked.

"We caught Marcus here inside the battery shed. He'd unhooked one of them and was in the process of shoving it into a duffle bag when we walked in on him," Connor said.

Myri crouched down to be at eye level with the young boy. "Why were you trying to steal a battery?"

A tear escaped the corner of his eye and rolled down his cheek. He swallowed before speaking in a near whisper, voice shaking. "I can't tell you."

"Why?"

"Because… he…" The boy lost the tenuous control he had and choked out a sob. "He has my sister."

"Who has your sister?" Myrikal tried to control the anger in her voice.

The boy shook his head and wiped his nose on the shoulder of his ratty T-shirt. He was definitely from outside the Compound.

"Will you tell me if I promise I'll find your sister?"

The boy sniffed. "He'll just kill you, too."

Myri looked down at the ground for a few seconds and took in a deep breath. She returned her gaze to the boy's. "Marcus, my name is Myrikal. I am *really* strong and whoever has your sister won't be able to kill me. I promise."

Marcus raised a shaky eyebrow at her. "Serious?"

"Very." She put her hand on his shoulder. "Tell me who has your sister and where I can find him."

"He'll kill her if he sees anyone coming besides me with the battery thing. You won't get a chance to save her."

"Then you'll just have to come with me." She stood. "We'll trick him."

Branch spoke up. "We have to run this past Cascus first."

Myrikal put her hands on her hips. "You can if you want to but I'm doing it no matter what he says."

Branch sighed and led the group back inside.

After Branch explained the situation to him, Cascus folded his arms and said, "This boy must face trial for what he's done. I deny your request."

For someone who insisted he wasn't the "boss" he sure sounded like he was ordering her around. "Excuse me, Cascus," Myrikal said. "But I wasn't asking for your permission. I apologize if that's how it seemed." She turned to Marcus and put her hand on his shoulder as she led him toward the door.

"Myrikal…" Branch hurried to her side and whispered, "What are you doing?"

"The right thing."

Branch stared after her but didn't follow.

"What do I do if he looks in the bag before you get inside?" Marcus's voice had lost its frightened quiver as he stared Myri directly in the eyes. He adjusted the bag's strap on his shoulder. They'd found a rock about the same size and weight as the battery

Marcus had wanted to go back to the shed and get a real battery—and return it later—but Myri didn't want to push her luck with Cascus.

"He won't. I'll be in position before you go in and I won't give him a chance to get that far." The man holding Marcus's sister was hiding out in the bell tower of an old church. The roof of the building next to it was within jumping distance to the open belfry—jumping distance for Myri, anyway. "You ready?"

Marcus swallowed. "Shouldn't I give you a head start?"

Smiling, Myri shook her head. "I'll be ready and waiting by the time you climb all those stairs to the tower."

The boy nodded. With one last look over his shoulder, he exited the alley down the street from the church. Myrikal waited until he entered the building before she left the alley from the opposite end, turning down the cluttered street a block over from the church.

She ran to the designated building, trying to push down the anger rising in her chest. People that messed with kids made her furious. A successful rescue depended on precise timing, and she didn't want her anger to interfere with it. She leaped onto the fire escape ladder on the side opposite the church and climbed to the roof.

Now glad for the clouds that had interfered with the sun earlier in the day, Myrikal made her way to the edge of the roof facing the bell tower, hunching down, out of sight. Marcus should have been at least halfway up the tower stairs at this point, and Myri was counting on the kidnapper to be focusing on him. She'd told him to make a racket as he climbed. She peered up over the crumbling four-foot wall surrounding the roof. Most of the man's body was hidden by the bell, somehow still hanging from the belfry. His back to her, he moved toward a door that likely led to the stairs.

Should she jump now? The plan had been to wait until Marcus got there, but the guy's position was perfect. She watched the door, deciding to wait. She didn't want to risk injuring the boy if he came through the door at the wrong time. She'd rather know his position before the leap. She wished she knew exactly where the girl was positioned, too. She figured he wouldn't keep her right by an opening, though.

Myri's senses perked up as the old door squeaked open. Before Marcus even had a chance to speak, the man asked, "Did you get it?"

"Yeah."

"Did anyone follow you?" The man pushed him to the side and leaned through the doorway to look down the stairs.

Myri jumped. She flew through the window and Marcus dove to get out of the way. Her feet barely touched the floor before she leaped again and tackled the man, pushing him through the open door. They tumbled together down ten or so stairs before Myri grabbed the broken banister and stopped their frenzied descent. The man, stunned but not unconscious, lay limp beside her. She grabbed one of his arms and dragged him back up to the belfry as he groaned and cussed at her.

She slid him across the floor. His back hit against the rotting barrier around the bell.

"I'm gonna' rip…"

He pushed against the floor to stand, but Myri moved beside him and planted her booted foot in the middle of his chest, pinning him to the floor. Without removing her gaze from the man's face she said, "You alright, Marcus?"

"Uhh… yeah. Yeah… I'm okay," he stammered.

She turned her attention back to the man. "Where's the girl?"

"I don't have to tell you anything." He pushed at her foot. It didn't budge a millimeter.

Without saying a word, Myrikal urged little electrical impulses to the surface of her skin, covering herself with intense static. She increased the pressure of her foot on his chest and leaned toward him as little yellow lights darted across her fingertips. His lips peeled back in a grimace and his hair straightened, standing on

...d. Eyes wide, he shook his head while trying to push it further ...to the floorboards.

"Okay!" he shouted. "I'll tell you!"

Myri released the energy but stayed crouched close to his face.

"What are you, anyway?" he asked.

"I'm Myrikal. Where's the girl?"

"Down... down the stairs, on the top floor..."

"Show us." Myri grabbed him by the shirt and roughly lifted ...im to his feet.

"You're... umm... a really strong girl," the man said.

She pushed him toward the door. "I'm a really strong *person*. ...ow shut up and take us to the girl."

Marcus tugged on her arm and whispered, "He had a gun... ...efore."

The man bolted out the door. Myri rolled her eyes and jumped, ...nding right behind him. He squealed like a hungry piglet as she ...icked him up by the waistband of his pants and slammed him to ...e floor. With quick, rough movements, she searched him for ...eapons. She pulled a gun out of the big pocket of his cargo pants ...nd a knife from a sheath at his belt. She needed to remember to ...eck for weapons in the future. They wouldn't hurt her, but they ...uld injure or kill innocent people nearby.

She emptied the bullets from the gun and handed the weapons to ...arcus. "Put those in your bag. I'll show you how to use them later."

His eyes widened and he smiled.

"Now," Myrikal said to the man. "Get up and take us to the ...irl. Any more nonsense from you and I'll rid myself of you and ...nd her myself." She could easily have found Marcus's sister on her ...wn, but she wanted to take this loser back to Cascus in exchange ...or Marcus. She definitely wasn't sure about the clan leader—she ...asn't even sure he was human—but she didn't want to jeopardize ...er standing in the new community. She wanted to be where ...ranch was. And, besides, this slime-ball deserved to go to "trial."

The man slowly climbed to his feet and, head drooping, started down the stairs. Even though he seemed defeated and cooperative, Myri still kept a close eye on him. They reached the top level of the church—more like an attic than an actual floor—and she grabbed his wrist and pulled him back when he reached for the doorknob of an off-sized door. "She'd better be in here. And she'd better not be hurt."

The man swallowed and wrinkled up his face like a baby getting ready to wail. "She's in there and she… she's not hurt… too bad."

Myri squeezed his wrist, bones crackling beneath her grip.

"Ow! Shit! That hurts!" He tried to pull away. Like a flea tugging on the mooring line of a large ship.

"Shut up." Myri turned the handle on the door and pushed it open. She sucked in a sharp breath as her gaze landed on a little girl, curled up in a ball inside a medium-sized dog kennel.

Marcus pushed past them and ran to the cage. He landed hard on his knees and fumbled with the lock. "Annie! Are you okay?"

The man, still attempting to pull his wrist from Myri's grip, whined, "I… I don't know what I did with the key."

Myri pulled him down to the floor. "Stay put. I don't need a key."

He rolled to his side, toward Marcus, as Myri knelt and grabbed a hold of the small lock. Without even looking at him, she reached her other hand down and seized his wrist, slamming his hand on the floor. He let out a howl of pain as she smashed her knee onto his knuckles, pinning his hand to the splintering hard wood. She ignored him as his knuckles snapped beneath the pressure.

With a twist of her wrist, the lock broke in two. She dropped the pieces and pulled the door of the cage open. The little girl, no older than eight, Myrikal guessed, pushed up to a crouched sitting position. One eye swollen shut, the other one widened as it took in Myri and her lightning-bolt unitard.

"It's okay, Annie. I'm here to help. Marcus is with me." Myri moved away from the opening, positioning herself between the girl and the man who now lay clutching his mangled hand to his chest.

Marcus dropped to his knees in front of the kennel, arms spread wide. The girl's face twisted up and she let out a sob as she lunged for her brother. "Annie, are you okay? Can you get up?"

She nodded, her face pressed up against his chest.

"Okay, come on, then. Let's get out of here." He glanced up at Myri with raised eyebrows. "*Can* we go?"

Myri tilted her head to the side, ignoring the moaning kidnapper at her feet. "Do you have somewhere to go? Somewhere safe? Parents?"

"No parents, but we live in a compound. It's safe."

"Okay. But I still have to teach you how to use those weapons. Wanna' tell me where I can find you?"

Marcus looked down at the kidnapper then back up at her.

"Ahh. Yeah," Myrikal said. "Probably not a good idea to tell me in front of him. Let's step out into the hallway."

He described the same compound where she'd taken the kids and dog the day she'd left her father. "I know where that is. I'll stop by in a couple of days and teach you some stuff."

"Thank you, Myrikal." He hesitated before hugging her around the waist quickly then turning to go down the stairs, holding Annie's hand as he led her.

Turning to the kidnapper, Myri said, "Get up."

"Why?" A bit of his earlier defiance crept back into his voice.

"Because I'm taking you back to the compound where I live." She still couldn't quite bring herself to call it "my compound," even though she had a house high up in a tree and had been there for over a month. She questioned whether taking him there was the best option, but she was sure she didn't want someone like him loose in the streets, a danger to more children. Handing him over to Cascus seemed to be the best—the only—option. There was no form of jail out in the city, only street justice, and that rarely turned out to be on the side of good.

"Why? What are you going to do with me?" He still clutched his hand to his chest, no attempt to get up off the floor.

The bruises on Annie's face flashed in her memory and anger flashed in her chest. "No more questions. Get up."

"And if I don't?" He swallowed and looked away from Myri's face, his bravado weakening.

Myrikal slammed her open hands down on the empty kennel. The metal bars crumpled like paper, the large cage flattened to the shuddering floor.

His lips disappeared as he clamped them together and scrambled to stand.

"And don't even think about running." Myri pushed him between the shoulder blades and he stumbled toward the open door.

⚡

PEEKING over his shoulder at her for about the hundredth time on their two-and-a-half mile walk back to Central Park, the kidnapper and would-be battery thief cringed when Myrikal raised her hand to gesture toward the west gate.

"Go in," she said.

He lowered his head and slumped his shoulders as he shuffled through the opening.

"Hey, Myrikal. Who's..." The guard stepped closer to the kidnapper. "William, you aren't allowed inside the compound."

"You know him?" Myri asked.

"Yeah, he used to live here. He got banished for fighting."

"Just fighting?" Myri raised an eyebrow. She'd seen fights break out in there before and no one had gotten banished for them.

"A lot of fighting," the guard said.

"Well, now he's done something worse." Myrikal grabbed

William by the arm. "I'm taking him to the Central Building for lock-up so he can stand trial."

"Lock-up?" William dug his feet into the ground, forcing Myri to pull him along like an obstinate two-year-old.

Myrikal ignored his query. "You can either walk or I can drag you by the hair."

He stumbled as he tried to keep up with her. "You… you can't lock me up. There… there's no *law* anymore. You can't just…"

Digging her fingers into his arm, she kept walking in silence as he squirmed.

Branch met her at the steps to the Central Building, coming from the direction of his house. He looked from her to William and back again. "Myri, why do you have William? Where's the boy?"

The gravel crunched under her feet as she twisted to face him more fully. She put her free hand on her hip. "*Marcus* and his sister are safe. I never said I was going to bring him back." She jerked William forward. "This is who you want. He's the one who kidnapped the little girl and forced her brother to attempt to steal the battery."

Branch pursed his lips and snuck a peek at the large door. "I'll go in with you."

Her hair whipped as she pivoted to start up the steps. Part of her wanted to ask him how mad Cascus had been that she'd defied his wishes. But the bigger part of her didn't care. She swallowed down the strange unease touching the door gave her and pushed her way inside, trailing William along behind her.

Cascus, hands tucked into the sleeves of his gown, stood in the same area he'd been when she'd left with the boy as if he hadn't moved from the spot. "What do we have here?" He raised an eyebrow, his face blurring in Myri's sight.

Shoving the kidnapping, child-abuser toward him, Myri released her grip. "This is William. He kidnapped a little girl then forced her brother to come and try to steal a battery with the threat of killing her if he didn't."

"I see. Take him up to a cell, please. Then I'd like to have a word with you. If you'll allow." Cascus's fetid breath wafted through the air.

Myri held her breath and nodded. She ignored William's whining as she prodded him up the stairs. It had been a long day and all she wanted to do was go to her house atop the tree and spend some quality alone time. She shoved William into the cell and slammed the lock into place.

Deciding to hurry and get the talk with Cascus over with, she took the stairs in one leap, landing on the main floor in a slight crouch. Branch and Cascus looked up from where they sat. Myrikal joined them, sitting on the small couch next to her friend. She tried to arrange her face into a less defiant configuration than she felt at the moment. The same as she'd felt ever since Cascus had suggested they put a child in a cell and put him through a trial.

"Myrikal," Cascus began. "First I want to give you my utmost gratitude for apprehending several criminals today. Thank you. You are every bit as amazing as Morgan said you were." He paused, as if waiting for a response.

She attempted to smile, but worried that it came across more as a grimace. "Thanks."

Nodding once, he continued, "I would, however, like to discuss the issue of the young boy."

Myri stiffened. "There really isn't much to discuss."

His mouth blurred into a smile and he held a hand up toward her. "I would just like for you to hear my thoughts on why he should have been kept and tried." He continued quickly before she could say anything. "It matters not what the reason behind breaking a law is. We must be consistent in treating all broken laws the same. Otherwise, people will come up with all kinds of excuses in order to get away with infractions. That's how this world delves into chaos. Chaos is what we're trying to prevent here."

Myri leaned forward, ignoring the odor of Cascus. "A child's life is more important than any law. In fact, preserving human life no matter the age of the human, should always be the goal wherever possible. We came close to losing it all with the 'quakes and the sickness. Every human life is precious." She stood and looked down on him. "Especially those of children."

"Myri…" Branch whispered.

Cascus interrupted. "Your position on the matter is duly noted. My intention was never to harm the boy."

"No," Myrikal said. "Maybe not. But by keeping him here, great harm—greater harm—would have come to his sister."

"I only wish you would have given me a little more time to express my opinion on the matter before sweeping out of here." Cascus got to his feet across the coffee table from her.

"A little more time could easily have resulted in the death of the little girl." Myri took a breath, calming the tone of her voice. "Look, Cascus, we're going to have to agree to disagree on this one. I was raised by a man for whom life held no value. I won't—*can't*—be that person."

Cascus sighed. "Very well then. We will amicably disagree. Thank you again for your assistance today. I hope to see you at the trial tomorrow morning."

She nodded.

A glimpse of the undulating green beneath his skin came into her view. He shrugged a shoulder in a quick motion and the blurry façade returned to cover it. "It's been a full day. I believe I'm going to retire a bit early tonight. See you both in the morning." He disappeared down the stairs.

A whoosh of air forced its way out of Branch's lungs. "Myri, you're going to give me a heart attack."

She smiled down at her friend. "I won't go against my instincts anymore, Branch. Not even for you. I am sorry I stressed you out, though."

He stood and they walked to the door beside each other. "I don't want you to go against your instincts, either, Myri. It's just… I don't know… Cascus is a good and kind person. I *know* he is. And I want you to see that in him, too."

And I wish you could see what I see in him, Myrikal thought. "It might take me a while to believe that." She bumped his shoulder with hers and smiled. "I have a few trust issues, you know."

224

The seven prisoners plodded single-file down the stairs, led by Branch flanked by other members of DefCo. The leader of the group—the one who'd held a gun to Branch's head—tensed up, his eyes darting around the room, as they neared the bottom of the stairs. His gaze landed on Myrikal, standing midway between the stairs and the exit of the building, arms crossed over her chest. His tense muscles instantly deflated, his shoulders slumped, and the hopeful gleam in his eyes faded to a hateful glare.

Under normal circumstances, Myri would have laughed at the dejected countenance of the would-be attempted escapee. But she found no humor in the situation. Cascus had been too vague about possible punishments for the crimes. No matter how bad she wanted to trust him for Branch's sake, she couldn't.

Like a parade of sad clowns, Branch led the group to a bench set up in front of a podium and motioned for them to sit. The leader hesitated, glancing back at Myri and twitching his shoulder, before joining his crew. Myri narrowed her eyes at the jailbirds' backs.

Branch came and stood by her side. She leaned toward him and whispered, "Where's William?"

"Separate trials. We'll do his after these guys."

She nodded. Her attention moved from dark thoughts of the kidnapper still upstairs, to the podium. Cascus appeared from around the corner, his gown flowing behind him as he glided to the wooden stand. "Welcome to this trial of lawbreakers."

A hushed murmur traveled through the crowd of people who'd come to watch this novel occurrence. There weren't many seats, so most of them stood, packed into the room.

The trial ended quickly. Cascus called the guards to testify, strangely leaving the DefCo team out of the proceedings. He asked only one question of the accused. "For what purpose were you attempting to force your way into our community?"

Six faces turned to look on their leader. He sneered and said, "I don't have to tell you nothin'."

Cascus smiled, his eyes sweeping over the accused. "It does no matter anyway." He looked pointedly at Myrikal. "The law was broken, the excuse for which matters not." His gaze returned to the leader. "I was merely curious."

The leader spat on the floor.

Cascus sighed. "You have been found guilty. You are sentenced to death. The sentence will be carried out this evening in the central square."

⚡

"I won't do it, Cascus." Myrikal spun around and reached for the door.

"Talk to her, Morgan," Cascus said quietly.

Myri slammed the door behind her, not waiting for Branch. After Cascus had pronounced the sentence, the room had fallen eerily quiet for several seconds. Then all six of the condemned erupted with shouts of protest and the spectators talked in hushed voices.

Myrikal had watched in stunned silence as the DefCo team escorted the six back up the stairs to their cells. She hadn't even had time to process Cascus's declaration when the team returned leading William down the stairs. His "trial" proceeded much quicker than the last. Cascus pronounced him guilty of kidnapping and attempted theft and sentenced him to die that evening, too.

"Myri, wait!" Branch called to her.

The bitter wind thrashed her hair out behind her as she ran. She didn't stop until she reached her tree. She climbed all the way up and sat atop her house, looking out over the compound to the city beyond the walls. She sat, still as stone, as she seethed at what Cascus had asked her to do.

She didn't even twitch as Branch, huffing for breath, climbed up beside her ten minutes later. "Myri, listen…"

"I'm not going to do it, Branch. It's wrong."

"It isn't wrong. They're bad people. We can't make this place better if we allow bad people to get away with crap." He grabbed her arm. "Look at me, Myrikal."

She jerked her arm from his hand and whipped her head around to glare at him. "I won't kill people."

His face reddened. "You were going to kill for your dad!"

"But I *didn't*, Branch. I didn't kill for him. And I'm not going to do it for Cascus, or you, or anyone else."

Branch looked down at the shingles of the roof. He whispered, "You helped him kill my old clan."

"No. I tried to stop him…"

"But you didn't stop him, did you Myrikal?"

"I tried," she whispered again.

"We need you. Cascus's whole plan depends on your participation. We have to show everyone that breaking the law won't be tolerated. It's all for the greater good. So we can have a better world." His voice softened as he regurgitated the words of his perceived savior.

Myri swallowed, unable to respond.

Branch continued. "Just do it tonight. They say it's easier to do the next time and the next, until it just becomes a job."

A tear slipped down Myri's cheek. "I won't do it. Human life is so precious."

A frustrated huff blew past Branch's lips. "But they're all bad people!"

Turning to face him more completely, Myri said, "That's what my dad said, Branch. He was wrong. And you're wrong. And Cascus is wrong."

"He isn't! He's going to change the world. We're going to go out into Manhattan and rid it of all the bad people there next." He gripped her hands. "We need you, Myrikal."

The warmth of his hands touching hers calmed her anger a few degrees. She met his gaze and blew out her held breath. "Branch, I should have told you this the first time I noticed it, but I wasn't sure about what I was seeing."

"What…"

Squeezing his hands, she interrupted, "Cascus isn't *human*."

Branch narrowed his eyes, eyebrows coming together in confused unibrow. "What do you mean, he's not human?"

Myri swallowed and looked past Branch, out over the walls of the compound. "I can see through his human form. Not all the time, but enough that I know it's some kind of disguise. Not only that," she hurried to finish before he interrupted, "he *smells* funny. It's disgusting. I've never known what it feels like to be nauseated before coming here and smelling his odor. The stuff his building and the batteries are made out of gives me that same unsettled feeling."

"What are you talking about?" The confusion turned to irritation, she could hear it in his voice. "Of course Cascus is human. What else would he be?"

"I don't know what he is, but he is definitely not like us." She realized the irony of that statement as soon as it slipped across her tongue.

Branch noticed it, too. "*You* aren't like *us* either, Myri. More so than Cascus." His fingers worked at a loose piece of bark on the tree.

"But I'm human on the inside. He's something else. Something green and oozy and nauseating…" She trailed off, not knowing how to describe it to him. Not knowing how to make him believe her.

The chunk of bark broke off in Branch's grip and he chucked it out over the roof of her small house, into the surrounding trees. "This is crap, Myrikal. I know that you don't like him, but making stuff up is just ridiculous."

She'd already lost him. He couldn't see what she saw and there was no way to convince him otherwise. She touched his arm and waited for him to look at her before speaking. The disgust in his eyes made her wince. "Branch," she sighed, "I'm leaving. Come with me. We'll find a new place. Make our own rules. Rules that don't include killing anyone."

Branch's face flushed red. Not the pink-tinged red of embarrassment, but the purplish red borne of anger and frustration. He stood, nearly toppling off the small roof, steadying himself against the thin upper trunk of the tree. "I can't believe you," his voice low and seething. "Cascus *saved* my life after your dad turned my clan into a pile of ashes. I was near starving with nowhere to go. I'd already fallen prey to the underbelly of the city. More than once…"

"What do you…"

His head spun in her direction. Spittle flew from his rage-filled face as he let loose on her. "What do I mean? Is that what you were going to ask? I *mean* that a young boy wandering the streets alone is a prime target for perverts and those illustrious entrepreneurs who make a living supplying them with young boys to… to do with as they please." He slumped back down, his rear-end hitting the roof with a solid thud. Hiding his face in his arms folded atop his bent knees, his voice quavered as he mumbled, "Cascus saved me. From that."

Myri raised her hand to hover over his shoulder, wanting to comfort him but afraid to touch him. "Branch… I… I'm so sorry. don't…"

"Just leave, Myri. Just go. You will never understand what it's like to be vulnerable and helpless to someone stronger than you. I get it now. I understand why you refuse to accept that Cascus is a good man who only wants to rid the world of scum." He raised his head to look her square in the eye, eyes sparking with disgust. "You don't have to worry about being a victim so it isn't important to you. It's easy for you to say, 'let them live' because they can't hurt you."

She dropped her hovering hand to her lap.

With one last disgusted scowl, Branch looked away and whispered again, "Just leave."

She wiped a tear from her face. She waited several minutes after Branch climbed down from her treehouse before she swung down to the porch. She gathered a few things into her backpack, looked around one last time at the small home she'd built with her friends, and stepped out onto the porch, shutting the door softly behind her. She thought briefly about stopping by Alyssa's to tell her good-bye, but decided against it.

Myrikal stepped off the porch twenty feet above the ground, landing with a slight bend to her knees before taking off at a run. No idea where to go, she ran. Out of the city, across a crumbling bridge, farther away from Manhattan than she'd ever dreamed of going.

PART FOUR
JUST MYRIKAL

$\xi 23\xi$

The goggles hung limp around her neck as the clouds obscured even the faintest hint of light from the moon or stars. Myrikal had run at full speed for several hours. Every time her imagination wandered to the things Branch had been forced to endure after losing his first clan—bringing horrible pictures to her mind—an anguished scream would tear from her throat and she'd force a new burst of speed from her feet and legs.

Dozens of miles farther from Manhattan than she'd ever been, she finally collapsed in a field overgrown with weeds and trees bent at odd angles. Truly alone in the world, she sat curled in upon herself, rocking back and forth like some of the crazies she'd seen in the underground tunnels. At least she wasn't talking to herself yet. Not out loud, anyway.

What was she doing? Where was she running to? She'd promised to teach Marcus how to use the gun. She should go back.

Should she go back?

What would Russ do if he found out she was no longer there to stop him? She knew what he'd do. The same thing he'd done her whole life. He'd kill people and get paid to do it. Unless Cascus taught him. She wasn't sure how she felt about that, convinced that both men were equally evil, but not comfortable with the thought of either of them doing away with the other.

She had to go back. But not now. She needed some time to

think. Laying her backpack on the pressed down weeds, she laid her head on it and closed her eyes, trying to push all thoughts from her mind.

$$\frac{1}{2}$$

MYRIKAL'S EYES flew open but she stayed still where she lay. Something had awakened her. She held her breath, listening. The soft *whoosh* of rustling grass alerted her to the whereabouts of… something. Myri shot up to a crouch and turned to face the sound. She was met by a flurry of teeth, claws, and black fur. She grabbed the attacker by the fur and skin around its shoulders and flung the *rawring* animal away from her. A *thunk* and a rush of breath told her the animal had smashed into a tree. Fumbling for the goggles around her neck, Myri squinted in the cloud-covered morning sunlight streaming through the leaves above. She pushed the goggles in place, snapping the stretchable band beneath her hair at the back of her neck.

A panther. A black panther.

She approached the unmoving animal with caution. There had been the occasional wild animal sighting in Manhattan, but she'd never seen a real giant feline before. Her dad had explained to her that during and after the 'quakes, the wild animals that had been kept captive in zoos and by eccentric rich people had all escaped. Most of them headed out of the city, away from all the people. Apparently, at least some of them had survived and multiplied. Myri knelt next to the large animal and pressed a hand to its chest. Blood dripped from its nostrils, matting the fur on its face.

No up and down movement of a living creature drawing breath. Crashing into the tree had killed it instantly.

"Oh," Myri said, noticing the fullness of the cat's teats. "You have babies somewhere. I'm so sorry." She hung her head for a few seconds, devastated that she'd killed such a magnificent creature.

A soft mewling caught Myri's attention and she stood and

moved toward the sound. It led her to a felled and decayed tree. She knelt before a crooked opening in the hollowed out trunk and reached inside. The invasion of her hand was met with a juvenile hiss and a swat from sharp claws. Myri gripped the edges of the opening on each side and ripped a bigger hole. A black ball of fur —about half the size of Dal's German Shepherd—backed up, hunching its spine as its tail-end pushed against the rear of the hollowed trunk.

Smiling for the first time in days, Myri laughed at the brave hissing fit of the small feline. She sat next to it, legs crossed in the tall grass. "I'm really sorry about your mom, little one. I can't just leave you here to fend for yourself. I don't think you'd last very long. You're gonna' have to accept me as a friend." She reached for the cub, unconcerned with its teeth and claws, and spoke in a soft, soothing voice. "It's okay, baby. It's okay. I won't hurt you. We're going to be friends. I'll take care of you."

Myrikal ignored the cub's vicious attack as its claws raked her impervious hands. She cradled it close to her chest until it wore itself out and fell asleep in her arms. Myri turned carefully, so as not to awaken her new reluctant friend, and leaned her back against the downed tree. She closed her eyes and tilted her head back, enjoying the peace and quiet. She'd rarely been somewhere where there wasn't constant noise and people nearby.

The cub was warm against her chest. She smiled as it purred in its sleep. How was she going to feed her new charge? What did you feed a panther cub who wasn't yet quite weaned from its mom? Just under the surface of this new dilemma, lurked the sadness and rage from earlier. It was a good distraction, just not good enough to rid her mind completely of the pictures Branch's words had put there.

Eyes still closed, the cub scooted up to Myri's shoulder and nestled its face into the crook of her neck. Its breath and whiskers tickled her skin, and she smiled again.

Myri thought they must have sat like that for at least an hour. The cub's purring and cuddling caused a calmness to fall over her such as she'd never felt. She even fell asleep for a short while, leaned up against the fallen tree.

The calmness disappeared as soon as her young charge awoke, however. High-pitched cries of what Myri assumed to be hunger replaced the sweet little breaths and intermittent purrs. Myri stood, one arm wrapped around the wiggling cub. Time to figure out what to feed him. Or her. She lifted the cub in line with her eyes and moved its tail out of the way to have a peek. Him. She was *pretty* sure, anyway.

She walked toward an area even thicker with trees and brush, listening as the soothing sound of water running down a creek bed delighted her ears. Her mind shifted to the time Branch had taken her fishing a million years ago. Back when they were young, before time and circumstances had changed everything. When a river creature had tried to bite Branch's arm off.

Fish. *Cats eat fish. Right?*

"Okay, baby," she said to the crying cub. "I think I know what to feed you for dinner. And I think I'll officially name you Baby." She rushed through the brush to the edge of the stream and followed it to a spot where it pooled before falling over some moss covered logs blocking its path. "There should be some fish in here, don't ya think?"

The cub answered with a spitting hiss and a rake of his claws. He was in no mood for questions, it seemed. "Well, I guess we don't have time to find supplies and fish like my friend taught me. She couldn't bring herself to say his name out loud. "I'll have to improvise."

Not wanting the cub to wander off, Myrikal quickly threw together a small caged-in area using rocks. She hadn't thought Baby could protest any louder until she put him inside the rock cage. "Wow. You really have some lungs on you."

Myri concentrated for a brief second. Electricity crackled from her fingertips and into the shallow pool of water, lighting it up with an ear-splitting *crack*. She tipped her head in a satisfied nod as the first of the fish floated to the surface, belly up.

"Oh," Myri exclaimed. She splashed into the knee-high water as the fish floated toward the little waterfall. The first one slipped past her, but she was able to scoop up the other five as they followed the current toward her.

"I hope you're hungry, Baby. I didn't mean to zap this many." She waded out of the pool and deposited her catch on the grass near the cub's cage. He stopped mewling and sniffed the air, moving cautiously closer to Myri where she sat just outside the rock prison. He sniffed again, then started in with more desperate crying while he clawed his way up the quickly constructed barrier.

"Okay, I get it. You're hungry." She pulled her backpack to her and dug inside for her knife. The blade glinted in the sparse sunlight as she pulled it from its protective sheath. She grabbed a fish by the tail and scraped the scales off, unsure of the best way to feed it to the cub. She filleted a slice of meat from the side of the fish and cut it into bite-sized pieces atop a flat-ish rock.

Setting the knife aside, Myrikal reached for Baby. If they were going to be friends, she was sure the first step would be for him to associate her with feeding time. She held him close to her chest and grabbed a chunk of meat from the rock, holding it under his nose. A pink tongue flicked out and snagged the fish. Myri laughed as he chomped, probably swallowing it more intact than not.

He *mewled*, ready for more. They sat near the stream, Myri feeding him from her hand, until he'd finished off the first round of chopped fish and almost all of the second round. His belly bowed out where it rested against her arm. Her mouth twitched at the corners as she watched him lick his paws and clean his whiskers.

Baby took a short nap on Myri's lap before waking up ready to play. As he ran around attacking her from different angles, rolling away from her when he tripped over his too-big paws, she thought about how easy it'd been to gain his trust. It was all about food and feeling safe. Not so different from people. Not so different from the children she'd saved.

Myri frowned. She'd promised Marcus she'd teach him how to use the gun she'd taken from his sister's captor. She would like to check on Dal and Chansong, too, to make sure they were doing okay with Changsong's clan. Maybe she shouldn't wait to go back. After her conversation with Branch, she couldn't deny that people did horrible things to children if they knew they could get away with it. She should go back. At least for a day or so. She'd make it known that anyone wishing to harm a child would have dire consequences.

Isn't that what Cascus is trying to do? Bring some order and consequence to Manhattan? Myri shook her head. That's what Branch and the others thought. But Myri couldn't shake the strong feeling that Cascus had ulterior motives. She didn't know what those motives were, she just knew they were bad.

Mind made up to go back, she filleted and cut up the rest of the fish then cooked it on a heated rock, thinking it would keep better if cooked. She filled her canteen with water from the stream and waited for Baby as he lapped up his fill from the pool. Baby sniffed around in the grass to find the perfect spot to do his business. While he crouched there, Myri changed out of her lightning unitard and into normal clothes. She made room for Baby in the backpack, folding the slick rayon outfit and laying it on top of the odds and ends in the bottom of the bag.

"All right, little dude." She scooped him off the ground and settled him into his new carrier, leaving the zipper open so he could poke his head out. "Let's go check on the kids."

Not wanting to jiggle Baby around too much, Myri walked back at a pace much slower than the frantic speed with which she'd fled the city the day before. Having a young cub to care for required frequent stops to feed, water, and allow him potty breaks and frolicking time. They were still quite some distance away from their destination as night fell. Worried that he might wander off

yri tied a thin rope around Baby's neck then tied the other end to
er wrist, then laughed at his histrionics when he felt the leash tug
n him.

Mad at her, Baby laid down to sleep as far from her as the rope
ould allow. He growled low in his throat as he chewed on his
straint. His need for warmth or fear of being out in the open
nquered his irritation, as he soon belly-crawled over to Myri and
irled up next to her, his warm breath tickling the sensitive skin of
er neck.

⚡

CRASH of thunder brought Myrikal and her charge abruptly
vake. Baby's black hair stood on end all over his body, his ears
astered against his head, and his green eyes opened impossibly
ide as he clawed at her skin. A rush of intense, unexplainable joy
rged through Myri. She tucked Baby partially into the backpack
id, leaving it on the ground, jumped to her feet, face turned up to
e blackened sky.

She rushed to a small clearing just as the skin on her bare arms
arted to tingle, the tiny hairs standing at attention. She stretched
er arms out wide to the sides and, just as she'd done outside
ranch's compound on the day she'd left her dad, she called the
ghtning to her, accepting the bolts of pure electricity in through
er hands. Accepting the pure exultation into her heart. Into her
ul, as it connected with her at the level of the atoms that made
 her being. She'd never felt so strong or so alive as the lightning
ntinued to pulse into her, longer than any lightning strike she'd
er been witness to.

Was that because of her? Was she now *causing* the lightning to
ntinue pouring from the sky? When the pulsing in her head told
er she'd reached full capacity, she *released* the electricity with a
ep exhale of breath. The dark clouds lit up for a brief time as
ey took back what she'd pulled from them.

Hands clenched at her sides, Myrikal closed her eyes a[nd] lowered her head, remnants of static electricity buzzing throu[gh] her frizzed-out hair. She inhaled deeply and held the breath [,] wanting the feeling to last.

Incessant meowing and ripping noises coming from her bac[k] pack broke the spell. Myri released the held breath and ran h[er] hands over her hair, trying to tame it somewhat. She smiled as s[he] glanced at the backpack where Baby had crawled out and now h[ad] one of the straps in his jaws, yanking it around like a whip. He w[as] probably hungry. And they should be on their way back [to] Manhattan.

Myrikal pulled on the backpack, but Baby refused to let g[o.] The ferocious young panther finally released his grip when his fe[et] no longer touched the ground, rolling gracefully on the grass befo[re] landing in a crouch. Myri laughed, wondering if her still sligh[tly] sparking hair matched the hair standing on end along Baby's spin[e.]

She held a handful of dried fish out to him, happy that, after[a] slight hesitation, he ate it right out of her hand. "Alright little o[ne.] Let's get on the road. We should be able to make it to the city [by] lunchtime."

⚡

MYRIKAL SCOOPED up an exhausted Baby and settled him into t[he] backpack, his head and shoulders extending out the top. He galloped and played alongside her most of the way, weari[ng] himself out by the time they reached the outskirts of Manhatta[n.] Her stomach lurched in small stops and starts as she neared the t[all] buildings. She desperately hoped not to run into anyone fro[m] Cascus's clan. Or her father.

Luckily, the Repopulation Clan's compound was near the ed[ge] of the city where few people ventured. Myri knocked on the ga[te.] She could easily have climbed over the surrounding wall, b[ut] thought knocking would be better received by the leaders. Cha[nce] song's mom peeked around the edge, peering through the iron slats. Recognition blossomed on her weathered face and her eyes crinkled up into a smile.

"Myrikal! It's so wonderful to see you. Come inside. The children will be thrilled to see you. They talk about you all the time."

"Thank you." Myri stepped into the compound, closing the gate behind her. "How are the kids? Chansong? Dal? Marcus and Annie? Are they doing okay?"

"They're doing well. See for yourself." She swept her arm in an arc toward three kids, running full-bore toward them.

"Myrikal!" Dal reached her first, his long legs outpacing the others. He wrapped his arms around her waist in an exuberant hug. "I thought you forgot about us."

"Dal, you've grown. I guess I don't have to ask if they're feeding you enough." Myri knelt to receive hugs from the two girls. "Where's Marcus?"

"He'll be here in a sec," Annie said. "He went to get his gun. He wants to show you something." She rolled her eyes as only an unimpressed little sister can.

Myri stood and looked across the large grassy compound. There he was, running toward her with a big grin spread across his young face. She waved.

Much had transpired in the few days since she'd rescued Annie from the dog kennel William held her in. And rescued Marcus from whatever punishment Cascus had planned for him for attempting to steal a battery.

Marcus slowed to a stop in front of her and gave her an awkward one-armed hug. "Hey, Myrikal. You kept your promise." His eyes flicked up to hers before returning to stare at the ground.

"Yeah." She ruffled his hair. "I told you I would."

He shrugged. "People don't always keep their promises." He met her gaze, then, and smiled. "One of the dads here showed me how to use the gun you gave me. Wanna' see?"

"Of course I do." Myri looked around. "Where do you practice?"

"Anywhere, really. We have to save the bullets so I've just been practicing without them." A tinge of pink touched his cheeks.

"Let's see it, then. Show me what you've learned."

Marcus started by telling her about the safety steps—don't ever point the gun at someone you don't intend to shoot, always treat it like it's loaded and ready to go. He showed her how to click the safety on and off. How to clip the magazine into the grip and pop it out again with the push of a button. With a slight bit of difficulty, he pulled the slide back, showing her how to chamber a bullet, if there had been any in the magazine.

The gun was big for his small hands, the tip of his index finger just resting on the trigger as he closed one eye and aimed toward the back wall. "You have to line up the front sight and the back sight on the target before you shoot," he explained. He pulled the trigger and the slide closed on the empty chamber.

"Looks like you have a great teacher. You might need to grow into this gun a bit before you can shoot with accuracy. Because of the way your finger rests on the trigger, I'm afraid you'll pull up and out when you fire a real bullet."

"That's what Larry said, too. He told me I should adjust my aim to make up for it." Marcus's eyes lit up. "He said we could spare three bullets during the next thunderstorm so I can fire it for reals."

"Why during a thunderstorm?" Myri asked.

"He doesn't want anyone outside of our clan to know about the gun. He said the thunder will hide the gunshots."

Myri nodded. "That's smart."

Baby wiggled at her back, and popped his head up over her shoulder.

Chansong clapped her hands together and pointed at the panther.

"Oh, a kitty!" Annie exclaimed.

Myri laughed and swung the backpack off her shoulder, laying it gently on the ground. She held Baby aloft. "Not exactly. He's a black panther cub." Her lips drew down into a frown. "Orphaned."

Eyes pleading with Myrikal, Chansong held her hands out then gestured in a petting motion.

"He's still pretty wild. I just found him two days ago. His teeth and claws aren't super big, but they're sharp." Myri set the wriggling cub on the grass, keeping hold of the scruff of his neck.

Chansong dropped to her knees. Myri was pretty sure the girl hadn't heard a word she'd said. The girl held her hand out toward Baby and the heretofore ferocious little beast army-crawled to her and licked her little fingers. Within minutes, Baby's head lay in Chansong's lap, eyes half closed, purring as she stroked his fur.

"So much for the wild beast I found in the forest." Myrikal stepped back to watch the four kids shower the cub with affection.

"What's its name?" Annie asked.

"His name is Baby."

She screwed up her tiny face with a look of consternation. "You know he isn't going to stay little, right? He's already bigger than our cat."

"Right," Myri laughed. "From the look of his paws, I'd say he's going to be quite large, in fact. But I like the name Baby."

Annie smiled. "Me, too."

"Uh-oh." Chansong's mom looked past the children, back toward the large building. "You'd better get your dog, Dal, before he sees Baby."

Dal jumped up and spun around, intercepting the large dog halfway across the compound. "Hey, Lobo." He rubbed the dog's ears and back. "Where you been? Out hunting? Let's go get you some water." Dal led the dog away, turning to wave. "See you later, Myri!"

As she raised her arm to wave back, a large blast sounded nearby, outside the walls, but close enough to shake the ground where they stood. A plume of smoke rose into the air a block or so away. "Chansong, you're in charge of Baby until I get back."

Myri ran toward the wall, gripped the edge with her hands and catapulted herself over the top. She hit the ground, running toward the screams.

Flames rose from the smaller building that could have been a pizza restaurant in the time before the 'quakes. The front of the building lay in a mess of jumbled bricks and broken glass. Flames shot out the opening. A soot-covered woman with burns to her hands and face stumbled toward the wreckage, stopping with a cry when the heat became too much to bear.

Myri skidded to a stop in front of her. "Are there people in there?"

The woman nodded, tears streaming down her cheeks. "My friends."

Arms covering her face, Myrikal jumped through the flames and into the crumbling building. Right away she realized it was too late for the first body she came to. Charred beyond recognition, there was no saving them. Coughing came from further back, so she made her way toward the sound, slapping at the flames that had taken hold of her jeans. A woman laid on her stomach behind a piece of the counter that still stood. Blood seeped from a wound in her head, but her back rose and fell with labored breaths.

Myri knelt next to her, searching for another way out. She couldn't carry this woman back through the flames. She spied a metal door at the back of the room. Myri lifted the woman and carried her over her shoulder. She tried the door with her free hand, but it wouldn't budge, like someone had blocked it from the outside. Myri raised her foot and kicked it square in the middle. The door bowed at the center, cracks opening up at the edges near the doorframe. A couple more kicks and the door buckled in half, tearing free of its hinges and whatever had been blocking it from the outside.

Most of the smoke and flames converged near the front of the building, so the only smoke in the back alley came from what the wind pushed over the rooftops. Myrikal made her way around, wanting to get to the lady out front, to ask if there were any more people inside. She rounded the corner of the building and stopped, nearly dropping the injured woman. Four similarly clad people stood back a safe distance from the burning building, one of them with an arm draped around the crying lady's shoulders. Lightning bolt patches emblazoned the right shoulders of their uniforms.

Crap. They were the last people Myrikal wanted to see. Especially the tall one. It was too late to do anything about it now though. Branch had already seen her. The scowl on his face made that much clear.

She straightened her shoulders and readjusted the unconscious woman she carried. Attempting to keep a neutral expression on her face, Myrikal strode over to the group.

"Hey, Myrikal." Ya gave a slight bow.

"Hi, Ya."

Branch refused to look her in the eyes. "You can put her down now. And leave. We have this under control." He pulled a flare from his belt and shot it into the air.

His words stung. The sparking hatred in his eyes was like a knife in her back. She swallowed down the rising bile in her throat and laid the woman in the street with a gentle swing of her arms. Not wanting to see similar looks in the eyes of the others, Myri turned and hurried away.

She whipped her head around as something glinted off the light of the flames. It flew through the air right toward the small group she'd left standing in the street. Right toward Branch.

Myrikal leaped, intercepting it mid-flight. She curled her body around the familiar metal object and crashed to the ground, rolling. The small bomb exploded.

"Myri!"

Branch's voice echoed inside her head as she skidded to a stop on her right shoulder and hip. She blinked open her eyes, glaring light blinded one of them. Too bright. She touched the goggle lens on that side and found nothing but the frame and a few jagged remnants of the lens.

"Go after him!" Branch yelled.

His voice sounded distant, as if he stood at the end of a long, stone cavern. Myrikal, keeping her uncovered eye closed, glanced down at her shredded clothing. She almost expected to see blood even though she'd never bled before. No blood. Just shredded cloth and the metal fragments of the explosive device she'd been able to keep her body wrapped around.

The shrapnel fell to the ground as Myrikal sat up. Branch dropped to his knees next to her. "Myri, are you okay?"

His voice still sounded far away, yet he was right next to her. She tilted her head, slow with a response. "I… I think so." She cupped her hand over the broken lens. "I broke my goggles." She shook her head, trying to clear away the fuzziness.

"Can you stand up?"

That thought hadn't occurred to her yet. *Yeah. Stand up. That's probably a good idea.* She stood, looking around through her goggled eye. Something just happened that she should be responding to. She looked at Branch, his face reddened as he jerked his gaze away from her body to search an area across the street. She looked down. Oh, yeah. Shredded clothing. There were more holes in her shirt than actual material. It didn't cover much. She liked that shirt, too.

"The others ran after him." Branch waved a hand in the direction he stared.

"After who?"

"After your dad." He grabbed her by the shoulders. "Myri, are you sure you're okay?"

"My… my dad?" She closed both eyes and forced her mind to think. The bomb. Someone had thrown a bomb. She'd caught it. No wonder her clothes hung on her like threadbare rags. She opened her eyes, ignoring the brightness in the uncovered one. "My dad threw a bomb at you. Are you sure it was him?" She hadn't seen who'd thrown it.

"Yes, Myrikal. I'm sure it was him." He sounded exasperated.

In a flash, her mind snapped back together. She remembered Branch telling her to leave. Remembered his anger. "I should go help them." She took off in the direction he'd pointed, not waiting for him to answer.

She heard the struggle before catching sight of them. Her father was a great fighter, but he was no match for three DefCo team members. Team members she'd trained in hand-to-hand combat. Heck, he was barely a match for Ya, who really hadn't needed her training in the first place. By the time she reached them, they had her father's hands cuffed behind him. He cursed and spat blood onto Donna as she propelled him forward.

"Myrikal," he almost smiled. "Get these assholes off me."

"The assholes you just tried to blow up, you mean?" Myri asked.

"You don't understand, Myrikal. They're trying to take over the city. They think they're better than everyone else out here."

"Throwing explosives at people is a way to prove you're 'better' than them?"

His bloody face contorted into a hateful scowl. "Screw you *daughter*! I should have known you wouldn't help me."

"Yeah. You should have." Myri rounded a corner back the way she'd come and stopped, her stomach lurching. Cascus stood next to Branch and the injured women from the burning building. She could smell his rotten odor from a half block away.

"Myrikal," Cascus said as she neared them. "I thought you'd left the city."

"I came back to tie up a few loose ends."

"Well, we have this little problem under control. You can leave now." He narrowed his eyes at her, his true form undulating just beneath the surface. "For good this time."

One glance at Branch told her he agreed with his alien mentor. "I'll leave when I want and return whenever I choose." She jerked her head toward the three DefCo members dragging her dad across the street. "What are you planning to do with him?"

"You'll be happy to know that I took your thoughts on the death penalty to heart, dear Myrikal. We've come up with other ways to ensure compliance with our laws. Your father will be one of the first we try it out on. We won't kill him. He may just wish we had." Cascus's lips turned up in a gruesome smile.

"What…"

"Don't worry about it, Myri," Branch interrupted. "You left us. You've already proven you don't want to be a part of creating a better world. Just go."

"Yeah! Go!" Russ yelled. "You're a worthless piece of junk."

Ya turned on him and punched up into his diaphragm, exploding the breath from his lungs. "Don't talk to your daughter that way."

Myri gave Ya an appreciative nod then turned to Branch. "The score's ten to one now, by the way. See you around."

Branch grunted in response as Myri turned and walked away.

She returned to the repopulation compound just long enough to change her clothes and get Baby and her backpack. This time, she meant her goodbyes. She was never coming back to this place.

⚡25⚡

The sunshine, unobscured by clouds for probably the first time in her life, warmed Myrikal's skin. Was it always like this out here, days away from Manhattan? She and Baby had taken their time when they'd left. And why not? They had nowhere to be, no destination in mind. Myri made sure to stay near a water source, which were all blissfully cleaner than what she was used to.

It had been a week, maybe more, since the bomb incident and the short reunion with her father. She'd tossed the useless goggles, determined to train her eyes to accommodate the brightness of daylight. They weren't cooperating. Especially in the unaccustomed sunshine unfiltered by clouds. After an afternoon's worth of squinting, eye watering, and holding her hand up for shade, Myri fashioned a visor by weaving together some long grass. Alyssa would definitely have something smart-alecky to say if she'd seen it. But it helped. And her eyes were adjusting somewhat. That wasn't to say she wouldn't snatch up a pair of tinted goggles if one happened to become available, though.

"Not that I don't appreciate your company, Baby, but it'll sure be nice to talk to a real person or two." Myrikal stooped to examine a shoeprint in the soft earth. The semi worn trail they followed hinted that they neared a town of some sort. "Let's go check things out."

Baby had stayed within a dozen feet or so of Myri while they traveled. She'd only carried him when his young legs tired out and only tied the rope to his neck the first couple of nights. They had officially become surrogate family to each other, and she no longer worried about him wandering off. He knew where his daily meals of fish came from.

The trees and brush opened up to what had once been a small suburb. There were remnants of such all over the place, Myri had passed through or near many of them. The homes had all been in shambles, most of them overgrown heaps of wood and brick atop crumbling foundations. This one was different. The sounds of life—human life, not insects and small woodland creatures—tickled her ears.

Her breath caught in her throat as she surveyed the area. Homes. Real homes. Someone—some *people*—had restored the homes here. Not just that, they'd built a town. A small town, one that Myri could take in almost all at once with just a slight turn of her head. But it was a town.

Children's laughter caught her attention and pulled her toward it. Right in the center of the town at least two-dozen children of all ages played outside a single-story building. A hand-painted sign hung neatly over the door—SCHOOL. Myri smiled. She'd never seen this many children gathered together. She didn't even know if there were this many children in all of Manhattan. She watched the children play some sort of chasing game, closely watched by three adults. One of the kids stopped, pointed at Myrikal, and yelled, "Stranger!"

The three adults—two females and one male—pivoted in her direction, putting themselves between her and the children. Their faces showed concern and alertness, but not anger, thankfully.

Myri waved. "Hi?"

The older of the three, a female that looked to be about Russ's age, told the others to take the children inside and get started on their next lessons. She turned to Myri and smiled as she walked over to her. "Hello. My name is Katherine. And who might you be? We don't often get visitors here."

"I'm Myrikal. You can call me Myri if you want. I'm sorry." She looked toward the school. "I didn't mean to scare them."

"Oh, I don't think you scared them. They've been taught to alert us and each other of any strangers in town. It happens so rarely, they find newcomers fascinating." She inhaled deeply and put her hands on her hips. "So, what *does* bring you here, Myrikal?"

How should she answer that question? "Just passing through, I guess. Exploring." *Running away from my past.*

Nodding, Katherine said, "Miracle, huh? Your parents must have really wanted you. Loved you."

Myri huffed and looked down. "Just the opposite, actually. *From now on I think I'll stick with telling people my name is Myri.*

The woman gasped and stepped back, causing Myri to look up, senses at high alert. "What?"

"Is that…" She pointed toward Myri's legs. "Is that a *panther*?"

Baby sat next to her, leaning against her leg. "Yes. His name Baby. I think he might be a little shy." She'd been amazed at how fast he grew. She guessed him to be almost twice the size he'd been when she rescued him. She preferred to think of it that way as opposed to thinking about being responsible for the death of his mother.

"Yes. Well, you probably should tie him up or something. He looks to be mostly wild and I wouldn't want anything to happen to him."

Baby hissed when Myri reached down to pick him up, swatting at her hand. His flattened ears and the hair standing up along his spine showed him to be at high alert. Nervous about these new surroundings. Myri lifted him, held him close to her chest, and soothed him with strokes to his fur and quiet words. "It's okay, Baby. No one's going to hurt you." She pulled a rope out of the backpack and slipped it around his neck before setting him back on the ground.

"I can't believe you can just lift him like that, he looks so heavy," Katherine said. "How long do you plan to *explore* here?" She smiled as she spoke, seeming kind and welcoming now that the wild animal had been dealt with.

"I'm not sure. Is it a problem? Is there a time limit on how long someone can visit?" Myri said the last part jokingly.

"Actually, yes, there is. Joseph will explain it all to you." She gestured for Myri to follow her. "He's the current Committee Leader."

They had rebuilt the homes in concentric rings around the center of the town. It looked like they'd gathered up usable supplies from all the destroyed homes and used them to rebuild. Remnants of concrete from the foundations of old homes spotted the landscape. It looked like they'd rebuilt one out of every three homes in three large rings, leaving open spaces between them for individual gardens. And—Myri gazed out beyond the homes—was that an orchard? She decided to save her questions for the Committee Leader, hoping he didn't turn out to be another Cascus. This place looked amazing. But so did Cascus's Central Park.

Katherine led her to a building on the far side of the school, where she knocked on the door before opening it and entering. "Joseph? I brought a visitor to see you."

A diminutive older man scooted a wheeled office chair back from a desk in a room with the door wide open. "Welcome! It's been a while since we've had a visitor. Are you alone young woman?"

Myri nodded, smiling at his cheerfulness. Baby let out a loud feline cry, causing all three of them to jump. Myri's face reddened. "Except for my noisy friend, that is." She pulled on the rope, encouraging Baby to step out from behind her.

Joseph's eyes widened as his eyebrows shot up to his receding hairline. "Well, well. Does your *friend* need a drink of water or anything?"

"He just drank from the stream before we wandered into your beautiful town. He should be fine for now."

Joseph stood and gestured to a chair facing his desk. "Have a seat., uh…"

"Myri," she said.

"Have a seat, Myri. Let's talk." He turned to Katherine. "Thank you for escorting our guest to the Community Building, Kate. You may stay if you'd like."

She shook her head, looking warily at Baby. "No, I'd better get back to the school. The children have probably formed a coup and have Crystal and Bernard tied to chairs by now."

"She's joking, of course," Joseph said as Katherine's footsteps echoed toward the exit. "The children here are all wonderful."

Moving her backpack to the front, Myri sat, resting it on her lap.

"So, Myri, you're probably wondering why Kate brought you here."

She nodded, surprised he didn't start right off questioning her.

"Our little town is modeled after a kibbutz. Do you know what that is?"

"I have no idea." She reached down and stroked the top of Baby's head. Whether it was to calm herself or him, she wasn't sure.

"They were all the rage in Israel a century or so ago. The concept is that a community works together for the survival and hopefully, the betterment of the community. We have joint ownership of the property. Everyone's home is the same size. We all have assigned work."

"And, you're the leader? The boss?"

Wrinkles at the corners of his eyes scrunched up as he laughed. "No, no, no. The town runs by committee. Everyone takes turns being on the town committee and we elect a new leader every two years. No one gets to be the committee leader more than once every four elections."

"So everyone gets to decide how things are done?"

"Yes."

"What happens to people who disagree?" Myri thought about people who'd been kicked out of Central Park for disagreeing with the way Cascus ran things.

"Well, sometimes we have some pretty heated debates, but eventually, everyone agrees to go with the majority vote."

Myri nodded. "What about punishment? Crimes?"

He tilted his head to the side and raised a single eyebrow. "Thankfully, there isn't much of that around here. Everyone is trained to defend themselves and we have a militia of sorts in case of threats from outside."

She decided to ignore the suspicion that his last comment was meant for her along with the fact that he'd basically skirted around her question.

"May I ask you a question now?" He leaned forward, resting his elbows on the desk.

"Of course."

"What brings you here?"

Even though she knew this question was coming, she hadn't really prepared an answer. She decided to just forge ahead, using the same vague excuse she'd given Katherine. "I'm just exploring. I've never been outside Manhattan, and I was—am—curious to see other people. See how they live."

"Is there a specific reason you chose to leave your home?"

Myri snorted derisively. "I never really had a home. But I chose to leave Manhattan for a lot of reasons. Let's just say it was time to get away."

"Okay." She could tell Joseph wasn't happy with her evasive answers, but he didn't push it. "You're welcome to visit with us as long as you agree to our terms of visitation."

"And those terms are?"

"We only allow visitors to stay a maximum of two weeks. You will need to pitch in with the work while you're here, though you can choose your work assignment. You will be provided a place to stay and meals to eat in return. The Committee reserves the right to ask you to leave at any time and you have to agree to do so without argument."

"That all sounds fair enough. Why only two weeks, though?" Baby slapped playfully at her hand, growling.

"Any longer than that causes problems."

"What if I decide I would like to stay longer?" *Maybe live here forever.*

"I'm afraid that isn't possible. We have a full community at this time." He leaned back and rummaged around in a desk drawer for a few seconds. He held a small chunk of dried meat out to her. "Would your little friend like a snack? He looks like he's getting antsy."

"I believe he would, yes." Myri took it from him and held it in front of Baby's nose. "What do you mean by 'full'?"

"Our system only works well in small numbers. No more than two hundred may live here at a time, and right now, we're at our capacity. You're welcome to visit, but you can't stay."

Baby attacked the meat with gusto, making little growling noises as he chewed. "Okay, then. Two weeks. What are the work assignments I can choose from?"

"You agree to the visitation terms?" Joseph raised a bushy eyebrow.

"I do."

"And it's just you and the cub?"

"Yes." Myri tilted her head and frowned. "I think I already told you I'm traveling alone."

"I just want to be sure. It's my duty to ensure the safety of our community. It's not typical, or safe, for anyone to travel alone these days. Particularly a girl of your young age."

"I guarantee you that I am alone." *Really, truly alone.* She stroked Baby's back. "And I can take care of myself. I don't need a traveling companion." She didn't want to give away too much about her abilities. The less people knew about what she could do, the less they'd find ways to *use* her.

"The most common visitor assignments are: working in the fields by weeding, planting, harvesting,; food preparation, we eat morning and evening meals together; tending to the animals; or, this time of year, helping harvest fruit from the orchards."

She noticed that helping out with the children was not given as an option. Probably a good policy, to not have strangers hanging around the kids. She wanted to choose something she could truly be helpful with, but not show off her abnormal abilities. "I'd like to help in the orchards, if that's okay."

Joseph smiled. "Good choice. We need all the help we can get out there." He leaned forward and raised his eyebrows. "I hope you aren't afraid of heights."

Myri smiled. "Nope. Heights do not scare me."

"Okay." He stood and stretched his hand out toward her. "We have a deal." They shook hands. "I'll show you to the guest house and let you get settled. You can join us for dinner in the communal dining room when you hear the dinner bell ring. Someone will stop by first thing in the morning to show you to the orchard."

The leashed Baby walked next to her as she followed Joseph through the cracked streets. The single story guest house was slightly larger than the surrounding homes. Joseph opened the front door and hollered, "Nancy? Are you here? I have a guest for you."

An elderly woman shuffled around a corner, into the entryway. "Nice hat," the woman, Nancy, snorted. She looked down at Baby, hiding behind Myri's legs. "That thing better not do its business inside. You'll be cleanin' it up if it does, 'cause I'm sure not gonna'."

Myri touched her hastily crafted visor and tried to hide a smile. She was going to like Nancy. "I'm not used to this much sun. This thing was the best I could do with my limited abilities. Don't worry about Baby, I'll make sure he goes outside to 'do his business'."

The deep creases in Nancy's brow softened almost impercepti
bly. "Well, maybe I'll show you how to weave a real hat while
you're here. Come on." She turned her back and waved an arm.
"I'll show you to your room."

Myri waved to Joseph and followed the woman down the hall
way. Baby scurried alongside her, swatting at her pants-leg and the
rope with each step.

26

Sleeping in a real bed with soft sheets and a thick comforter made it really hard to get moving in the morning. Myri stretched, pushing Baby to the edge of the mattress, where he let out a little *hiss* and jumped to the floor. She followed suit, stretching again as she rolled to her feet.

She dressed in jeans and a T-shirt, tied her hair into a sloppy ponytail, and plopped her ill-made visor on her head before proceeding to the communal dining room to grab a bite to eat before heading out to the orchards. She filled her plate, taking care to add items she could slip under the table to Baby. She breathed in the scent of fresh cooked eggs and bacon. She could get used to this.

She frowned. No, actually, she couldn't. She wasn't staying here.

The rising sun peaked over the horizon and shined through the open side of the large building. Myri squinted as she searched for one of the three people she'd met yesterday. Not seeing any of them, she looked for an open spot at one of the long tables. She met eyes with a young girl. Young-ish. Actually, she could have been Myri's age. Myri just felt old. Ancient really. Not physically, only emotionally.

The girl smiled and scooted over to allow room for Myri to sit on the wooden bench.

"Hi. My name's Grace. I heard we had a visitor, but I didn't catch your name." Grace reached a hand down and dropped a small piece of bacon next to Baby.

"I'm Myri." She smiled as she watched Baby pounce on the treat.

"Where will you be working today?"

"The orchard." Myri shoveled a forkful of scrambled eggs in her mouth.

Grace's eyes brightened. "Me too! I'll walk there with you when we're done eating."

⚡

After a quick trip to the stream where he drank his fill, Baby napped contentedly, bulging belly and all, beneath the apple tree Myri worked from. Grace occupied the branches of the next tree over. They had this section to themselves, as most of the group had been dispensed to harvest from the peach trees, which were quickly becoming too ripe to wait.

"Just wait until you taste a peach. I'll make sure we get some when we break for lunch." Grace stretched to reach an apple farther out on a thin branch. "I mean, apples are good, but they taste like dirt compared to a fresh-picked peach."

Myri could not even imagine something that tasted better than the sweet apple she'd eaten earlier. Living where the sun shines more often had some distinct advantages, even if the brightness irritated her eyes. "I don't believe you." She raised an eyebrow at her new friend.

Laughing, Grace dropped an apple in the pouch that hung at her side. "You will."

Myri dropped to the ground, careful to do so from a "safe" distance, and emptied her bag into the large basket set between their trees. "How often do you get visitors here?' she asked as she climbed a new tree on the other side of Grace's.

"Not very often. We've probably had less than ten in the last five years." She stopped and wiped the sweat from her forehead. "How do you climb so fast without even using the ladder?"

Myri shrugged, she'd have to remember to slow down, use more caution, maybe use the ladder leaned up against Grace's tree. "Have you had any interesting visitors? Any that wanted to stay?"

"Well," she smiled, "you're all interesting. Living with the same group of people your whole life can get pretty boring." She tilted her head and scrunched her eyebrows together in a thoughtful gaze. "Most everyone that's visited has wanted to stay, but it seems like we're always full at those times. Except for two-and-a-half or three years ago. We had some visitors that were invited to stay and they declined."

"You had room for them then?"

"Yes. A large family that had been here for decades decided to move south and start their own kibbutz, since they were getting so big." She climbed carefully down to empty her bag.

"Who... what kind of people didn't want to stay here?" Myri asked.

"It was a man and a boy." Grace grunted as she hoisted herself back up the ladder. "About two or three years ago. The boy was a little older than me, I think. He was real quiet, haunted looking almost. I think he wanted to stay, but the man he was with declined the offer. I would have liked for the boy to stay, but I was glad the man didn't. He gave me the creeps."

Myri's senses prickled. "Why?"

Grace shrugged. "I'm not entirely sure. Maybe it was the way he talked. It was like he hadn't been speaking English long, but he didn't have any type of accent. I think after his strange response to the offer, the leader at the time was glad he didn't stay, too."

"What was his response?" Myri stopped pulling apples from the limbs of the tree, and leaned toward the other girl.

"He said, 'there aren't enough humans here for the plan'." Grace shook her head. "I heard him say it, I'd been sitting next to the boy at dinner, trying to get him to open up a little. Creepy." Grace reached for another apple. "Morgan didn't seem too happy about leaving, but he left with the man anyway."

Myri slipped as her heart leaped into her throat. She snagged her arm around a branch to keep from falling to the ground. She cleared her throat of a sudden mucousy obstruction. "The boy's name was Morgan?"

"Yeah. I think he'd been through something traumatic, the way he acted. That's what Katherine said anyway."

$$\lightning$$

MYRI AND BABY ended up only staying for a week. After hearing about Cascus's strange response to the leader of the kibbutz, she made a decision to backtrack, to see if she could figure out where he—or *it*—had come from. Further questioning of Katherine had revealed that Morgan told her he'd met up with the *man* in another town a couple days' walk from there. She said her goodbyes after breakfast, promising to come back and visit, hoping she'd be able to. She'd felt more at peace there than she could ever remember feeling.

As Joseph hugged her goodbye he said, "You're welcome to come back anytime. Be careful at Hilton, if that's where you're headed. The leaders there aren't nearly as nice as we are."

Myri nodded. "Thank you for everything."

She didn't know if all the extra food people had slipped Baby under the table was the reason for his growth spurt or not, but she swore he'd again doubled in size the week they'd spent there. He definitely no longer fit inside her backpack. He was getting spoiled and probably needed to learn how to hunt for himself. So, as they traveled northwest—the direction Katherine had guessed Cascus and Morgan had come from—Myri caught small rodents and let them loose for Baby to chase and play around with. Within two days, Baby was bringing them to her and they weren't always *small*

"Baby," Myri rolled over and sat up, pushing against the soft ground, "what do you have there?" A rusty, brownish-gray rabbit struggled to escape the tight clamp of Baby's teeth around its neck. The rabbit grunted and squealed, kicking at the cat with its large hind feet. Myri leaned up against the trunk of a tree and watched, wincing every time her panther's prey squealed. She forced herself to let Baby continue. He needed to learn hunting skills.

When Baby decided the game was over, he pinned the rabbit down with his big paws and ripped its throat out. *Hmm,* Myri thought, *when did his grown-up teeth come in?* Her impenetrable skin made it impossible for her to tell the difference when he chewed on her arms or ankles playfully.

"I suppose you aren't going to share that with me, huh?" she said.

Baby replied by growling low in his throat and dragging his kill a few feet away. Myri sighed, "At least I won't have to start a fire to cook it on." She unzipped her pack and pulled out the package of food Nancy had sent with her.

"You're really making a mess over there." Baby looked up at her and licked his bloody whiskers before returning to his feast. Myri bit into her last peach. Grace had been right, apples were good, but nothing compared to the dripping-with-juice peaches fresh off the tree. They should be getting close to the next town, if they were still headed in the right direction.

Myri washed up in the stream then stood, shouldering her pack. "Come on, killer. Let's get on the road." She had to do some coaxing to get him to leave the carcass of his first solo kill behind.

⚡27⚡

From the looks of the outskirts, Hilton was definitely not a
friendly as the kibbutz. It also appeared to be much large
Ragged tents housed bedraggled people—old, young, families—i
an area that had been decimated by the 'quakes and what cam
after. From her perch in the top of a huge evergreen, Myri looke
over the large city-town that centered around a tall building wit
the word "Hilton" still dangling from the top.

People milled about the crumbled streets and in and out of
number of buildings that still mostly stood. The city showed n
obvious signs of improvement—no planted fields, no cleanup
the streets, no new construction. It reminded her of Manhatta
only somehow worse. The only area that looked even remote
cleaned up was the Hilton itself, and the surrounding block arour
which a barricade had been built. *Built* was not exactly right, mo
like *piled*. That's where she should head first. That's where th
leaders would be.

She tried to get Baby to stay back, hiding in the trees, no
that he was too big to hide in her backpack, but as soon as sh
got a few yards away from him, he bounded out to swat
her legs.

"Panther!" came a yell from the street ahead.

A couple of people screamed and ran. Two men and a wom
nearest her grabbed weapons—a shovel, an axe, a club. Th

didn't charge, thank goodness, they just stood their ground, eyeing Baby.

Myri held up her hands, palms out. "He's with me. He's tame. He isn't going to hurt anyone."

As if to defy her proclamation, Baby leaped in front of her and crouched, wiggling his butt back and forth. A sign, Myri knew, that he wanted to play, but the people bearing weapons didn't know that. Baby roared. A deep, barky, roar. The loudest she'd heard from him yet. A roar like a grown panther, instead of the meager juvenile attempts he'd made before.

The group of armed citizens stepped back. "You sure he's tame?" asked the man holding the axe.

Myri reached down and picked Baby up. His hind legs hung nearly to the ground now. "He's tame. That was just his way of saying 'hi'."

"Maybe you should tie him up or something, just in case?" The woman lowered the shovel in her hands.

"I'll just hold him for now." The wriggling cat apparently didn't feel the same way about that decision.

"He looks heavy," the woman said. "You sure you don't want me to get you a rope?"

Myri shook her head. "I've got one if I need it."

"Okay." She didn't sound like she believed her. "Where you headed anyway?"

Myri's eyes flicked to the Hilton. "There."

The woman's eyes widened, as did her two male companions'. "Why?" she whispered.

"I'm looking for some information and instinct tells me that's the place to get it." *That's where Cascus would have gone. Straight to the traders.*

"They won't let you in." The woman still whispered, like she was afraid the people in the big building several blocks away would hear her.

Myri smiled. "I'm going to try anyway."

"They have weapons." The man lifted his axe a little. "Real ones. Like guns and stuff."

"Where did they get them?" Myri asked.

"Max, the self-appointed governor, owned a big gun store before the 'quakes hit. He gathered what remained of his friends and family in the aftermath and they hauled 'em all to the hotel. Threatened or killed anyone that tried to get in."

"Yeah," the second man spoke up for the first time. "Unless you had something to bring to the table. Pretty much all the food storage, money, ammo, batteries, generators… if it was something they deemed necessary or *worthy*, they let you join them."

A couple of children slunk out of hiding, eyes wide as they stared at Baby, still trying to escape Myri's hold on him.

"Hmm…" Myri said. "That sounds beastly."

A bitter laugh escaped the woman's mouth. "That's a great way to describe it. They rule this city. They hand out just enough crumbs to us to keep us around. Order us around like they're kings of some kind."

Myri knew better than to ask why they put up with it. She knew about survival. She knew what it was like to feel as if you had no choices. "I'm going to go talk to them anyway but maybe I should leave Baby here." She pointed her chin at him. "If I tie him up, will you keep an eye on him? I'll bring you something back from Palace Hilton." Myri was bullet proof, but Baby wasn't.

The man with the axe *harrumphed* and the woman rolled her eyes. "I doubt that. I doubt that you'll even make it back alive with that overly-confident attitude." The woman pointed to a blue tent tied to a tree. "But I'll keep an eye on him for you. Tie him over there."

"Thank you." Myri smiled. "He'll probably fall asleep shortly. He had an eventful morning."

After securing him, protesting, to the tree, Myri asked, "What would you like me to bring back for you?"

The woman scoffed. "Food. Always food."

Myri pursed her lips and nodded before setting out at a jog for the Hilton.

⚡

RATHER THAN DEALING with the armed guards posted at the small opening in the ten-foot high wall made up of the piled remains of buildings and homes, Myri climbed over it in a spot where she wouldn't be easily seen.

Unlike at the kibbutz, she really didn't care if she made a good first impression here. These people sounded like jerks.

She landed in a crouch and glanced around. No people in sight. The place was a disorganized mess. She noted a few plots of ground where vegetables grew amongst poorly tamed weeds. Some sad looking strawberry bushes wilted against the wall. Her ears perked up.

"What do you think you're doing in here? Your kind aren't allowed on this side of the wall unless we need you to do something for us."

Myri searched, sure right away that the person belonging to the voice wasn't directing his comments to her. A glimpse of movement nearer the building led her to the speaker and the young teen boy who was being spoken to.

"You know what the penalty is for stealing food, don't you?" The man, in his mid to late thirties, held a black rifle pointed at the boy's head.

"Yes, sir." The boy didn't whimper or plead. His voice remained steady as did his eyes as he looked at his tormentor. "It was worth the risk. People are starving out there."

"Survival of the fittest." The man gestured with the rifle. "And the fittest are those with the weapons and food. Now, to your knees, thief. The penalty will be enacted immediately."

"No!" Myri stood and crossed her arms in front of her chest. "It won't."

The boy, already halfway to kneeling, stood and jerked his head around, wide eyes catching Myri's. The gunman whirled toward her, eyes narrowed, rifle pointing at her chest. Undeterred, she strode toward him, not rushing now that the gun was pointed at her and not the boy.

"Who are you?" the man growled.

"I'm Myri, and you're going to let this boy go. I have some questions for your leaders. Take me to them."

The man laughed, but Myri caught a trace of fear within the scowl he threw her way. "Oh, really? Well, seeing as I'm the one with the gun here—"

A giant leap landed her right in front of the muzzle. She ripped the weapon out of his hands before he even registered she was there. She held it there, intending to break it in half. But, instead she handed it to the boy and said to him, "I think this place needs to be a bit more balanced. I'll meet you at the outskirts and bring you some more items to help even things out around here."

"You… what do you think you're doing?" The man looked from his now empty hands, to Myri, then to the kid with the gun. "That's mine."

"Not anymore." Myri nodded to the boy. "Go. I'll catch up to you later."

The boy's mouth twisted up into a half-smile and he nodded before turning to run back behind the building.

"You can't…" The man lunged toward the retreating boy. Myri stuck her arm out and clotheslined him then stood over him as he lay on the ground gasping for air through his damaged trachea.

"I can." She dragged him to his feet. "Now take me to the leaders of this pitiful compound."

He drew in a hoarse breath and stared at her with bulging eyes, one hand protectively covering his neck. Myri gave him a little nudge and he started walking toward the front of the former hotel.

A middle-aged woman lounged in a chair just outside the entrance. "Who you got there, Marco?"

"I'm Myri," she answered for him. "Marco is taking me to have a little chat with your leaders."

"Marco? Is that true?" The woman hefted herself out of the chair, and stepped closer to Myri and her new "friend."

Marco, eyes wide but no longer bulging, nodded at the woman.

"Hmmf. I think I'd like to come along and see how this goes." The woman motioned for Myri and her escort to proceed through the door ahead of her.

An older woman dressed in rags, mopped the former lobby of the hotel. "Lacy," Marco called to her, hoarsely. "Go get Liam."

Myri gave Marco a push. "You go get Liam. I'd like to talk to Lacy for a minute."

The woman who'd followed them inside raised her eyebrows, but kept quiet, lips pursed. Marco stumbled around a corner and down the hallway.

Lacy continued mopping but followed him with her gaze, a slight smile playing across her wrinkled mouth. Myri stepped up to her, standing far enough away to not get slopped on by the mop. "Hi, Lacy, I'm Myri. Can I ask you a couple of questions?"

Shrugging, Lacy said, "Sure."

"You seem to be from out there." Myri bobbed her head to indicate outside the barriers set up around the hotel. "And you seem to be working for the people that live in here. What's it like in here compared to on the outside?"

The slip of a smile disappeared from her face and her eyes darted to the woman from the porch. "I'm very lucky to have the privilege to work inside The Hilton. They treat me fairly and provide food for me and my son."

"You're scared to tell the truth," Myri whispered so only the mopping woman could hear.

With a slight nod of her head, Lacy dunked the mop back in the bucket and turned away from Myri. "If you'll please excuse me, miss, I have a floor to finish cleaning."

Myri stepped back out of her way and cocked her head as

approaching footsteps alerted her to the arrival of Marco and Liam. Her enhanced ears picked up parts of their hushed conversation as they shuffled down the hall.

"Why're you so freaked out if she's just a young girl? You shoulda' just thrown her ass out," a man, who must have been Liam, said in hushed tones.

"I don't know, man. There's something up with her. She's strong and didn't seem at all scared of my threats. And she took my gun."

"Are you freaking kidding me? I'm just going to throw her out."

Several seconds passed with no answer from Marco. The two men rounded the corner into Myri's line of sight and stopped a few feet in front of her. Liam stood at least a head taller than Marco with bulging biceps exiting the short sleeves of a too tight T-shirt. His right hand rested on the handgrip of a pistol shoved into holster at his hip. "I'll give you one chance to turn around and get out of here," he said, his fingers tightening around the handgrip of the gun.

Myri rolled her eyes, stepped forward, and grabbed his hand as he attempted to pull the gun free. Her grip tightened as she stared up into his widening eyes. Bones crunched beneath her fingers and Liam squealed like a newborn baby. She lifted his slightly mangled hand and snatched the gun from its holster with her other hand.

"What do you want?" Marco backed away, staring at his friend's pained face.

"I want a couple of questions answered." She looked down the gun in her hand. "And I want to even a few things out in this town before I leave."

"Wh… who are you?" Liam cradled his injured hand against his chest.

"I'm Myrikal." She didn't know why she used her full name for the first time in weeks. It just felt right. "Now it's my turn to ask the questions."

"Lacy," Marco said. "Go get the others."

Lacy glanced quickly at Myri, fear evident in her eyes, as she rushed down the hallway.

"Sit." Myri gestured with the gun to a couch and a couple of chairs.

The men sat on the edge of the couch, perched as if ready to bolt. Myri remained standing. "First, how long have you two been here?" She needed to establish whether or not they would have been around when Cascus and Branch came through.

"Since before the 'quakes," Liam sniveled.

"A few years ago, a man visited here. And a boy, about fifteen years old. They came separate of each other but left together. Do you remember?"

"Yeah." Marcus's eyes shifted to the hallway where Lacy had disappeared then back to Myri. "The guy was strange. Weaseled his way right into the hearts of the elder-leaders."

"And the kid," Liam added. "He showed up a few days after Cascus—that was his name, the guy—half starved, a little crazy in the head. The elder-leaders wanted to," he glanced at Marco, "uh… they wanted to get rid of him. Said he'd be nothing but a drain on our resources."

Marco leaned forward, glancing again at the hallway. "It was weird. The kid didn't even talk at first. His clothes were all torn up, he had scrapes and bruises everywhere. That Cascus dude took him on as, like, a special project or something."

"Why did they leave?" Myri could hear the approaching footsteps of "the others" Marco had sent Lacy to gather. She needed to get her information before all hell broke loose.

"It was weird." Liam winced and then scowled at her as he tried to use his injured hand to gesture. "The elder-leaders were all smitten with him, even allowing the useless kid to stay in The Hilton. Rumor was he had some grand plan to fix this place up, inside and outside the wall. They asked him to stay, even going so far as to tell him he could be the supreme leader or some such bull."

"Why did they leave?" Myri asked again as the footsteps drew closer.

"I wasn't there when it happened," Liam said. "But I heard that Cascus turned them down and said something really strange. Like, 'not enough humans here,' or something crazy. Him and the kid left right then."

"Which direction did Cascus come from when he arrived?"

"Northwest. The opposite direction the kid came from." Liam's eyebrows shot up and he tensed.

The "others" came into view, quickly spreading out. The woman nearest Lacy pushed her to the side. She fell to her knees with a grunt and slid a couple of feet across the pitted tile.

"Stay down, Lacy," Myri yelled as she stepped toward the line of ten people pointing various guns at her chest.

"Stop or we will shoot you," an elderly man holding a rifle said.

Myri shrugged. She'd had enough of these bullies. She drew in a deep breath and continued to walk toward them as electricity tingled at her fingertips. A shorter man, about the age of her father, pulled the trigger first. Liam and Marco, still behind Myri, yelped and dove out of the line of fire, tipping the couch over.

The first bullet struck Myri in the center of her chest. She caught the slug as it dropped, the tip flattened from the impact with her impenetrable skin, and flung it back at the shooter hard enough to leave a nice, big bruise. Her intention wasn't to kill anyone. She only wanted to even things out for the people struggling to live outside the walls of The Hilton.

She followed the flung bullet with a mild arc of electricity aimed at the metal barrel of the gun. The strike lit up the man's face as he swore and dropped his weapon.

The others opened fire. Myri continued to step toward them as they backed up. The bullets that hit her fell to the floor around her. She reached the line of bullies, their backs now snug against the wall, and kicked the dropped rifle over to where Lacy cowered on the floor. "Hold onto that for me, please."

Lacy laid a shaky hand on the weapon, tears falling from her wide and frightened eyes.

Myri gathered all the weapons into a pile and cornered the town leaders into the non-functioning elevator. Still facing them with her body, she turned her head to look at Liam and Marco, slinking toward the exit. "You two. Get over here with your friends." They hesitated, looking from her to the door. "Don't make me show you what a couple jolts of electricity slamming into your bodies feels like."

They slunk over to her and wedged themselves into the packed elevator.

"Now, listen closely." Myri took turns staring into the eyes of her captives while she shot little lightning bolts from one hand to the other and back. "Things need to change around here. I'm going to even it up a little by taking some of these weapons and ammunition and giving them to the people outside your little wall here. I'll also be taking some food and seeds to them and anything else I find here that they may need."

"But," the short man who had fired the first shot said, "we'll starve!"

"And those losers out there will kill us," Marco said, eyebrows raised so high they hid beneath his bangs.

"I'm not going to take everything. Everyone should be able to defend themselves—*everyone*—not just you guys. Everyone should share in the harvest as well as the work, too. Figure out a better way to do things around here."

"Like what?" a lady said, sneering.

"I don't know. Like hold elections every couple of years to see who gets to lead and make decisions that affect the community. Like splitting up the work that needs to be done and making sure everyone has a job to do—one that's suitable to their abilities." Myri narrowed her eyes at the group. "And I mean *everyone*. No one gets a free pass in this post 'quake world."

"Does this mean you're staying here?" a voice from the back
the elevator asked.

Myri shook her head. "I won't be staying. I have other things
need to get done." She paused. "But I will be stopping back
And if things haven't changed for the better around here, there w
be consequences." She released the pent up energy she held in h
hands out a large broken window. A huge ball of electric flan
crashed into a crumbling stone fountain, the explosion sendir
rock shrapnel flying in all directions.

"I need you all to stay put while I go gather up those supplies
talked about." She squeezed the elevator doors shut and wedged
couple of broken-off chair legs between the floor and the doors.

28

The woman who had agreed to watch Baby for her stared wide-eyed at the stack of food, weapons, and ammunition Myri and Lacy dropped at her feet. "How?"

They met up with the young teen, Jimmy, that Marco had been ready to shoot when Myri first arrived inside the walls of the Hilton. Jimmy's eyes filled with tears as he thanked Myri for saving him.

"Lacy and Jimmy here are in charge of handing this stuff out. I can't stay, but I'll tell you the same thing I told the people at The Hilton. Figure out a better way to live and get along. Lacy heard that I told them and she has some pretty good ideas."

"Did you take all of their weapons?" a man asked, a glint of vengeful hope in his eyes.

"No. I didn't. No one group of people should be able to hold power over another. Switching places isn't the answer. Working together is the answer." Myri turned to Lacy. "Lacy. Jimmy. You guys take it from here. They'll be asking for volunteers who have knowledge of how to safely use guns and how to plant and harvest food, and a bunch of other stuff. Share your knowledge. Work together. I'll be back to check on you."

She untied Baby, pulled her pack onto her shoulders, and headed off in a northwest direction.

⚡

T HEY PASSED multiple deserted and destroyed towns between Hilton and the next inhabited town. They ran into an occasional loner here and there, living off the land, taking shelter in broken and abandoned buildings. These people chose to be alone and looked upon Myri with great suspicion. She learned quickly that interacting with her—or anyone—was the last thing they wanted to do. She left them alone, wondering if solitude, either forced or chosen, always ended up with the lone person evolving into something a bit wild.

On the third day after leaving Hilton, Myri and Baby spotted the next town as they crested a hill. Myri raised her eyebrows. Were those actual, functioning *stores* she saw along the main street running through the middle of the little valley?

She'd been working with Baby, training him to stay by her side, to sit and wait when she stood still, to not roar at people. "This your big test, Baby. Stay next to me. Let's go." She slowed her step as they descended the hill, not wanting to scare anyone.

Leaving Baby outside picking the meat off a bone she'd saved for just such an occasion, Myri entered a building beneath a recently painted sign that said "Mercantile." She picked up an apple from a basket sitting atop a shelf full of produce and vegetables, turning it in her hand as she examined it before laying it back down.

"Can I help you?" a young man, maybe a few years older than Myri, said.

Myri smiled. "I'm just passing through. Can you tell me a little about your town? About this?" Myri gestured around the store.

"Sure," the man smiled. "I'm CJ, what's your name?"

"I'm Myri."

"Well, Myri, I assume this is the first cooperative-slash-capital town you've come across in your travels?"

"Yes, I guess it is."

"Welcome to Winchester. The quick explanation of how things work here is that everyone works to provide either goods or services necessary for the survival of our town. My wife and I run the store here. The farmers, seamstresses, and other people sell their goods on a commission basis. Basically, they split the money with us."

"Money? You use real money, then?" That was something Manhattan had started doing again over only the last couple of years. Before that, everything was bartered and traded for. Or the strong just stole from the weak. That *still* happened.

"Yes. We are a self-sustaining town and the monetary system works well here."

"What about people who have no goods or services to offer?" Myri was thinking about the beggars and orphans in Manhattan and the destitute people living outside The Hilton compound.

"We have very few here who are unable to work in some capacity. We have a system where everyone donates a small amount of goods or money to what we call the storehouse. Those people are taken care of using those donations." He cocked an eyebrow at her. "Anyone who's able-bodied is expected to pull their weight. The storehouse is only for those who can't."

"Like…"

"Like the elderly. Or the crazy guy, Chomper."

"Crazy?" Myri asked.

"Yeah. He hears voices. No one knows his real name and he's too far gone to tell us."

"He isn't from here originally?"

"No. He wandered into town a few years ago, half-starved and rambling on about a giant chasm opening up and swallowing his family. Mumbling over and over about a creature crawling out of the abyss."

"Was it true?" Myri asked. "Did anyone else see this chasm?"

CJ shook his head. "Chomper either came a long way from here this happened, or it only happened inside his head. Some of us tried to backtrack the way he came, and we didn't find anything after traveling several days from here."

A strange feeling tickled the back of Myri's brain. "Where is he now? Has he been able to tell anyone more about where he came from or anything?"

"He's always close by Main Street, trying to convince people of his story. He always mumbles the same things over and over: 'I crawled from the endless chasm that swallowed my Lilly and Tommy. Heat. Flames. Dark. Evil.'"

"He never says anything else?"

CJ plucked an apple from the top of the basket and handed it to her. "Only once. A couple of weeks after his arrival here we had another visitor. A man that gave off some pretty weird vibes himself. He didn't speak much, if at all, the first couple of days he was here. It was almost like he was observing us, learning how to talk and act." CJ shook his head. "That sounds a little paranoid on my part, but that's what I remember thinking."

"Chomper spoke to this man?" Myri prompted him to go on.

"No, not exactly. Chomper freaked out when he saw him, yelling—no, *screaming*—'that's the monster! Kill it! Kill it before it kills us all'!"

Myri's stomach flipped and she looked down, trying to hide her anxiety as she asked, "What did the strange man look like?"

CJ narrowed his eyes. "Why?"

"Just curious. I mean, what was it about him that set Chomper off, do you think?"

"I don't know for sure. He made my skin tingle." CJ looked down. "And to tell you the truth, I can't tell you what he looked like. When I try to picture his face, it's just a blur." He looked back up and shrugged. "I can tell you that he wore a long robe, though."

MYRI WANDERED DOWN MAIN STREET, Baby staying glued to her

heels. People were friendly but gave her a wide berth when they passed by, eyeing the black panther with apprehension. A young girl carrying a basket of eggs walked toward her. She stopped abruptly, eyes wide as they fell on Baby. "Is that a *cat?*"

Myri smiled. "Sort of. He's from the same family as a cat, only bigger. He's a panther."

"Is he friendly?"

"Yes, although sometimes he likes to growl or roar, and that can sound pretty scary."

"Can… can I pet him?" The girl's eyes never left the big, black cat.

"Sure. But you might want to leave your eggs there. He might think you're bringing him dinner." Myri crouched and laid a hand on Baby's back. "Baby, lay down. Stay." He obliged.

The girl sat her eggs in the street and approached, her footsteps slowing as she neared them with her hand outstretched. She swallowed and looked at Myri. Myri nodded encouragement and the girl reached out and patted Baby on the head. He purred as she scratched behind his ears. The girl smiled so big her eyes crinkled up at the edges. "My cat loves this, too."

Since this girl was the first person to get close enough for her to talk to, Myri asked, "Do you know who Chomper is?"

The girl nodded.

"Do you know where he is?"

"Yeah." She turned and pointed back the direction she'd come. "I just saw him down by the mill. He was getting a drink out of the stream."

"Thank you. Maybe I'll see you later and you can play with Baby some more."

Her eyes lit up. "That would be awesome!"

Myri waited for the girl to pick up her eggs before continuing on toward the mill.

She knew the man leaning against a tree by the fast moving stream was Chomper. His hair grew in a matted mess around his sun-worn face mostly covered with a scraggly beard. And he greeted her by saying, "It crawled from the endless chasm that swallowed my Lilly and Tommy. Heat. Flames. Dark. Evil." The intensity in his eyes gave the impression that whatever disaster had befallen him, had just happened. Not years ago as CJ described. But just moments before.

"You poor man," Myri whispered.

A low growl from Baby didn't even cause the man to flick his eyes in the big cat's direction. He continued staring right through Myri and into her soul.

He leaned closer, his rancid breath blowing in Myri's face. "I crawled from the endless chasm that swallowed my Lilly and Tommy. Heat. Flames. Dark. *Evil*."

Myri laid her hand on his arm. "Can you show me where?"

Chomper's eyes widened. "You… believe?"

She nodded.

He mimicked the motion of her head, nodding, before turning to splash across the stream. He looked back once to make sure she followed him as he led her away from the town.

⚡

As DARKNESS FELL, Chomper finally stopped his hurried foray away from Winchester. He turned to Myri and looked her in the eyes for the first time since before crossing the stream at the mill. He pointed in the direction they'd been heading. "It crawled from the endless chasm that swallowed my Lilly and Tommy. Heat. Flames. Dark. Evil."

"I believe you. Show me the chasm."

Fear sprang up in his eyes and he shook his head and pointed again. "Five days. Maybe six. Good luck."

In an ambling gallop, he took off back toward the town of Winchester, mumbling, "It crawled from the endless chasm that swallowed my Lilly and Tommy. Heat. Flames. Dark. Evil."

⚡

ONLY STOPPING when Baby dropped to the ground, refusing to go another step, Myrikal made good time. As the panther fell into an exhausted sleep, Myri lay next to him on a soft cushion of grass. Her mind raced, preventing her from getting even a moment's real rest.

The creature who crawled from the chasm had to have been Cascus. She knew he wasn't human. She'd been able to see his true form beneath the human façade he'd somehow constructed. *Evil.* Chomper knew it, too. So had CJ. *Too bad Branch refused to recognize it.*

She allowed Baby to rest for a couple of hours before waking him up and continuing in the direction Chomper had pointed her. As the fourth day dawned, Myri saw dark smoke rising in the distance. As she neared the smoke, a familiar stench filled her nostrils and her stomach clenched.

Cascus. It smelled like Cascus.

29

Myri pulled her spare shirt from her pack and tied it aroun
her mouth and nose. It barely stanched the odor, but mad
enough of a difference to settle her stomach. Baby growled low i
his throat, the hair on his neck and back raised.

"You don't have to come with me," Myri whispered dow
at him.

Baby wasn't the only one with raised hackles. Myri stole towar
the smoke-emitting crevasse, eyes darting back and forth, taking i
her surroundings. The ten yards of ground surrounding th
crevasse was void of vegetation and sprinkled with bones. Bab
predator-crawled just behind her, occasionally nudging her fo
with his nose. She tightened the knot of the shirt fastened aroun
her face and swallowed. As nauseating as being near Cascus ha
been, this was at least ten times worse.

As she drew in another stomach-turning breath, Myri realize
something—she could hold her breath for an extended period
time. "Duh, Myri," she whispered, rolling her eyes. Taking one la
deep breath, she untied the makeshift balaclava and let it fa
behind her.

She dropped to a crawl near the edge of the gaping chasi
dust billowed around her as her arms and knees hit the dead eart
The smoke coalesced into a thick ribbon and shifted to envelo

Myri as she moved to peer over the edge. Green flames licked at her face and hair.

This one is different.

Myri gasped in the whirling smoke as a deep and ancient voice reverberated in her head. Not just in her head—in her chest, her limbs, her soul.

It's not burning. Not screaming.

She *felt* the confusion of this new voice inside her pounding head.

"Who are you?" she asked before holding her breath again.

Prisss… cussss. This voice came to her as a hoarse murmur, cracking and wheezing.

"*What* are you?" she whispered.

The voices bombarded her. Pounded against her brain. Disturbed the regular rhythm of her heartbeat.

Ancient…

Trapped for eons…

It's our time…

Only Cascus escaped…

Even through the immense heat, Myrikal shivered.

The smallest amongst us…

Sent to conquer…

… return for us.

Lower life-forms to serve us…

… or to be eradicated.

It took every ounce of strength, both physical and psychological, for Myrikal to pull away from the chasm. She scrambled backward, away from the evil inside the pit. Baby had a hold of her pant leg, pulling her away. The strange hold on her mind didn't fully release until she moved well beyond the perimeter of dead earth. She rolled to her back and sucked in a breath of rancid air. Baby pounced on her chest and roared into her face.

"I know," Myri choked. "We need to get away from here." She

pulled him to her in a tight hug as her heart calmed to a normal pace. "We need to get back to Manhattan."

30

The DefCo uniform felt surprisingly good, familiar and non-restrictive with her movements. The time had come for Myrikal to fully embrace her powers and quit trying to pretend she was just like everyone else. Wearing the uniform was the first step.

Baby ran beside her, his legs stretching in long strides. He'd grown considerably since she'd first taken him under her wing. He could now stand on his hind legs and put his front paws on her chest and stare into her eyes. She figured he weighed over a hundred pounds. And he wasn't done growing.

It had been about a week since they'd run from the chasm filled with unspeakable, evil beings. Myri had no idea how long, at this pace, it would take for them to reach Manhattan. She hoped it wasn't too late, though she couldn't even imagine the timeline needed for Cascus to fulfill his—their—plan. She was just grateful he'd been the only one of those things that had been able to escape from whatever prison held them beneath the earth.

Lost in her own thoughts, it took Myrikal much longer than it should have to see the approaching figures, really only noticing them when Baby let out the most vicious growl she'd ever heard. By the time she snapped out of her thought-trance, he'd bounded ahead of her.

"Baby! No!" She jumped, reaching him just as he crouched to

leap at a blur of brown and black fur running toward Baby. Myrikal grabbed Baby's tail.

"Lobo!"

Myrikal jerked her head up. She knew that voice. And that name. She narrowed her eyes and focused in on the boy, still twenty yards back, running toward them. "Dal?" she said. She flung Baby backwards and jumped between him and the large, oncoming dog. She caught the dog, mid-leap, around his torso, holding him snug against her chest as he barked and snapped his teeth.

"Myrikal!" Dal stumbled to a halt then bent and put his hands on his knees, gasping as he tried to catch his breath.

She turned and gave Baby the hand signal for "stay" then lowered Lobo to the ground next to his boy. Dal grabbed the loose rope that served as Lobo's collar. "Sit!" he commanded.

Continuing to growl, the dog obeyed, eyes never leaving the enormous feline.

"Dal, what are you doing here?" She was sure she was still a couple of days away from the city, even at the fast pace she'd been traveling.

"I came to find you." The quiver in his voice seemed more than just oxygen deprivation.

Myrikal bent down to look into his face. "What's wrong?"

"It's Cascus." He scowled. "You have to come back. He's out of control."

"Did Branch… Morgan send you?"

"Hmf," Dal snorted. "Not *even*. Morgan is his Number Two. He's just as bad."

Myrikal flinched, her throat tightened, making it difficult to speak. She wasn't really surprised, but had been holding out hope that Branch would somehow get over his worship of Cascus and see the truth. She swallowed and cleared her throat. "What's going on?"

Dal slumped to the ground and pulled on Lobo's rope-collar. "Lobo, shut up! I'm not gonna' let you fight Baby, he's ginormous.

now." He looked up at Myrikal and sighed. "He holds 'court' everyday with people his goons caught breaking his laws the day before. I don't even know why he goes through the motions of a court. Everyone is found guilty no matter what."

"What does he do to them?" Myrikal clenched her jaw as she recalled the punishment Cascus had wanted her to mete out.

"I guess at first he had a couple of them killed, but Morgan talked him into something else." He picked up a dirt clod from the trail and threw it against a tree. "Now he brands them on the forehead and makes them work like slaves. Even kids."

Myrikal tightened her hands into fists and sucked in a sharp breath.

Dal continued, "He's separated the boys from the girls in the compound. They aren't even allowed to talk to each other outside of their work assignments. And Myri," he turned to her, "he's building something. Strange lights and sounds come from the building all hours of the day and night."

"Are the people still following him with all this going on?"

"Most of them. They're afraid not to. I took off, though, when he threatened Lobo. Apparently, he doesn't like to be growled at every time Lobo smells him coming."

"You moved to the park? Why?"

He shrugged. "The leaders of my compound came to an agreement with Cascus. We all moved there."

Myrikal stayed silent for a few moments while she thought. Did she have the strength to take out some sort of ancient being? She didn't even know his strengths or weaknesses—or if he even had any weaknesses. He obviously had some special abilities, that much was evident by the human façade he wore over his true form. Myrikal shook her head. It didn't matter. She had to find a way to get rid of him.

She patted Lobo on the head and stood. "Baby and I are going to hurry back to there. Are you two going to be okay? What's your plan?"

Still holding onto his dog's makeshift collar, Dal stood, too. "I[f] you're going back, I'm going back."

Myrikal smiled and nodded. "Okay. I guess you made it this fa[r] on your own, so you'll have to make it back on your own. I'm goin[g] to be traveling fast. I have a feeling the trouble Cascus is causing i[s] only getting worse with each passing day."

"We'll be fine. Lobo is a great protector."

"I know he is." She wrapped her arms around the boy in [a] quick hug. "Stay safe. I'll see you back in Manhattan."

⚡

BABY HAD GROWN strong with all the quick traveling and infrequen[t] rest. His endurance nearly matched Myrikal's. It took two days fo[r] them to arrive at the bridge over which she'd escaped the city. Sh[e] paused but a moment there, with a hand on Baby's head, to loo[k] out over the huge and crumbling buildings. "You watch my back i[n] there, Baby."

The panther *chuffed* as if agreeing to do just that.

Walking with determined strides, she picked her way across th[e] dilapidated bridge, Baby at her heels. The people she passed on th[e] streets in the gray early morning light stared but didn't speak. Sh[e] didn't hesitate as she walked up to the front gate of the Centr[al] Park compound. She barely recognized one of the guards th[at] scrambled to step in front of her.

"You… you can't come in here." His voice got higher as h[e] spoke and his eyes darted back and forth between Myrik[al] and Baby.

Myrikal leaned toward him. "Stop me, then." She brushed hi[m] to the side with a swipe of her arm and continued on through th[e] gate. People whispered and pointed as she passed them, but no[ne] approached her. She headed for Alyssa's, hoping she still resided [in] her tiny house. Hoping she hadn't gotten on the wrong side

Cascus during Myrikal's absence. Myri shook her head. It scared her even more to think of Alyssa being on the *right* side of Cascus.

Her heart dropped as she stepped onto Alyssa's porch. The place looked deserted. She knocked anyway, hoping.

"If you're looking for that girl who used to live there, she ain't there."

Myrikal turned to see an elderly man, hauling a wagonload of vegetables behind him. "Do you know where I might find her?"

"Seeing as this is the men's side of the compound now, I'd have to assume she's over on the women's side. Probably out in the fields." He jerked his head to indicate the direction.

"Thank you." Myrikal stepped off the porch.

"Yep." The man tugged on the handle to the wagon. "Don't let one of Cascus's men catch you over here."

"I'm not afraid of Cascus or his men." Myri turned to Baby. "Let's go, Baby."

The potato field was full of women, digging up the vegetables with small shovels and dumping them in wagons interspersed throughout the rows. Myrikal didn't have time to search for her, so she stood to the side and yelled, "Alyssa!"

Some of the women looked frightened but a few of them quirked their mouths up at the corners as they looked up at her.

"Myri?" Alyssa dropped her shovel and jogged over to where Myrikal stood. "Where have you been?" Her half-smile turned down into a worried frown and her voice dropped to a whisper. "Why are you back? Cascus ordered everyone to let him know immediately if you showed up and I don't think it was so he could invite you to dinner."

"I came back to stop him. I just wanted to get some information from you, first."

Alyssa looked around nervously. "I can't talk to you for long. I'm sure someone's already on their way to tell him you're here."

"I'll make it quick. Do you know what he's building? Dal said there's a new structure, top secret, and Cascus is building some-thing in there."

"Dal? Isn't he the kid with the dog? Where did you see him? I thought he took off… hoped he'd taken off instead of…."

"He's fine. I saw him outside the city."

"I don't know what he's making in there, but I can tell you where it is. He only lets his closest followers anywhere near it though."

"Anything else I need to know?"

Alyssa ducked her head. "Morgan… he's changed. He goes along with everything Cascus says. The courts, the prisoner-slaves, the separation of males and females. He's pretty ruthless."

Myrikal winced and nodded.

"Oh, and there's another, smaller building they put up a couple of nights ago while no one was around. You'll see it by the bigger one. I have no idea what's in there."

"Thanks." She turned in the direction Alyssa pointed.

"Myri?" Alyssa asked. "Is that a… a *panther*?"

Myrikal smiled. "Yep. His name is Baby. He's watching my back." She patted him on the neck and walked away.

⚡

QUEASINESS FILLED her insides as she got within a few feet of the large building. Determined, Myrikal swallowed and pressed forward. Holding her breath would do no good in this instance, the building itself made waves of unease cycle through her body. Four guards stood watch outside the garage-like door that appeared to be the only entrance. The guards weren't members of Cascus's elite DefCon team she'd helped train—*they* were meant for much more important things than simple guard duty. These guards did carry weapons though, in addition to the flare guns that, she assumed, would summon help, likely in the form of her friends. Including Branch.

"N… no one's allowed in here," a female guard stuttered.

"No one's allowed anywhere near here," a powerfully built man said, stepping closer to Myrikal.

"Uh… Dante?" The girl put a hand on his arm. "You… uh… you probably don't want to mess with her." She lowered her voice to a whisper, as if that would keep her words from carrying to Myrikal just a few steps away. "That's the one we told you about. The one who can call lightning and stuff."

He narrowed his eyes, and moved his hand minutely toward the gun strapped to his waist.

Myrikal smiled. "No need for that."

A murmured whisper came from one of the other guards, "Not that it would do any good anyway."

"I'm just checking things out." The smile disappeared and she leaned in, mere inches from the guard's face. "But you might want to warn the next shift that I'll be back. It'd be a good idea if they decide to take a break when they see me coming." She'd come back at night to break into the building, hopefully less people would be around just in case things got ugly.

Myrikal reached around the muscled guard and touched the face of the building. The wall pulsated beneath her fingertips like a living being. Each beat of the alien substance sent an unnerving tremor through her heart. She stepped away and nodded to the guards. "I'll be back."

She had a strong feeling that if she stopped Cascus, the alien building and whatever was inside it would cease to be a threat. It was directly connected to him and whatever ancient power he possessed.

With that thought, she headed for the Central Building, where she hoped to find Cascus alone. Electricity gathered along the surface of her skin. She held her arms at an angle away from the side of her body as the small bolts crackled up and down, increasing in size and intensity even as she tried to hold back.

"Stay," she commanded Baby, who instantly sat on the street in front of the building.

Myrikal, now sparking like an electric storm, marched up the stairs to Cascus's quarters and pushed open the door.

"Cascus!" Her voice rang out like thunder. She thrust her hands straight out in front of her, the electric pulses merged and stabbed several feet out from her fingertips.

31

A flicker of movement caused Myrikal to turn and focus at the top of the stairs visible from where she stood just inside the entrance. Her heart dropped, but her hands didn't.

"Myri, what are you doing?" Branch pointed a gun in her direction, a crazed-like anger sparking in his eyes.

"I'm not here for you, Branch. Where's Cascus?" Myrikal didn't dare say more, afraid her voice would betray her. Seeing her best friend looking at her with such animosity threatened to break her resolve. Threatened to break her, period.

He squared his shoulders. "You're going to have to go through me to get to him, Myri. Are you willing to do that? Is your misplaced anger so strong that you're willing to kill me in order to get to him?"

Was she? No. She knew she wouldn't hurt Branch. But did he know that? She nodded and stepped forward.

Branch's eyes widened just a fraction and his finger twitched on the trigger of his gun. Cascus stepped into sight, directly behind Branch in such a position as to make hitting him a very dangerous prospect for Branch.

"Myrikal. I thought we'd decided you don't belong here." His human camouflage no longer fooled her eyes. "Did you have a change of heart?"

"Step out from behind Br... Morgan." The electricity pulsed brighter.

"Wouldn't you like to talk first?" His mouth twisted into a horrible semblance of a grin.

"Are you willing to tell me what it is that you're making insid your well-guarded building?"

"Of course not. That's none of your business."

Myrikal side-stepped, trying to get a better angle on Cascus Branch moved, shielding him further.

She focused her attention on Branch. "Do you know what he i Branch?"

An intensified glare was his only answer.

"I do." Myrikal stepped closer. "I know what he is. I kno where he came from." Closer. "I know what he wants."

Branch's face twisted into a rage-filled sneer as he opened fi on her. She shielded her face with her arms out of instinct.

"Go. Away. Myrikal!" he shouted. "Why do you have to ru everything good in my life?" He fired off another round of usel shots.

That hurt. Branch was so far under Cascus's spell, he refused see the evil truth. She lowered her arms, pulling the bolts of ele tricity back inside her. "Okay, Branch. I'll go." *And I'll come ba when I'm sure you aren't here to protect him.*

His shoulders slumped but he kept the gun pointed in h direction. "Stay gone this time. Please." The last word was a wh pered one, but Branch knew her well enough to know she'd hear i

Sorry, friend. That isn't going to happen. Myrikal turned her back them and strode to the door. Ya and Miguel met her on the porc She quirked an eyebrow at their uniforms that still included t lightning bolt patch that symbolized one of her powers. "I thoug he'd get rid of those." She nodded at the patch on Ya's pocket.

"What's going on in there?" Miguel ignored her remark.

Not wanting to rehash the betrayal she'd felt from Branch wi her friends who were obviously still part of Team Cascus, s sighed and said, "Nothing." She whistled for Baby to come, and turned away from her former friends.

Ya jogged over to her as she hurried away. He touched her arm and kept in-step with her. "Myrikal," he whispered. "I'm with you when you make your move. So are most of the others. All except Miguel and Vicky. And Morgan."

Myrikal pursed her lips and nodded. She patted his hand that still rested on her arm. "Thanks, Ya. It won't be long."

Making her way to the front gate, Myrikal stifled a short cry as a small, dark-haired girl ran toward her, arms flung wide. Myrikal dropped to one knee to receive the embrace. "Chansong. What are you doing here?" She knew the girl wouldn't answer, but she did look behind her and gesture toward her mother who was hurrying in their direction.

Huffing to catch her breath, Chansong's mom reached to pull her away from Myrikal with a terrified look over Myrikal's shoulder. "The Repopulation Clan joined with COP." Her voice quivered and her eyes darted over Myrikal's shoulder again.

That's right. Dal told me that. Myrikal stood and glanced behind her as Changsong's mom ushered her quickly away. Cascus stood at the open door of the Central Building. Ya, Branch, and Miguel stood as shields in front of him. The lift of his eyebrows and smug smile on his fake face as he looked from the retreating child and her mother, then back to Myrikal sent an icy chill down her back.

32

The treehouse she'd built and called home for too short a time stood as she'd left it. Myrikal could see if from her perch in a tall tree outside the walls of the compound. The cloud cover was particularly thick, causing the darkness of the night to be overwhelming to most. Myrikal rested her head back against the trunk, trailing her fingers through the silky fur of Baby's back where he rested in the crook of a branch just below her.

Cascus would expect her to come in the night. He'd be prepared for that. So she'd make her move during the day, after watching to make sure Branch was off somewhere else, doing his bidding. She closed her eyes and drifted off to a light sleep.

⚡

"Myrikal!" the whispered yell was enough to bring her immediately from sleep to complete awareness.

"Alyssa?" Myrikal peered down between the branches, over the wall into the compound.

"Ah. I've been looking for you all night. You have to come…"

The thick cloud-cover from the night remained in the pre dawn, making her eyesight focused and clear. "What's happened?"

Alyssa looked over both shoulders and lowered her whisper

even more. "He… Cascus… he took Chansong. He has her in a cage hanging above the smaller building I told you about."

Myrikal crouched on the branch then jumped to the top of the wall.

Alyssa looked at her with pleading eyes. "I know it's a trap, Myrikal. But you have to come. He said if you don't show up before sunrise, he'll drop her in."

Jumping down beside her, Myrikal asked, "What's in there?"

"I don't know. No one knows. But he made it clear that whatever it is, Chansong won't survive." Alyssa rubbed her arms. "They dragged her mom away in cuffs when she tried to climb the walls to reach her."

"Who's guarding her?"

"About half of DefCo." Alyssa jumped and let out a little scream as Baby dropped down next to her.

"Ya?"

Alyssa nodded.

I hope he meant what he said. "Will you stay hidden where you can see what's going on?"

She nodded again, fear and determination battling it out in her eyes.

"I'll leave Baby with you. If I get into trouble, give him the command to go." Myrikal showed her the hand signals then knelt down to be eye-to-eye with her panther. "Baby, you're going to stay with Alyssa. Be good." He raised up and put his front paws on her chest, raking his rough tongue across her face.

Just minutes before sunrise, she had no time to make a plan. She ran straight on, toward the four-foot wide, ten-foot tall building. Ya gave a slight nod of his head as she made eye contact just before jumping over him to the thin rim running around the narrow roof. Chansong jerked, tears streaking her dirty face, causing the small metal cage to swing.

"It's okay, Chansong." Myrikal ignored the heavily locked cage-door and instead, grasped two of the metal bars making up the cage. She pulled them apart just wide enough for the girl to fit through. She reached inside and barely got a grip on the girl's wrist when the roof of the building dropped, splashing into a thick green liquid and immediately dissolving with a smoky hiss.

Myrikal tottered on the rim, barely able to keep her balance. The chain holding the cage released from the apparatus that held it and the cage plunged toward the death-trap just a couple of feet below. Myrikal jerked on Chansong's wrist, knocking her against the widened bars of the cage as she pulled her free. "Ya!" she yelled, swinging the girl over the outer edge of the rim.

Ya dropped his weapon and raised his hands. Myrikal released her grip, Chansong's eyes widened but not a sound escaped the silent caverns of her throat. Before Myrikal could see if Ya made the catch, bright flashes of light blinded her un-goggled eyes and an explosive burst of air hit her from the side. Crouching at the odd, twisted angle necessary to drop Chansong to safety, she didn't have time to right herself.

Myrikal plummeted into the green liquid below.

334

Ceiling flaps closed above her, plunging her into a darkness so complete, even her super-sight couldn't pierce it. The acid-like liquid sizzled against her skin, but didn't seem to be doing any damage. She kicked her feet until her head surfaced at the narrow space at the top. This small bit of open air lasted only a few seconds, as the green liquid quickly gushed to meet the ceiling.

Holding her breath, Myrikal hit and kicked against the walls, but the strange material gave not an inch. She braced her shoulders against one wall and pushed with her feet and legs against the other. Again, with no results.

Panic welled up inside her like her gut and chest were filling with cement, ready to burst outward. She forced her muscles to relax and she sunk to the bottom, resting against the floor to think. She knew she could hold her breath for about an hour—any longer than that and she'd start to get dizzy and see spots. She wasn't sure what the time limit was after that, but she was sure it'd be short. And that was in water. Who knew what this green goo was doing to her?

Just as that thought seeped into her mind, her limbs began to shake. Overwhelming weakness penetrated every fiber of every muscle in her body. She wilted back against the wall. Just the act of lifting her arm took all her strength. Her stomach, and everything else inside her, revolted, making the queasiness she'd felt near

Cascus—and even the crevasse—seem like the fluttering of a butterfly. She doubled over as massive cramps rolled through her abdomen. She'd never known physical pain before. Her ability to think seized up, just as the muscles in her arms and legs did.

All concept of time and space blurred into one continuous internal shriek of pain. Myrikal had no idea how long she'd been trapped in the life-sucking liquid. It could have been anywhere from a few minutes to an hour. The earth rumbled beneath her. The tight ball she'd curled herself into unwound as the ground shook violently. She slammed into the walls of her prison over and over again, tumbling around until she had no idea which direction was up.

Take control, Myrikal! She yelled inside her head. *Ignore the pain. Something bigger than your circumstance is happening right now.*

Myrikal thrust her arms and legs out to the sides, making contact with the walls. Forcing her muscles to obey, she pushed the stabbing pains to the back of her mind. She couldn't get out through the walls, so she'd have to find another way. The only other option lay at the top, with the trap-like doors.

Not entirely sure she headed up and not down, Myrikal pushed onward as the world trembled around her. Her head bumped into the ceiling doors sooner than she expected. She'd forgotten how small the building was. She braced herself with her feet each pressed against a wall, thrusting the waves of agony to the back of her mind, a distraction to clear thought. She pounded her fists against the doors, fit so tightly together they may as well have fused when they closed. Not one tiny crack of light shone through.

Panic rose in her chest as spots danced behind her closed lids.

Her head swam with dizziness.

Her hour was up. Myrikal needed oxygen.

She stopped pounding and tried pushing. Not a budge. She ran her fingertips along every inch of the doors, searching in vain for a weak point or a finger hold with which she could gain some purchase to pry the doors apart. Nothing.

Bubbles floated from her mouth as she released the last bit of air she held in her lungs in a silent roar of rage. The spots turned to surges of light behind her eyes.

Flashing lights…

…that slowed to…

pulsing lights…

…that slowed to…

an occasional flicker…

…that faded to…

darkness.

One small part of her brain remained aware as she pounded a fist one last time at the doors. That small part of her brain, aware that her legs had relaxed, demanded with a feeble command that they hold on. Too feeble to reach the synapses that controlled the muscles there.

Her hands fell to her sides as she slipped toward the bottom of the tank.

34

Myrikal's eyes flew open. Something happened. Something changed.

Light.

That awareness hidden deep within her dying brain surged with one last effort, and this time, her body obeyed. Myrikal raised one arm, hand flopping loosely, above her head as she continued to slowly descend.

Something gripped her wrist tight and raised her from the depths of a sure death. Her rescuer struggled to keep hold of her wet, slick skin. He pulled her up enough that he could submerge his head, shoulders, and arms and grab her under her armpits. He heaved with such great power, as she emerged from the goo, they both flew back over the edge of the building and crashed to the ground ten-feet below.

Myrikal landed on top of her rescuer and rolled off him with an incoherent *grunt*.

"Myri." It came out as a half-rasp, half-gurgle. "Myri." He reached toward her.

She gasped for air. It took a few moments for her mind to respond to the fresh intake of oxygen. She blinked at the raspin figure lying next to her. With the fuzziness of her brain and the green ooze dripping into her eyes, she had a hard time focusing.

"Branch?" she whispered. She lifted up on her knees an

moved toward him. "No! Branch!" A sob tore from her throat. His shirt had been eaten away and his skin bubbled. His arms, face, torso—bubbling, burning, right before her eyes.

"Myri." He reached out again, blind eyes searching to no avail. "I promise… I promise I didn't tell him. I kept your secret." A racking tremor passed through his tortured body. "He guessed. He just guessed you could drown."

She wanted so bad to hold him in her arms, but she was afraid to touch him. His bubbling skin turned black and sloughed off in large chunks, revealing the muscle and sinew beneath. "I know, Branch. I know." Another sob tore through her.

His hand found hers and his fingers curled around hers. "I saved… you. How… many… points?" His muscles started turning to liquid, pooling around his bones.

Myrikal laugh-cried. "You win, Branch. This gives you *all* the points. You win." She leaned in next to where his ear had been a moment before. "I love you."

His lips and tongue dissolved. His eyeballs rolled around in skinless sockets before popping and liquefying with a *hiss*.

With a roar of anguish, Myrikal leaped to her feet and rounded the corner of the small building in which she'd been trapped.

The scene before her stopped her as if she'd hit a wall. She turned her head from side to side, trying to take it all in at once and make sense of it.

Ya, Connor, Donna, Bryan, Aaron, and Sandeep formed a protective semi-circle—facing outward—around three figures. Myrikal shaded her eyes with her hand and peered between them. Baby lay still, except for the heavy lifting and dropping of his chest as he struggled to breathe. Chansong knelt at his side, holding pressure to a chest wound, her hands and arms bloodied up to her elbows. Chansong's mom held Baby's head in her lap as she rocked back and forth.

"Baby!" Myrikal cried. The panther raised his head and

mewled, then scrambled as he tried to get to his feet. "No. Stay, Baby. Lay down," she commanded.

Myrikal turned to see what force the DefCo deserters faced. She gasped. Where the larger building had stood just prior to her splash into the dunk-tank of death, now stood an enormous machine, the same green liquid that had killed Branch running through transparent tubes. Miguel and Vicky stood about six feet in front of the machine and the quickly widening gap in the earth Myrikal assumed was being caused by said machine.

Her eyes locked on the figure standing behind them, right on the edge of the chasm.

Cascus. In his true form.

That explained the wide-mouthed stares of those who faced toward him. Myrikal dropped her hand, the dim sunlight no longer a problem to her rage-filled mind.

"Cascus!" Her voice boomed like thunder.

Without so much as a flinch, Cascus said, back still facing everyone, "Ge-et. Rrrid. Of. Herrr." The words came out slightly garbled and with a deeper, older voice—his true voice, unhindered or unchanged by the human façade he'd worn.

Miguel and Vicky whipped around to stare at their inhuman boss. The fear in their eyes and draining of blood from their faces as they turned back to face Myrikal proved that had been their first glimpse of the real Cascus. His transformation must have taken place only moments before.

"Choose now, Miguel and Vicky," Ya yelled. "Do you stand with this alien species, or with us?"

With one last look back at the writhing, multi-limbed, semi-transparent Cascus, they both dropped their weapons to their sides and pushed off like speed runners to join the others. Two clawed limbs stretched to grab each of them about the waist. Amid screams of terror and agony, Cascus lifted them ten-feet into the air and threw their now severed bodies into the chasm. Dark, whirling smoke tendrils *reached* from the crevasse. Cascus let out a joyful whoop. "I've reached them."

The same voices from the crevasse Myrikal had found a few days prior, now filled the air.

Cascus...

...needs to be wider.

Almost there...

...freedom is nigh.

Myrikal stretched her hand out in front of her, little bolts of electricity turned to huge bolts that coursed up her arms, quickly surrounding her entire body. She had to stop Cascus. Had to stop the *others* from reaching the surface. She sensed her loyal DefCo teammates spreading out behind her. "Give it all you've got!" she yelled back at them.

Guns blared and bullets whizzed past her as she blasted the inhuman figure with electricity. She smiled grimly as guttural noises escaped its mouth. The smile dropped from her face as she realized the noises were an alien form of laughter instead of cries of injury and pain.

She poured more power into her blasts. Its gelatin-like body just absorbed them, seemingly without any damage.

Two limbs whipped out, their claws grabbing two of the defenders behind Myrikal. Cascus slammed them to the ground with bone-crushing force then swept the lifeless bodies into the chasm. More of the dank-smelling smoke rose from within, along with the ancient voices, cheering Cascus on.

With a primal roar full of anger and grief, Myrikal rushed toward Cascus. Part of her recognized a wild snarl and a slew of shouts from behind. Her focus never waivered. She lowered her shoulder and crashed into Cascus full-force, the momentum carrying both of them over the edge of the chasm.

‡35‡

Sharp teeth clamped into the tight-fitting uniform and the flesh beneath. Myrikal's body jerked back as Cascus plummeted into the crevasse. Myrikal tumbled to the ground and scrambled backward to distance herself from the edge. And the rancid smoke. And the *voices*.

Baby collapsed onto her chest as she rolled to her back. Blood oozed from his side and he breathed in deep, rasping breaths.

"Myrikal." Ya hurried to her side and knelt down, speaking in a low tone. "The slit in the earth… we must… we must close it. Or cover it. Or fill it in." He pulled his shirt up to cover his mouth and nose. The smoke and accompanying odor had intensified.

And… the voices.

I see light…

…freedom is nigh.

We can compress enough…

Cascus, why art thou…

Myrikal drew in a deep breath and gently pushed the injured Baby off of her. "Get Baby back away from here." She looked up at the approaching crowd of people. At her friends. "And them too. Get everyone back."

Weariness as she'd never known it seeped into the marrow of her bones. She climbed to her feet, walked a short distance away from the chasm, then turned to face it.

Thoughts of Branch filled her head.

The young Branch she'd saved from bullies.

The angry Branch, leaving her because of her father's sins.

The happiness they'd both felt at finding each other again.

Myrikal's face contorted in anger as her thoughts turned to Cascus. How easily a young, traumatized Branch had been conned by him. By *it*.

Branch's last act of bravery and loyalty as he lost his life to save hers.

His *skin* dissolving and pooling around him as he died.

Burning anger replaced the weariness inside her, filling her with a strength beyond her own. Every cloud in the sky above Manhattan converged above her as Myrikal raised her hands into the air. Every particle of electricity stored in the clouds, in the atmosphere above the clouds, in the huge machine built by Cascus, and in any and all items containing batteries or other man-made power within a hundred miles of Myrikal—coalesced above her.

The massive electric storm crackled and thundered as it hung in the sky, waiting to be released by the power that called it.

Not a sound escaped from Myrikal as she circled her hands in the air. The power soaring above her followed her movements, whipped into a frenzied electrically charged vortex. She threw her hands down, directing the storm to strike the chasm and the machine that created it.

She held the firestorm there, staring into the maelstrom with unblinking eyes. The machine exploded, its splintered pieces falling into the chasm. Unaware that she was even doing it, Myrikal directed the power to push the sides of the crevasse together, instead of just filling it up with the surrounding dirt. The earth trembled as the fault lines beneath it moved back to their former positions.

One last blazing white bolt of lightning, as big around as a car, struck the now closed crack at Myrikal's silent command. The ground sizzled and the pyrotechnics ended, the dark clouds slowly moving away.

Myrikal stood, frozen, as Ya and some of the others stepped up behind her.

"*Qiji*," Ya whispered. He stepped closer and crouched down where the chasm had been only moments before. "The ground is hard as stone. Smooth as glass." He looked up at Myrikal, tears in his eyes. "You truly are *qiji*. Miracle."

She smiled, then swayed before collapsing to the ground.

36

Alyssa helped Myrikal to the nearest house where she showered, getting the Cascus-goo off of herself.

Alyssa stood just outside the bathroom, new clothes in hand, as Myri exited with a towel wrapped around her.

"Thank you." Bone-deep weariness pressed down on her as she reached for the clothes. She turned back and looked at the filthy discarded unitard, then back at Alyssa. "Why didn't my suit dissolve in that stuff?" She grimaced as she recalled Branch's clothes disintegrating before her eyes.

Alyssa shrugged and drew her eyebrows together. "Maybe because it isn't made of organic material? I don't know."

Myrikal closed her eyes, trying to gather strength from an empty well. She reached to steady herself against the wall. "It doesn't matter. Gather the DefCo team, please," Myrikal said, eyes still closed.

"Myri, you should rest," Alyssa pleaded.

Myrikal shook her head. "No time for that. Please gather the others so I only have to explain once."

"No."

Myri opened her eyes and looked at her friend.

Alyssa softened her voice and reached out to squeeze Myri's arm. "You need to get some rest. Whatever it is, it can wait. It has to wait."

Myrikal lowered her chin to her chest and sighed. Her friend was right.

"Get dressed. I'll go turn down the bed for you." Alyssa squeezed her arm again, a sad smile flitting across her lips.

⚡

MYRIKAL CURLED into a ball on the stranger's bed, exhausted but unable to sleep. Losing Branch before had hurt. But she'd known he was still alive then. She'd known there was still a chance of reconciliation. This was a whole new kind of pain. She wept into the pillow. She'd heard people say the death of a loved one left you feeling like there was a hole in your chest. She wouldn't describe it that way. Her chest wasn't empty. It was bursting. Like her broken heart was pushing to escape the confines of her body. Like it had grown—swollen and inflamed—to ten times its normal size, collapsing her lungs and pressing against her other vital organs like a vise.

Her thoughts turned to Baby. Alyssa assured her that Sandeep bandaged his wound and took him home to care for him, Chansong and her mom never leaving his side. *He has to be okay. I can't lose two friends in one day.*

Fatigue won out, and Myri slipped into the deep sleep of the physically, emotionally, and mentally wrecked.

⚡

"EVERYONE'S HERE, MYRI." Alyssa peeked around the door into the room where Myrikal paced back and forth.

With a heavy sigh, Myrikal joined the shell-shocked group of DefCo members and friends crowded into the small house. The crowd parted as Sandeep and Ya entered, carrying Baby between them. Myri rushed to meet them and fell to her knees beside the panther as they gently laid him on the floor. "Baby?" She held her breath, watching for the movement of his chest.

Baby let out a weak growl and pulled himself the couple of inches it took to lay his head on her leg.

"Oh, Baby. I'm so glad you're alive." Tears sprang to her eyes as she ran her hand over the fur of his head. She looked up at Sandeep. "Thank you so much for taking care of him."

Sandeep nodded, lips pursed and brow furrowed.

Myri knew she should stand to address the crowd, but she wanted to stay next to Baby. She swallowed the huge lump in her throat. She didn't want to have this conversation. She released the breath she'd been holding. "What did you do with Branch… Morgan's body?"

Ya lowered himself to the floor and sat cross-legged near Myrikal. "We wrapped him in a quilt and laid him in a casket that Bryan and I built. The casket is in Morgan's house. We didn't want to do anything further until we consulted with you."

Myrikal leaned forward and patted Ya's hand. "Thank you." Another deep breath. "I'd like to hold a simple service and bury him. Today."

Ya nodded once. "Do you have an idea of where to lay him to rest?"

"I do."

⚡

THE SURVIVING members of the DefCo team, Alyssa, and Channing and her mom, stood with Myri around the casket that had been lowered into the open grave next to Myri's treehouse. Next to the tree where they'd first met. Further back from this central group, stood a multitude of people from the compound.

Myrikal's shoulders shook as she looked down at what remained of her friend. The only sound that of shuffling feet and an occasional sniff.

Myri squeezed her eyes shut and drew in a deep breath, trying to gain control of her emotions. She released her breath through tight lips, opened her eyes, and raised her head, not looking at anything in particular, just staring out in front of her, not seeing anything but the past.

"I wouldn't be who I am today without Branch." Her voice hitched. Dang it! She needed to be strong. Alyssa stepped closer to her side and grasped her hand. Myri squeezed back, grateful for the support. "He was my first save." She looked up at the tree and smiled sadly. "My first friend. The first besides my father to know of my special abilities. The first to give me real clothes, the first to celebrate my birthday. He gave me my first taste of strawberries, took me fishing for the first time. That one didn't turn out so great, though."

A low chuckle passed through the crowd.

"Branch was the only light in my life filled with darkness. He showed me that I could be more than what my father raised me to be. He showed me, through his actions, that kindness exists in the world. He brought laughter into my life. And love."

She looked down at the casket again. "You saved me long before your insane act of bravery in pulling me from that monster deathtrap. You won all the points, Branch. You won and I lost. I love you."

The group silently shoveled the dirt over the casket until a small mound covered Branch's final resting place.

A loud bark and the crunch of running feet made Myri turn toward the sound. "Dal!" She smiled and hurried to meet him. She hugged him tight with one arm while scratching Lobo behind the ears with her other hand.

"Myri, you're squishing me."

"Sorry." She pulled back and looked at him. "I'm just so glad you made it back safe."

"Me too. The guards at the front gate told me what happened." Dal frowned. "I'm sorry about Morgan." His eyes glistened with tears. "But I'm really glad you're okay."

✦

"I HAVE TO LEAVE." Myrikal sat next to Baby, her friends gathered around her.

"No, Myri! You just got back," Alyssa cried.

"I have to. And it has to be soon. Like now. I should have gone right after closing the chasm." Her fingers dug into Baby's fur. "There's another one of the crevasses. It's the one Cascus crawled out of after the 'quakes. I have to go close it before he gets out again."

The crowd, eyes wide, stood in silence. No one urged her to stay this time. They now had an understanding of Cascus's abilities, if not precisely *what* he was.

Myrikal gave quick instructions. She left Baby's care in the hands of Chansong and her mom. "Please do all you can to help him sur… survive," her voice broke on the last word.

"You should take some of us with you, for backup," Sandeep said, eyes downcast.

"No." She smiled her appreciation at the offer. "You'd only slow me down. I think I can get there in a week if I don't stop or slow down."

Dal wiped his nose on the sleeve of his dirty shirt. "But you're coming back, right?"

Myri stood and put her hand on his shoulder. "I'll try my hardest, Dal."

With a lightened load in her backpack, Myrikal ran toward the nearest gate out of the compound.

As she gathered speed out into the city, Dal yelled, "You come back when you're done, Myri! You be safe and come back!"

The pressure around her heart eased just a touch. Being wanted, needed, and loved was the only thing likely to heal her broken soul.

EPILOGUE
JUST RUSS

Russ escaped the compound shortly after his daughte
dispatched Cascus. He wasn't about to stick around to se
how things turned out. Myrikal could rot in hell for all he cared
Today was the day he had a meeting with the scientists. He'
contacted them back when Myrikal had refused to do what she'
been born to do, when he realized he would not be getting rich o
of her abilities after all. What a waste of time she'd been. H
should have just dumped her in the river when she was born.

His hope was to still get something out of the abomination hi
daughter was. The scientists had shown great interest in his tal
Enough interest to pay him a healthy sum in advance, with more t
come if things panned out.

A diminutive woman, slightly older than Russ, met him nea
where the Empire State Building once stood. "I'm going to tak
you to our lab, but you must promise not to reveal its location t
anyone. Understand?"

Russ nodded.

What looked like just a pile of rubble turned out to be a secr
entrance to a stairway. She led him down too many flights of stai
to count then down a well-lit hallway with doors on either sic
about twenty feet apart. Russ marveled at the lights. No flickerin

How did they have power for this? He hadn't noticed any solar panels or large batteries.

The woman stopped at a set of double doors and placed her finger on a print scanner. It beeped and the doors slid open.

"How do you have…" Russ gaped at the technology.

"Don't ask any questions," the woman interrupted. "Follow me."

Russ narrowed his eyes at her back but did as she said.

They entered a clean, well-equipped, gigantic lab. A group of men and women in lab coats greeted them as they approached the table where they sat. "Russ," Brad, the man Russ had been dealing with, said. "Have a seat and we'll get started."

Russ sat mid-table in the metal chair proffered him. He rested his elbows on the table and leaned forward. "Well? Were you able to find anything out?"

Brad nodded. "Yes. I think we have a good theory as to where your daughter got her powers. The sample of her hair you brought us revealed some very interesting changes in her DNA. Diane, do you want to explain our findings to, Russ?" He gestured to the woman who had led Russ to the lab.

"First, we tested her hair. We believe her invulnerability occurred as a genetic condition, likely inherited from the mother—something that changed within your wife that allowed her to survive the plague where so many others did not. We believe that, because of that invulnerability, Myrikal's stem cells were able to adapt to new powers in utero." Diane looked at Russ. "Does this make sense to you so far?"

"Mostly." His heart burned with anger. It was Karly's fault. She gave Myrikal her powers.

Diane nodded and continued, "What that means is that your attempts to abort the fetus resulted in more mutations in her cells. So, when you punched her in utero, her muscles adapted, gaining strength. When you infused saline solution into the womb it did two things, we believe it caused her skin to become impenetrable and also to make it so she can be submerged in water without drowning."

Russ ran his hands through his hair and suppressed a growl. So... not all Karly's fault. He played a hand in the birth of an abomination, too.

"The stem cells are the key, here." Diane tapped a finger on the table excitedly. "Your attempt to electrocute her gave her the power to draw electricity to her and shock other people without getting electrocuted herself."

"What about the radiation? Did that give her any powers?" Russ asked.

Brad answered, "We aren't exactly sure there. Are you sure you told us about all of her extraordinary abilities?"

"All that I know about." Russ strained to think of anything else. "I don't know. Maybe that's what helped her survive the green goo Cascus dumped her in. Everyone else that came in contact with it just melted away into a blob of liquefied tissue."

"Perhaps," one of the other scientists said. "We'd need a sample of said 'goo' to determine that, though."

"Well," Russ said. "I'm not going back to that place."

"We'll figure out how to get a hold of some. Do you have any other questions?" Diane asked.

"Yeah, will she be able to adapt further? Gain more powers?"

"We don't think so. If we're right about the stem cells, and I'm sure we are, her ability to adapt ended after she was born. She'll only be able to develop more powers if she was injected with more stem cells with the same properties."

"Well, that's good." Russ sighed. "So, what now?"

The lab-coated men and women looked at each other. Brad answered, "We'd like to—*invite*—your daughter to visit us here. We've even built her a special room with all the comforts she could possibly need." He smiled. "If you can arrange for her visit, we'll take care of the rest. And we'll compensate you well for your efforts."

Myrikal would never agree to anything Russ proposed. He'd have to find a way to lure her there. "I'll get her here."

"Great!" Brad clapped his hands together. "Diane will show you out, and remember, keep quiet about our whereabouts."

Russ nodded. He hung back just a little to try to listen in on their continuing conversation.

"… we found another female plague survivor. Chihiro is bringing her in."

ABOUT THE AUTHOR

Holli Anderson has a Bachelor's Degree in Nursing—which has nothing to do with writing, except maybe by adding some pretty descriptive injury and vomit scenes to her books. She discovered her joy of writing during a very trying period in her life when escaping into make-believe saved her. She enjoys reading any book she gets her hands on, but has a particular love for anything fantasy.

Along with her husband, Steve, and their four sons, she lives in Grantsville, Utah—the same small town in which she grew up.